the
ICE BRIDGE

ALSO BY D. R. MACDONALD

Eyestone
Cape Breton Road
All the Men Are Sleeping
Lauchlin of the Bad Heart

the
ICE BRIDGE
a novel

D.R. MACDONALD

COUNTERPOINT
BERKELEY

The Ice Bridge
Copyright © D. R. MacDonald 2013

All rights reserved under International and Pan-American Copyright Conventions.
No part of this book may be reproduced in any manner whatsoever without written permission
from the publisher, except in the case of brief quotations embedded in critical articles and reviews.

This is a work of fiction. Names, characters, places, and incidents either are products
of the author's imagination or are used fictitiously. Any resemblance to actual events or
locales or persons, living or dead, is entirely coincidental.

Library of Congress Cataloging-in-Publication Data
MacDonald, D. R.
The ice bridge : a novel / D.R. MacDonald.
pages cm
ISBN 978-1-61902-118-1 (hard cover)
1. Cape Breton Island (N.S.)—Fiction. 2. Love stories. I. Title.
PR9199.3.M23I28 2013
813'.54—dc23
2013001208

Cover design by Gerilyn Attebery
Interior design by meganjonesdesign.com

COUNTERPOINT
1919 Fifth Street
Berkeley, CA 94710
www.counterpointpress.com

Distributed by Publishers Group West
Printed in the United States of America

10 9 8 7 6 5 4 3 2 1

For Sheila, with love

Tri nithean a thig gun iarraidh—gaol, eagal agus eud
Three things that come without being asked—love, fear, and jealousy

—GAELIC SAYING

The boat has slipped its moorings and is leaving harbor to trust to the open sea; and no boat needs so much trust to put to sea as it does for one body to go human and naked and vulnerable into the arms of another.

—JOHN MCGAHERN, *THE LEAVETAKING*

part one

A KIND
OF COMFORT

I.

SHE HAD HAIR like Rosaire's, a black braid, brilliant in the cold sun. That he could see. Down near the shorebank of his back field she sat, in snow, legs tucked under, a wide pad of paper in her lap, and whenever she glanced up, her hand moved in quick strokes. Her red parka was bright against the ice-flecked sea, winter-dark and restless. The day had a feathering of snow over the brittle fields, peppered with dun stalks of grass and bush. What was she drawing? His weary gray barn, shaggy with icicles? Would she spot his old mug in the back-door window? She wouldn't know that for a few moments he'd made her into Rosaire, that a flush of foolish joy passed through him, just out of a nap as he was, his head furzy, blinking at the raw snowlight. She must have come along the shore.

They had talked once by her mailbox at the road, a few words in a cold wind. Anna, was it? Anna something. She had to be mad to move here at the rear end of February.

He rubbed his breath off the window glass and then closed the curtain to a slit. He watched her. Behind him the green whisky bottle sat like an empty vase in the centre of his table. Another day shot in stupor, stumbling through his past with Rosaire, things they'd done together, so achingly particular now. Torture to think of her in his arms. But here he was, in his own fusty, painkilling cocoon. Sprawled on the old kitchen lounge instead of awake and working, he sipped whisky to push beyond the last, wasting days of her life. Whatever he could find of what they'd had he found best in sleep, in the torrents of dreams.

A gust of wind got the whirligig chattering on the porch rail, that piece of whimsy Rosaire had bought him, a blacksmith bringing his hammer madly up and down, his muscled arm on the verge now of flying loose.

The cat mewed for the outside, Murdock held open the back door. "You're getting old, Mr. Cloud, you're on your own." Murdock watched him through the window, the poised, fastidious steps, the subtle bearings, belly low to the snow, his body freezing instantaneously when crows scolded him. He was not a lion, he could be prey and predator both, but he did seem more alive out there, alert, not asleep or sleepy like Murdock in the kitchen.

Over the sink he slapped cold water to his face and toweled off. He ran a comb, wincing, through his reddish-gray hair. His hands shook. His clothes were soiled and rumpled, what a sight.

Still, he ought to have gone to that woman at the shorebank, she was a neighbor now. He would have once, easily. Why was he so angry? He needed blame, but nothing satisfied it. Crazy. Of course it was. His heart had unsettled his wits. He was simply tired of himself, not just his face in the shaving mirror or his voice wheedling the cat, but his thoughts, places where his mind kept going and going.

He stood on the back steps in a bitter breeze. The field lay white and empty but for two waddling crows keen on something bloody in the snow. The sharp sunlight hurt his eyes. Cloud's tracks meandered below him, off on a hunt, an investigation. Rosaire's cat, thick-furred like a little gray bear, but he hadn't lavished on it the cooing, grooming lap time Rosaire had, though he fed and watered it, let it shelter in his own grief.

Had the woman seen him at the window, like some suspicious geezer?

A man could go mad grieving. Love was maddening anyway, the worst of it, and the best.

II.

HOW CAN YOU live alone *like you do, on the edge of that ocean? You couldn't get any further east if you tried,* her friend Melissa had written. Anna did not yet know any women here, or how living alone by choice might be accepted. Regardless, they would not likely frequent this shore in a winter wind, fretting over an animal cruelly killed. Or be living by themselves.

Stiff and cold, unhappy with her drawings—distracted sketches of a lifeless barn and sheds—she turned her attention to flotsam. Anything material, interesting matter of any kind. On the frozen beach, stones grouted with ice, the footing was poor, but almost every morning she walked, in all weather, punishing or otherwise. She'd thought the man in the house might come out if he noticed her, they could talk, she might innocently tell him that she'd seen a dog tossed from the distant bridge one night, late. She needed a local perspective, she didn't want that shocking sight to shade her feelings for this place so early. He was her only near neighbor, his weathered house hidden around a spit just east of her, a small conifer wood between them.

But only the tracks of crows stippled the man's snowfield, looping through the furry pink bits of a rabbit. A movement of curtain? Maybe. Whatever she saw today seemed slightly unstable, shifting, uncertain. She would never have mentioned the dog to him anyway— she was new here, and hoping now that March would glide into the spring she'd expected. Winter still gripped everything hard, an east wind swept bitterly over drift ice far offshore. Harsh? She'd asked for it. A drastic relocation. Moods of a new landscape, while she struggled with an old one.

Anna glanced back at her odd, veering tracks in the shoreline snow: who would they mean anything to? Not her neighbor. No more than a gull's, a crow's, those of the fox she'd seen foraging.

She hiked on. Her first days here she had not wanted news from home, not from or about her husband Chet certainly or the familiar events of the college town that had so long been their life. But she'd awakened this morning to a simple need of conversation, another voice, someone who might feign an interest in her sufficient to tell them about a dog, to ask how aberrant that animal's death might be. The warm letter from Melissa had been welcome, a treasure in the cavernous mailbox, but had no bearing on the present. These two weeks by herself had been exhilarating at times, at others unsettling, lonely, fraught with doubt.

The dog nagged at her now, she'd sketched it furiously before breakfast. Helplessness, cruelty, betrayal. Difficult to capture with just lines, white space, shadow.

The cutting wind numbed her face, her toes were little stones. Oh God, she couldn't get sick, a bad cold or something worse would send her to that upstairs bedroom, feverish, alone, thrashing underneath quilts smelling of mothballs. Pneumonia. The sun was now a pale stain in thin gray clouds, and the strait, broadening out east into the Atlantic, was cold even to look at, gray as rock. Anna pulled up the hood of her parka, then yanked at a length of rusted chain the frozen stones held fast. A piece for junk sculpture when the weather improved? She'd wait for a thaw, whenever that would be. It couldn't be soon enough.

Anna crossed over to the long barachois pond that curved out of sight into the foothill trees. She poked among broken khaki stalks of grass and sea oats, cattail, wary of its disguised boundaries. Where wind had swept the ice bare, its gray translucence looked bruised. Would it take her weight? Her heart pumped harder, the risk was appealing somehow, and she ventured along the edges, stepping out here and there, further and further, far enough to make out a dead bird akimbo just under the surface, a black bird of some kind too splayed to guess at, head torn backwards. There was a ragged clump of wood near to emerging, and a knot perhaps of blackened algae. Yellow rope snaking down, the corner of a board, the bottom of a green bucket— storm flotsam she'd noticed in a brief warming spell when the surface shimmered with meltwater. Further out, a dark gash (why unfrozen, a spring underneath?). She didn't pursue a trail of paw prints, or check a black dollop of what might be scat.

Returning, she came upon a scrawl of dirty urine played out in the snow. What animal would pee like that? Boot prints, though they were not fresh. Okay, a man had pissed here, left a bold signature. The shore was not private, after all, though so far she'd seen only wildlife.

The path home to the red house cut into the shorebank, through a thin patch of snow-draped spruce where she followed her tracks up the hill, coming out into her open field above the pond. At the back porch was the view she'd seized upon in a nature magazine ad—a wide, river-like stretch of water moving between the long mountain behind her, gray with winter now, too steep for trees at its highest here at the cape, and the long hills of St. Aubin, dense with forest, a mile across the water. The strait faded westward beyond a steel bridge, past distant, misty heads, and was lost in the interior of Cape Breton Island, a great saltwater lake—she'd thought, yes, put yourself *there* and live and draw and sculpt in that far-off place. But of course the accompanying photo was a summer scene, sun-infused blues and dark greens.

After locating on a map Cape Breton, Nova Scotia—a large island, with an inland sea, that took up the northeastern third of the province—she'd written immediately to a Jenny Budd in Ohio whose family owned it, a woman who'd grown up on this cape, who said yes, she'd rent it to Anna for the year if she liked, it had been her grandparents' house, but winter might be an uncomfortable time to move in, you might have to rough it some. I'm not after comfort, Anna said on the phone, although there were days when she would have welcomed a little more of it. She had expected a village, but instead it was the remnants of what they called a settlement, Cape Seal, at one time small subsistence farms strung down a long dirt road that skirted the strait to the south and the foot of the thickly wooded mountain to the north, a feature the magazine ad had boasted of, "You've got the high side and the water side," as well as the Atlantic that yawned out to the east. No mention that the winding road dead-ended against the steepness of the cape not far from Anna's house, ensuring more isolation than she'd imagined.

The cultivated land had returned largely to forest, the houses often no longer visible from the road or fallen away or turned into summer retreats, Willard Munro, handyman and caretaker of Anna's house, told her when he came by to fix her water pump. He sat down expectantly at the kitchen table when his work was done, so Anna offered him tea and supermarket cookies and he talked away as if she were an old neighbor. We had a school and two churches, and I live in one of them, used to be St. David's, that should tell you something.

My old house burned to the stones, somebody set it. That bridge way up there on the highway? Cost us our ferry, the good traffic, killed my dad's little store down there by the old wharf. We had a good life here, hard but good. Willard pointed out idiosyncrasies of the house—the electric water heater that had one of two elements burned out but you could still squeeze a bath out of it, the old fuse box and its coffee can full of fuses nearby like ammunition (I wouldn't run, like, that kettle while the heater's going), a register in the kitchen ceiling that wouldn't open anymore (You'll likely see it a little cool upstairs), the back-door lock whose key needed jiggling in a certain way, and the old root cellar underneath the kitchen floor, hidden under a large hooked rug that Willard peeled back so he could open the trap door and let Anna see the short, crude stairs descending into a dank darkness (You won't need it, he said, you have a fridge there, and Anna said, I'm glad).

Willard paused at the front door as he was leaving. Just a few of us left in the winter, old-timers, Scotch people like myself, the MacCuishes, Donald John and Molly MacKay toward the cape, Red Murdock MacLennan down from you there, don't see much of him these days, old Rory Gunn pushing a hundred, he don't walk anymore, but Connie Sinclair yes, on the road, coming and going, to a drink, from a drink. Yes, pretty thinned out, this end. We're dead or gone. Oh, and Breagh Carmichael, young woman and her little girl, rents Kenzie MacKillop's old place. Summer, things get a little busier, cottage people show up.

He gripped his black tool box that he carried around like a doctor's bag and went off into a light snowfall, fresh as it had been the day Anna arrived, so light on the ground puffs of it rose at her footsteps.

Before she'd put the key in the lock that day, she looked back at her dark tracks leading from the leased car: here she was, on this back road in winter, tired, a little terrified, but excited too by her very isolation—she had taken herself out of a life with her husband, out of his force field, because he had fallen in love with another woman, one much younger than she. That had wounded her, and she did not want to bleed where others could watch, and where her artwork had gone stale, trapped in distraction.

I'm going to Nova Scotia and I'm going soon, she had told Chet—a sudden decision that set him back on his heels, the dust of their relationship swirling around them, just beginning to settle. Impulsive, yes, but she'd taken solace in the shock of it, to him, and to herself. To both her women and men friends it seemed rash, if not for the same reasons. But his affair with a woman barely thirty seemed to call for a dramatic turn, beyond marriage, well beyond the college town it had soured in. She would do the new Anna alone, she and her art.

In the first days here, she couldn't bear idleness, such space and solitude let thoughts of home flood in, grievances, missed pleasures, the comforts of routine. She explored indoors, then out, as much as weather would allow, eager for material to draw. She took notes, photos, filled sketchpads. *Dear Melissa,* she wrote, *Look, new things every day, a fresh setting, I just respond to it. And if I want to lie in bed on a foggy morning and listen to the mournful Black Rock lighthouse, that's okay too. If I want to sketch a tall windfallen spruce sprawled across the pond ice, and the gray blemishes there that the wind has scoured (bad spots to walk on?), I can sit on a folded blanket until my butt is numb if I want to. I went up into the foothill woods across the road, until it got too steep, and the afternoon sun was so strong the shadows of the bare trees striped the snow, and I remembered it in pen and ink when I reached home and warmed myself. How different the woods will be in summer. Weekend merges into weekday here, Monday holds none of its inflated significance. I did a terrific pencil sketch of the old guy who looks after my house (sort of), mournful but strong features, big strong nose, chin, long, hollow cheekbones. Loneliness is always hovering after dark, but I keep busy, I keep it at bay.*

She had called Chet one evening after she was well settled in, he was still her husband, he had cared about her, listened to her, shared things with her she liked to think he had shared with no one else, he was not evil, not bad, just weak, and because she was lonely that night and fighting it, she told him about the big pond below her back field, separated from the sea by a snow-concealed barrier of sand and shingle and roiled stones, where she'd come upon a dead beaver on her first cold walk down there, strangled in a snare, thrashed to death, its comical teeth bared. The witless cruelty of that wire, more so when she later found where the beaver had lived, how easily the trapper had determined its trail up the bank to a comfortable den in the rooty, muddy cave of a fallen tree, its half-finished lodge of woven sticks and branches, a brown island near the bank, abandoned. She'd felt tears coming as she told him, but she didn't mention that. The beaver had been too intent, as wild animals often are, upon its innocent and driven enterprise, unaware that another world, another logic, overshadowed its own. She'd never seen anyone set a trap, not even footprints until today, and that bothered her.

"I have a new cat, a kitten really," Chet said on the phone, searching for a topic without flammable allusions.

"Don't you mean *we*?" Anna said, regretting immediately that she had acknowledged his girlfriend, adding gamely, "What's his name?"

"It's a her," Chet said. "I'll see what she's like and then name her. I wish I could do that with women."

"You have. And so have I."

"You like cats, we always had one until Luna died."

"Does your girlfriend like them?"

"Call her by her name, at least, Anna, call her Alicia. Please? Are you doing okay where you are?"

"You might have asked me that at home, oh, maybe a year ago, even earlier. But yes, my own kind of okay. Fine, in fact. It's not for everybody. But that's the idea, isn't it, that's the appeal."

The phone line was tinny and thin, she didn't want to offer details: details were the golden currency of a relationship, and she had no more to spare. A dog spinning slowly through moonlit air? Too strange, too exotic, for his ears.

III.

"THANK GOD TO be here," Red Murdock said at the door.
"Thank God for yourself," Donald John said, "come in, come in."

Murdock paused at the parlor door on his way past—there was a big rectangle cut into the seaward wall where two old windows had been. Clouded plastic was stapled to the fresh lumber that framed the opening. The plastic crackled and breathed with the wind. "Donald John, why in God's name you getting a window put in in this weather?"

"Cheaper. Kenny MacLeod'll be back with a new one tomorrow. *Picture* window, Murdock. Big."

"A good sou'easter, she'd blow out that plastic like a paper bag."

"Think of the view, Murdock, the view."

"I am."

Molly, Donald John's wife, looking up from her knitting, said weeks had gone by since they'd set eyes on him, anywhere. Murdock took in the lovely smell of baking and the warm kitchen, too often he warmed himself only with whisky and didn't care to eat.

"Not out and around much," Murdock said.

Willard Munro, seated at the table with a cup poised at his lips, had stopped in, wearing his big plaid coat, his tool box at his feet. Murdock joined them all at the table. Tea was simmering on the stove, dark leaves dancing in a clear glass pot.

"We didn't see you at the meeting, Murdock," Willard said, "last night in the church."

"For what? I don't go to church."

"The Mounties, they need our help," Donald John said. "The constable told us, You fishermen, beachcombers, anybody who's on the water, keep your eyes out for suspicious boats and the like."

Willard reached for a scone. "A lot of drugs pouring into Nova Scotia, by water, he says. I believe it."

"Right here?" Red Murdock said, looking out at the gray sea, the wind plucking up bits of white. Apart from a buoy tender, he hadn't seen a boat in a good while. "Not since rum-running."

"There's a new running going on," Donald John said, "and there's not much fun to it from what the constable says. Guns and thugs. Dope is what they're bringing in."

"Not for us they aren't."

"It doesn't matter about us, Murdock. They truck it away up the province. We got all these coves and bays for to bring it in, see. Down the States, they've tightened up the border in the south, so they're coming up here to smuggle it in, the constable says."

"Well, my father ran rum," Murdock said. "He had a boat. Lots bootlegging, in the hard times, family men trying to get by. The Mounties never found a jug of my dad's, in floor hides or anywhere else. It wasn't any popskull either."

"Even so, wasn't legal," Willard said.

"No one ever drew a gun. And nobody here got rich. Anyway, I haven't seen any dope. Have you, Molly?"

Molly smiled, smoothing her apron over her plump lap. "No, dear. Wouldn't know dope if I tripped on it."

"You'd know it if they dropped it in your teapot, girl," Willard said. "Make you weird."

Molly laughed. "It will?" She held up toward the window a half-knit sweater of tweedy brown wool. "I might walk around in this then."

"If it's weirdness around this end of the road, it'd be the young-sters anyway, and summer folks," Red Murdock said. "Who's left of us in the winter now? Handful."

"You haven't seen that little gang at Sandy Morrison's place?" Willard said. "They hung around the wharf last summer and I had to fetch my dog home more than once, raising such a fuss he was. Up to no good there and he knew it, they cursed at him, chucked stones. I never saw a face I knew. . . Taste of the devil in them."

"Young men anymore, they don't know what hard means unless it's in their trousers," Donald John said. "Say, that woman from away keeps to herself. Murdock Ruagh, do you know her now?"

"Met her once. I can't say I know her." He wouldn't tell them he had seen her seated in snow, calmly drawing, or that, for a few head-spinning moments, he thought she was Rosaire.

"Nice-looking woman," Molly said. "What would bring her here, though?"

"God knows, I don't," Red Murdock said. "Not drugs anyway."

"The woman's an artist," Willard said. "I seen her pictures on the walls."

"Those walls could use some pictures."

Murdock's cousin Jenny had written from Cleveland, *the renter's a woman by herself from California, so if you could kind of keep an eye out for her Murdo, seeing as you're so close by. . . .* He never had a word from Jenny unless she wanted something and none from her brothers, they owned Granny's house and he was on cool terms with them—many years since they'd cut themselves away from this place. He'd never answered Jenny, had enough on his mind without acting the handyman for them who never set eyes on the house anymore. Let them pay Willard for that. Murdock had painted it red one summer years ago, and framed the windows with white shutters, but that was for Granny, before she died, Something bright, she said, I'm tired of the gray shingles. His cousins would sell anyway when the time was ripe, to Germans or Americans maybe, shorefront was getting high money now. In the meantime he wasn't attending to Granny's house or anyone in it. He was the last of his family here, still holding family ground, but for how long? More distant cousins still lived on the Island, but as dispersed as stars as far as he was concerned. True, he hadn't done much to stay in touch these last years, but now just himself seemed more than he could deal with.

"Your color's not so wonderful, Murdock," Molly said. She was quick to detect illness or possible decline. "You feeling all right?"

"I was under the weather awhile, I'm good enough." He could see in the parlor the edge of a china cupboard he'd made for Molly, for the cups and saucers she collected, rock maple, dovetailed joints, glassed doors that shut solid as a safe. His closed-up workshop was strewn with unfinished furniture, some of it already cancelled, customers had given up on him. "How about I take a couple slices of that rum cake I'm smelling? That'll color me up."

"This'll color you faster," Donald John said, taking a bottle of rum from the cupboard.

"No thanks, too early." He had already had whisky when the sun was barely up.

"Is it the hour that matters, Murdock?" Willard said, pouring a good measure into his tea.

"Not to you, it looks like. Are you out fixing things today?"

Willard sipped the last of his tea. "That old house of yours . . ."

"Not mine. Jenny's and her brothers'."

"Family, even so. Something amiss in the wiring or plumbing or something."

"Best you figure out which is which, Willard."

"It's the woman living there. Anna something or other . . ."

"Going to fix *her,* are you?" Donald John said.

"Nothing broke in that girl," Willard said, "what I've seen of her. Like to see more."

Molly slapped his arm. "Willard!"

"Age damps the fire, it don't kill it. What's she doing for a man? Nothing."

"Ah, well," Molly said, "I'll tell you what a woman will do for a man. Tommy MacKinnon was fishing, this was some years ago, and his boat was in that gully, that kind of a tittle, they call it, between Goat Island and Sampson Rock, an awful force of tide there, rises up strong, and quite a breeze came up that day and capsized them, drowned them all, Tommy and the rest. The bodies got mixed up in ice and eelgrass, they washed to the shore a good ways off and they found them, but not Tommy's, never showed. His wife, Georgina, she said, I'm going to find him anyway, and she walked the beach every blessed day, long walk from her house, she had kids to care for, weather didn't matter, storming or not, cold, she prayed, she walked. One day, after a blow, there was a lump of eelgrass with a boot sticking out, she thinks, I know that boot, it's his, he's somewhere here. She felt it, you see, his body, that his body was there, somewhere. So she kept travelling the beach, and this day she went and she come on this big load of eelgrass in a big roll, and she got working, untwisting strands of it, and finally there was a hand, she worked him free of it, all of him, his whole body. Her husband. He wasn't pretty. But she wouldn't let him go. Did you know about that?"

Molly resumed her knitting. The men were silent. The plastic window in the parlor snapped in a gust of wind.

"I saw a pretty woman go by on the road a while ago," Willard said. "Breagh, and her little girl on a lopsided sled."

Red Murdock remembered the sled. Didn't Breagh ask him to straighten a runner on it? Lord, how many weeks ago was that? She had stopped coming by the time of that bad spell when he would pass out on the kitchen lounge and not hear the door, not care to hear it. He felt terrible about that now, he was fond of Breagh and her little Lorna, but he'd been so deep into himself, selfish with grieving. "How are they faring, Molly, those two?"

"Oh, Lorna is so sweet. I had her here the other day while her mother went to Sydney with that young fella, the one she's hot and cold over. Livingstone Campbell."

"She can do better than him," Red Murdock said. He knew the man since he was a boy, over on the St. Aubin side, but he didn't trust him, he had treated Breagh poorly at times, took her for granted, frosted her out. Not that she was a flower easily wilted, she could hold her own, when she wanted. But men she had a fancy for, she let them get away with too much sometimes. Breagh had that kind of straight beauty she didn't have to do anything with, it was just there, it hit you the first time you saw her.

"He's from a good family, Livingstone is," Donald John said.

"That doesn't make him good. He has to be more than his name. He was after renting my granny's place. Write to Jenny, I told him, anyway the woman from California is in there for a while."

"That buddy of his, Billy Buchanan with the fancy pickup truck? He's staying in Sandy Morrison's house. I seen him and Livingstone jawing with two fellas out front one day. I didn't like the looks of them," Willard said.

"Drug-runners were they?" Murdock said.

"I don't know just what they were. My dog knew. Now he's gone. You don't know what goes on at that house. Some awful rackets on weekends, cars coming and going? Way out here on this road?"

"And what *is* going on? Plenty of kitchen rackets when Sandy was alive. You're blowing it up, Willard. Nobody's there now, and we did the same things on that wharf in the summertime, a lot more of us too, raising hell. Rum for us, moonshine, whatever you had on your hip."

"Well, now, Murdock, I don't think we got crazy like that with drugs," Molly said.

Donald John laughed. "Thin ice you're on there, girl."

"Yes," Murdock said. "People jumped off the wharf with their clothes on. Danced like fools sometimes, didn't we?"

"Still, it wasn't drugs," Willard said.

"Booze was all we *had*," Murdock said. Out the window there was fresh snow in that sky, colder, and the open sea beyond the black cliffs had turned the hue of storm, rollers white-eyed, wind-driven. Far colder than that water was the day he'd realized for the first time that Rosaire's love was not there *for* him anymore, that it was no longer available, its comforts and pleasures and solace were slipping away for good, she was separating from the world. They could say all they liked about the lingering spirit of love, the grave cannot kill it and all that, but yet, but yet he had lost the woman who *loved* him, all her actions of love, and it had been no mean and easy thing to be loved like that, by her. No one exactly like her was left in the world, he was standing in their space alone. He had toppled backwards into a vast emptiness and she could never catch him up—there was no Rosaire love to be had, anywhere.

"Speaking of booze," Donald John said, "Connie Sinclair was on the road yesterday. Dressed for walking."

"He walks miles, that man," Molly said. "One end of the road to the other."

"He's looking for something, it seems like, and not just a drink," Murdock said. Connie stopped by Murdock's house now and then, they'd been boyhood friends and he knew he could cadge some liquor there, a few dollars, and a sympathetic ear. But Murdock had stopped answering the door, to anybody. "Hasn't a cent to his name anymore since he's come back home. We had some good times, Connie and me, when we were young fellas. He was smart enough, he just had that goddamn stammer."

"Used to be white shirt or nothing for Connie," Molly said. "Shirts are gray now. Who'd hire him? Lost every job he had."

"I seen him shoveling the driveway at Sandy's place," Willard said. "Livingstone gives him a few bucks, I guess."

"That's not hiring," Murdock said, rising, wanting suddenly to be by himself. He'd found it hard, going out and around after she died. A man who had come home years and years to an empty house and thought it fine, felt now, in a friend's kitchen, as if he wasn't quite there, that something of himself was so missing he couldn't feel comfort in company, only an aching hollowness. "Weather's turning. I should be getting on."

"Well, we won't be out on that water, neither of us," Donald John said. "Our fishing days are over, boy."

Murdock did not want to concede that, Donald John being older than himself. "I might have a boat again, even so," he said.

OUTSIDE, RED MURDOCK stood by his truck, the March wind teetering him, the little sack of rum cake warm in his hand. He could thread a needle, he could sew a patch. He had fished, here along the north side of the Great Bras D'Eau, out to Bird Island, years ago. He knew the raw rocks, where current and wave, combined against you, could tear out the bottom of your boat.

Sometimes he just stopped where he was and thought, where to now? as if any next step were pointless. It scared him a bit, that nothing mattered enough to take it.

IV.

S O DRAFTY WAS the house, cripplingly cold at windows and doors, Anna had early sequestered herself in the room off the warm kitchen, probably once a dining room, appropriating a worn but sturdy table of wide maple boards and an electric space heater, a boxy affair with glowering coils that looked to be out of the nineteen forties, always a few watts away from a blown fuse if she switched on the kettle or another lamp. But there was a wood stove too and here she did her drawing and her reading, the southerly light was good, and she wrote a few letters by hand at a small pine desk, its dark varnish dented and scarred. She read in the embrace of a stuffed armchair that gave out a mildewy sigh when she sat, so she'd draped it with a moth-holed blanket of some pale tartan.

Every room she'd explored, dug into cupboards and chests, trying to learn from what remained, to get a feeling for it, anything redolent of its past. A large copper boiling pot and, dropped inside it, a wash-board of corrugated glass, now cracked, on whose surface women had reddened their hands scrubbing clothes. The solid but well-made furniture, her spool bed, the pine commode, the old dresser in her bedroom, its maker's initials incised in the scalloped frame, *A* one side, *K* the other, the top drawer's hairpins and red ribbon and spent elastic smelling of stale face powder. There was a pitcher and washbowl decorated with violets. A blue-belled chamber pot. A roll of shelf paper with cherries on water-stained white. A set of china dinnerware in plain cream, one plate chipped, one with a hairline crack. A mirror that reflected a garbled, impressionistic image—more than adequate, she felt, a dreamy, timeless vision of herself.

She found in a tiny bedroom closet a garment bag containing a dress, dark burgundy through the foggy plastic. Why was this one left behind? A fragment of a woman's life, in this house and its occasions.

The first day of grinding cold and wind reminded Anna that winter here had force, it could kill you if you were careless. Cracking sounds from under the house turned out to be foundation stones contracting as the temperature fell. There was a high stack of firewood against the house where mice and woodlice had nested. Willard had the oil tank out back filled before she arrived, and he showed her how to operate the oil stove it fed in the kitchen, and bank the wood stove in her workroom so it would last the night. Its brand name amused her, the pure optimism—*Warm Morning*. Poorly insulated if at all, walls were cold to the touch when she got up. You'll survive all right, Jenny in Cleveland had assured her, our dad's family did, our grandmother to the end, no more than a kitchen stove for heat and a brook for water and the worst winters in Canada.

Survival, in that sense, had not been Anna's main concern, but still there was the scrim of ice in the bedroom pitcher she'd filled the night before, thinking to wash her face in the china basin—a quaint homage, she did not repeat, to those who'd awakened there. And the line of feathery snow whose gentle chill she brushed from the sill one morning. Yet, the first window frost lit with sun so delighted her she scratched into its patterns a rearing unicorn, the crystals pleasantly sharp under her fingernail. Other mornings, urging herself out of bed, she whimpered down the stairs, shivering in the bathroom while she waited for the water to run hot. It was not that she'd never known cold and demanding weather, she grew up in the fog belt of California's north coast, where, in that deep dampness redwoods loved, frost was not unknown, this was not sun and surf but hard-nosed California, a cold ocean you didn't wear a bikini in. But snow and ice, frosted windows? No.

Her father taught art in high school and moved there in his middle age to get away from city life, well before the hippies' movement, and built an A-frame house in the cathedral shadows of those enormous trees. Her first memories were the long, misty rays of sun slanting through their high branches, the sound of the fog they drank drizzling from needles onto the roof shakes, a night sound, soft and steady, the winter storms off the Pacific, violent and wild, littering the ground with redwood branches, clumps of sword ferns beaded with moisture in the morning, the air always cool somehow even in summer when the rain stopped but the fog still fed the trees in the evening, the vanilla scent of sweetgrass her father picked and dried and burned like incense when he smoked pot in his bedroom, playing his jazz LPs, his eyes closed. Anna's mother did not want her to know that he retreated to his studio sometimes not just to do yoga on an oriental mat but to smoke.

His wife had agreed, under his pleading, to move from San Francisco to this simpler life, he hated the hassles of the city, the raucous, strife-torn high school where he taught, but she was never happy on the north coast, with its village life, she longed for San Francisco's energy and activity. I like to see fog shroud houses and buildings, not just trees, she said, I like to see it on the street.

Anna even as a girl could detect her mother's discontent, her parents argued behind closed doors but whatever troubled them was moot

after her father died suddenly of a heart attack while building an addi-
tion to the house, a room with wide windows and skylights to amplify
the meager ration of sun, this for his wife, this offer of light. He had
encouraged Anna's love of drawing, his gentle comments and sugges-
tions as it matured, though her mother was disappointed when she
planned to study art, It didn't take your dad very far, she said. But
other things did, Anna replied, for she had loved him dearly, a man an
odd mix of free spirit and the conventional, okay with hippies when
they drifted in to set up homes in the woods, not keen to embrace all
their hang-loose ways, their permissiveness and lassitude, though he
did swap marijuana with them, and cultivate his own. I grew up in
Ohio, I'm pretty straight deep down, he told Anna once, but I'm okay
with that.

Her mother thought even less of her son's trajectory. Anna's
brother was almost twelve years older than her, and their dad had
taught him to play guitar which led him to seeking stubbornly a career
at electric bass and that took him out of Anna's life almost completely.
He played for warm-up rock bands in New York until he tired of that
grind and married a woman from upstate, ending up as a DJ in a small
town station. They exchanged messages at Christmas, but he was so
much older than Anna, he seemed more uncle than brother, nearing
sixty now. Her mother returned to San Francisco and remarried, an
act that cooled Anna's feelings toward her, even though she knew that
wasn't fair.

Sometimes she wondered about that house her dad had built, she
could see those long shafts of smoky light angling down through the redwoods. Unlike this house, its history was short, but it had been all their
own. Misty, damp, chilly even in summer, that place, but no, nothing

like this. Not long before he died, her father looked into her face and told her, Sweetheart, I have always loved you deeper than the sea.

TODAY ANNA WOKE early and the house was bone-cold. Willard was right. Whatever heat lurked downstairs never seemed to reach the second storey, so she slept beneath a heap of quilts, buried in their woody smell. She pulled her legs up and watched her breath smoke into the dim light. An icy floor awaited her, but she would dress next to whatever comfort the *Warm Morning* had to offer. She'd always liked to go to bed late, sleep late, and Chet had sometimes brought her coffee there. She missed those little kindnesses, indications that he'd cared about her, his concern for her even when she knew he was attracted to other women and the fun of pursuing them, whether he succeeded or not. Alicia Snow, of course, had changed everything.

All right. Anna had spent years with a man who proved a disappointment. Then again, what did that mean? What had she wanted from him that she should be disappointed when he failed to provide it? Not money certainly, not goods, her hardened feelings toward him did not lie in his being or not being "a good provider," a term Anna loathed, a favorite of her mother's, ever-practical Joan, who'd urged her daughter, if she was going to be mule-headed about sticking with art, to at least teach it in school like her dad. Yes. It made him so happy, Anna said.

Yet holding down a job those early years with Chet, she had languished as an artist, living in the background of her husband's needs. At that time all she'd really wanted from him was love, uncontested, felt, visible, completely theirs. But in the long haul of a married life, that might not have been possible anyway, she realized, with any man—or with the woman she was. She had had her own affairs, but they were harmless. Weren't they? And it had been a long time since she and Chet had been truly *close,* the clarity of that astonished her now. *Hadn't* they loved? Yes, passionately, once. But they had ceased to be intimate, entwined, long before Alicia struck Chet like lightning. Maybe that was better—disentwining was painful enough, the tighter, the worse. Or could that keep you together in the first place? She did not know anymore. She had a solitary streak in her, always, she'd often wanted to be alone, like her dad, though she had never been alone like this, and neither had he.

This morning seemed to focus cruelly all her doubts. She could feel tears coming and she gave in to them, cried softly. But soon the luxury of feeling thoroughly and unashamedly sorry for herself, under her covers, became a kind of tonic, and who would know anyway? After a few minutes, she wiped her face on the sheet and got up. The women who'd lived in this house would shame her.

Once comfortable in her fleece-lined boots, gripping a hot mug of tea, Anna stoked the *Warm Morning* with more wood and turned to the sketches she'd laid out across her big table, the disturbing immediacy of the dog. It seemed at times that it had been tossed *to her* somehow, that she was intended to witness its fall. Absurd of course. And sometimes she was not certain that she *had* seen it. Keeping control of her mind was crucial, she knew that, alone and isolated as she was, points of reference so unfamiliar. Charcoal figures on white paper, what could they say? A series of mingled perspectives—the dog in the air as a bird might see it, or its killer, revolving, diminishing, and from below as Anna had, but now its jaws yawning grotesquely as if to devour its own incomprehensible fate.

Spirits low or high, she had worked every day, landscape, seascape, all kinds of objects, still lifes, in pencil, pen and ink, charcoal,
oil pastels, a medium she liked, it could mimic paint, oil paints had
never attracted her. But her main project was still the dog in the air, in
moments of pure knowledge—*I am running, falling, I cannot fly. . . .*

WHAT MADE HER drive to the bridge so late that night? The unbe-
lievable stillness when she'd stepped out the back door? A white moon
above the cold black lines of the bridge, sending an icy shimmer over
the water of the strait? Restless, at least, that night, a bit down, she
had the urge to drive, to get out, but she'd gotten no further than the
bridge. . . .

After the third curve, she'd passed the defunct ferry wharf, its rotting timbers invisible, just west of it the cottage where sometimes cars
were parked haphazardly, lights on but no party ablaze that night in its
windows, and on the high side of the road the white-shingled former
church, now Willard's house, its steeple shorn, no lights in the tall gray
windows either. The dirt road, roughened by bad weather, rain and
old snow, jolted along the foot of the mountain, potholes, thinly iced,
shining like water in her headlights before the tires crunched them. Her
high beams caught the breakwater rocks protecting the road on the
water side, the strait beyond them black as the sky.

When she reached the dry highway and swept down the long,
forest-lined hill toward the bridge, she wanted only the sensation of
coming out of the trees and crossing it in the darkness, to feel a kind
of nowhere beneath its girders, free of this strange, demanding terrain.

But instead, just before highway rose into causeway, she wheeled
onto a service road closed off not far in by a cyclone fence, gated and

locked. She parked, waited until she absorbed more of the car's heat, then skirted the fence where it ended at the shorebank. She walked the unplowed road, the sharp squeak of her steps the only sound, until she was near that composition of girders and beams and shadows high above her. Were it not so cold, she would have brought a big pad and sketched out something rapid and rough that might have reflected her mood, the odd atmosphere and perspective, detailing it later, warm in her room. Just the idea of drawing in moonlight had pleased her, the mysterious form her lines might take, but already the cold was working into her limbs.

The stars were like ice-points, cold tingled her skin and she huddled deeper into her parka. Only faintly was she aware of a car curving down the mountain road she had just travelled, it seemed almost alien in the stillness, not fast, slowing as it gained the causeway, climbed to the bridge above, where, beyond her line of sight, it stopped and sat idling. She could hear the soft rumble of its exhaust, and then a door seemed to open to the sharp yaps of a dog. She looked up at the figure at the railing backlit by headlights, something in his arms. A trash bag? He paused, then flung it upward as if releasing a bird, and Anna saw a silhouette of legs scrambling in air, the animal giving out a single, tortured bark as it plummeted, turning over several times slowly before, with a tiny splash, it penetrated the sinuous currents beneath the bridge. Above, there was yelling, men's voices. Doors thumped shut. The car turned around, slowly, not in flight, just leaving, what they came to do had been done, and it returned down the causeway, gathering speed back up the mountain highway.

Crying out, Anna rushed to the shorebank but halted when she felt the slippery, unstable rocks, saw the hushed dark water moving, undisturbed. Gone, over. How could she have come here and seen a dog flung helpless from a high bridge? Was this a way of putting it down, was it hopelessly sick, unwanted, like newborn pups? How horrible if that man was its master. And if he wasn't, then why? What was she to do?

She had no connections here: who would she tell? The Mounties? And what could they do without a license, a description of the man, of the car? She didn't know even her nearest neighbor, and it could be a toxic story for a stranger to trouble him with. What would people think of her when it got around? That she made it up? And what had she been doing beneath the bridge at such an hour? Could she tell them she had to shake herself out of depression, out of doubt? No. This was hers, alone.

Inside her car, through the faint fog of the windshield, the atmosphere seemed stained with cruelty. Daylight would drive that away, wouldn't it? The dog was surely knocked senseless when it hit, it would have died quickly. Its terror lasted but a few seconds. But it swam through her mind, tumbling slowly, just one confused bark, then no sound as it fell, as if it had been too focused on righting itself, finding a purchase for its feet, or some way to fly. It was dead, forget it. Food for crabs, for fishes, its bones might wash up on the shore, picked white, she'd draw them, turn them into art. This was not for her to solve, there was nothing to work with except shock and pity, a dead end, forget it, an incident linked to nothing else in this place, to no one she knew.

She drove home in a daze, the deserted road rocking her numbly until her high beams picked out a man striding determinedly along the shoulder, his back to her, hands deep in the pockets of a dark topcoat, his hair damp and slicked as she swerved past him, he was not hitching, his hand was not out, but it frightened her, coming upon him, his long black coat and his black hair, bareheaded on a night like this, how could she have offered him a ride anyway, it made no sense, strangers, both of them, and even though he was much too far from the bridge even to have seen the dog in the air, Anna drove on, she was not capable of the kind of conversation that would have to take place, though yesterday she might have stopped, because after all, where could he have been going but to one of the few houses that had lights in them in the evenings, like the little house across the road from Willard's, lights in its windows now, late, a car out front that hadn't been there on her way out. Her whole body ached as if she herself had fallen from the bridge. . . . I live here. This is where I live. . . .

A small dog turning slowly through the night air had altered everything for a few days, she had to erase it, but that was proving difficult. She searched her own frozen shore for the corpse, hoping to find it, but afraid too to see it maybe mangled, half-eaten, bobbing in gray slush. She interpreted shapes wrongly, sometimes crazily, creeping up on a clump of driftwood sticks or dirty brown carpeting, her heart in her mouth.

V.

ANNA'S INSTINCT WAS to ignore the knock, as she would have back home in her studio, working, but now a rare and actual someone might be at the front door. Maybe only Willard Munro, caretaker cum handyman. A few things did need his attention.

Through the frosted pane she saw a splash of color, and she opened the door to a young woman with striking red hair curling from beneath a stocking cap of royal blue. In her arms she held a small child of maybe three or four.

"How are you today?" she said. "I'm Breagh Carmichael, from up the road? Will you look at that," she said, laughing. She pointed behind her to a small worn sled listing in the snow. "One of the runners came loose but we got a long way on it, didn't we, Lorna? Could I use your phone for a minute?"

The woman brought into the hallway a rush of energy and youth, her face bright with cold. The child wore a pink snowsuit with cheerful polar bears on it, the hood drawn tightly around her curious, brown-eyed gaze.

"The phone's in there," Anna said, "on the kitchen wall."

Breagh set the girl down while she dealt with the telephone. Her conversation, with someone she called Liv, was short and tense, Liv had not shown as expected. Anna knelt by the little girl who gave her a reluctant smile. Her cheeks seemed flushed. "Yes, I might be out in the sticks," Breagh said, "but I'm not about to sit around for you until you're good and ready," and she hung up.

"We were going to stop at our Uncle Red's," she said, "he's just over the way. Weren't we, honey? Not really our uncle, is he, but he's like one. Not home or not answering, I guess. We don't see much of him since his woman passed away."

"His wife?"

"Girlfriend. Well, she was more than that. It's been a big hurt, losing her." She bent down and kissed her daughter on the cheek. "This is my Lorna." She pulled out a tissue and wiped the child's nose. "She has a bit of a cold, don't you, honey, but you know, she never complains."

Anna introduced herself and urged them into the warm kitchen. Breagh pulled her daughter's hood away, her curly hair a darker red than her mother's, unzipped her snowsuit and set her loose. She wandered the kitchen with a shy smile before opening a low cupboard and carefully removing one by one the tin baking pans of different sizes, stooping to arrange them inside each other to her liking. Breagh moved to stop her but Anna, amused by the child's solemn concentration, said let her go, she never used the pans anyway, with their little dents and scorches from banging in and out of ovens.

"Oh, you're an artist!" Breagh said, getting up. "I draw too, but mostly figures, clothing." She moved close to the sketches Anna had pinned to the old wallpaper. "Is that our bridge?"

"They're just studies, nothing finished really."

"Is the dog flying or falling through the air?"

"I'm not sure myself sometimes."

They talked while the girl played with kitchen utensils. She seemed to enjoy the shape and motions of a flour sifter, a wooden masher, a set of tin measuring cups that telescoped into one.

"Maybe she'll be an engineer," Anna said, watching her.

"Or an artist. She loves drawing. Oh, she'll go on in school, I'll make sure of that. We'll move back to Sydney before then. I had to get away from there for a while." She smiled. "Men."

"Yes." Anna smiled.

"Red Murdock found us the house up the road I rent. You met Murdock?"

"Not really."

"The old fella, Dougal, died there, in our house and his wife's in a home, so it was available. Have you people here, Anna? Is that what brought you?"

Anna explained only as far as she felt like going, focusing on her artwork, how the landscape had drawn her here, the light, she'd read about Cape Breton and seen photographs, a research trip, really. She dodged personal details or made them up, which she found oddly enjoyable. Gossip was bound to be a hot commodity in this little corner and she wasn't about to donate her story to the cause. What would this woman, her life with men barely begun, understand about Anna and Chet's life together, what broke it apart? She apologized because there was no milk for tea or for Lorna but she did give her a cup of orange juice which she sat on the floor and drank in one go so she could get back to turning the crank on an iron meat grinder.

"The weeks I've been here and I still don't know half what's in the place," Anna said, pulling open a low kitchen drawer. "Okay, Lorna, it's all yours, sweetheart, there's nothing sharp in there."

"We should get home, Anna."

"Your husband's at work, I suppose?"

"I'm on my own. No husband."

"I'm sorry, I shouldn't have . . ."

"Don't worry about it. He wasn't fit for a husband or a father either, so no loss there." In May she and a friend would be opening a shop up on the east coast, in an old schoolhouse along the Cabot Trail, designing and sewing their own clothes. She was getting by on government money and some help from the man on the phone. She didn't have Willard's brogue, maybe because she'd grown up in the city, in Sydney.

"You shouldn't be alone down here so much," she said, shouldering Lorna at the door.

"Aren't you alone yourself?"

"Not all the time," she said. "Anyway I've got me girl." She peered into the front parlor Anna never used. "My boyfriend wanted to rent this house. I'm glad he didn't. Too close to home."

"Listen, let me drive you."

"Oh, it's not that far."

"Really, I'd like to. The weather's turning bitter and Lorna has a cold."

"When doesn't she? It's winter."

Breagh lived in a small house not far before the dirt road ended, up a hill that hid the sea down behind it. A glittering four-wheel-drive pickup Anna had seen at the house by the wharf was parked aslant, just off the driveway, its huge wheels sunk in the snow. "Oh, Jesus, Billy Buchanan is here," Breagh muttered. "He comes around on his own, buddy of Livingstone's. I bet he's in there with a beer in his hand."

"He just walks in?"

"If I'm there or not."

"You don't lock up?"

"Who comes down here, Anna? No drugs or money in our house."

A hand, clutching a green bottle, parted the parlor curtain and Anna could just make out a man's face there. "I wouldn't care for that myself," Anna said.

"Oh, I can handle *him,* he's a little thick. It's that I'm sort of tied up with Livingstone Campbell, and Billy comes here to meet him sometimes. They're partners in one thing or another, I don't ask. Anyway, Mr. Campbell is a no-show today. You see, Anna," Breagh said, hoisting Lorna to her shoulder and opening the door, "Livingstone is not for every day. He's a sort of occasion, and sometimes it's a good occasion and sometimes it isn't. But he's putting money up for our shop, and he always brings my darling a present. Doesn't he, sweetheart?" Lorna nodded thoughtfully. "Anna, come inside for a cup of tea. Billy's leaving."

"All right, yes. I'd like that." They waited by the car as Billy approached, waving his beer amiably. A stained peacoat was unbuttoned from a proud belly draped in a black T-shirt with a Kiss logo. He had a head of tight, uncombed curls that would keep him boyish for a long time.

"Liv been around, Bree?"

"He's hung up in Sydney, Billy. Business, he says. This is Anna and she lives down the road."

"How are you now, Anna? Listen, Bree, tell Liv we got a deal on the boat, me and the other fellas. Okay? She's a pretty good one."

"Going to sail around the world, Billy? Fish?"

"The world hereabouts, good enough. Motor anyway, not sail. From California, are you, Anna? Jesus, I'd like to go there sometime. Visit like. I lack the money, right now."

"I'm living here now," Anna said.

"Not much to do on Saturday nights, this time of year, eh?"

"I didn't really come for Saturdays."

"Which house is yours?"

"The old red one, above the point. It's hidden from the road."

"Yeah . . . I know it. Didn't know they rented it out."

"Livingstone knew, if you didn't," Breagh said.

"Did he? Ah, well, never know what that fella's up to, do we? See yous later." Billy tossed the empty bottle into the trees.

"Billy!" Breagh yelled, but he grinned, shrugged, and climbed into his hefty pickup, muscle trucks Chet called them, its huge chrome grille fierce against a purple-black paint job and more glaring chrome. The engine rumbled to life and the big tires backed it out of the snow with ease.

"He might grow up—someday," Breagh said. "Hangs on Livingstone's every word."

She toured Anna through the house she was hoping to fill with antiques, one here, one there, local things, she said, from the Island, so many had been carted away to the States when country people here didn't care about them.

"I never had family things, I mean that were really mine, from my own people, you know?"

"My mother never cared about them. I have a couple things from my dad."

There was a hanging oil lamp Breagh was proud of, with a parlor shade of white glass ringed with crystal pendants. Her sewing table, a pine drop-leaf, she'd bought from a lady bound for the old-age home.

"Uncle Red gave me those pressback chairs and a commode in my bedroom. He made the big table." She had her eye on old pieces in his house, if she could soften him out of them. "What's an old bachelor like him need with a big pine cupboard? He says, I store memories in it. That's good enough for me."

"Do you see him much?" Anna said.

"He's kind of closed himself away, Red Murdock has. No wood-work out of him for months. He was making a big desk for Livingstone. Expecting some money to burn, I suppose, Liv is like that. I always wanted me a fancy desk, he says, all kinds of special drawers and stuff. You going to do big business on it? I asked him. Exactly, he says, you pegged it, girl."

Breagh's furnishings gave the house a warmth Anna envied. She'd framed textiles and hung them on the walls, in wonderful colors and tones and textures that mirrored the clothes she was sewing, the second-hand fabrics piled on a table, hanging from wall hooks. They drank their tea slowly while Breagh told her about the road, how lonely it could be, she'd go off to Sydney now and then for a few days and stay with a cousin. "It's a thin place when the snow flies, Anna." Lorna plopped a storybook in her mother's lap and laid her head there, it was naptime, and Anna said her thanks and goodbyes, pleased at this chance to linger with this little family of women. Lorna and her mother had dispelled the sepia atmosphere that seemed to color Anna's house some days, an unknown but insistent past, long after she had first slid the key into the front door lock on a freezing February afternoon.

Driving home, she missed Melissa's girls, their lively visits, tumbling cheerfully into her studio where she always set them up with paper, colored pencils, a project to draw, some arrangement of animal figurines or flowers or odds-and-ends objects. But they were not her daughters, they ate her cookies and went home with their mother, there was nothing of Anna they would carry into their futures but some loving guidance as their hands tried to show the world as they saw it, felt it. Anna was not with them in the odd hours, the small, defining moments of their lives. That was the privilege of a mother.

Although she could not put a face to any name on a mailbox, she felt a bit less the outsider, she had visited and been visited. On the high side of the road, the gentle foothill accommodated a quiet house set back, here, there, barely visible or lost to sight, as the road curved, rose, fell toward Anna's. They were few and looked shut down in the wild, white, constricted fields, the bare hardwoods stark, hemmed in by spruce rising densely up the mountain before forest gave way to a steep, almost treeless slope.

She passed a dented mailbox: M. D. MacLennan in worn lettering. Her reclusive neighbor? His house, like hers, lay on the sea side, hidden by woods.

Someone coming on foot? Not MacLennan but the man she'd seen that night on the road, still in his long black topcoat, damp black hair, collar of a white shirt, necktie (Connie something?). It was as if he had never stopped walking since that night on the way back from the bridge. Despite his solemn expression, he waved mechanically without looking at her and she returned it. Did he remember her car? Not likely. The moonlit bridge shuddered through her, her helpless stumbling toward the dog.

Her own driveway snaked through snow-dusted spruce, and at the sight of the house, Anna sank with loneliness. Oh, that unexpected company, it had tilted her sideways. Breagh, her golden red hair, her sea-green eyes, yet no yearning, it seemed, even with her looks, to flee this tiny place. Did she ever question what had come her way, the available options and possibilities? But hadn't Anna, in her own ways, acquiesced, even as the nineteen sixties offered women a better shake? Yes, she had kept her name when she married, but along with it old attitudes that tied her down for far too long. Lorna there in the kitchen murmuring to herself in her own language, contented with found toys, what future for her?

Anna had a sudden, unexpected urge to call her husband, to reach for that exasperating but familiar link. Only twice had she weakened, the second time on a dreary Saturday evening when she longed for the frivolity of a weekend, that well-earned letting go. Long-distance, on a bad line, she wanted to find him appealing again, to joke with him, to hear gossip, to feel, in the gentle give and take of catching up, tension dissolve: but it was all voice, little was given by either of them, nothing new. She could feel Alicia Snow infusing whatever he said. They might have been distant relations touching base, no intimacy exchanged, no troubling information, no tender subjects broached, just a mutual, courteous coolness that depressed her deeply after she hung up.

Had Chet accepted that she was gone, separate from him now? It had hurt to think that he was carrying on smoothly with his own life, with a young woman, that Anna's absence might not matter anymore at all. When she was ill or down, he had taken care of her, he was good at that, he brought her medicine in bed, favorite food when she was hungry, lemon tea, the *New York Times* on Sunday. He fixed her broken things, if he could. She thought he did so because she mattered to him. Her mistake was believing that she mattered more than any other woman ever could, and so the infidelities she got wind of did not hurt her much, they were no deeper than her own, they burned out quickly before anyone's house caught fire.

All this of course was before Alicia Snow, the girl (as Anna preferred to think of her) Chet met at a health club where he was fighting off middle age. After a few weeks of flirtation (She's fun to talk to, he said, that's all), Alicia had persuaded him to join her on a caving venture, she was a spelunker and loved those labyrinthine, slithering, squeezing, ill-lit explorations underground. Chet, however, was violently claustrophobic, he could have a panic attack trying to get free of a turtleneck sweater. But he saw this as a test, he told Anna, he could not beg out of it, and by then Anna knew he was willing to do nearly anything to get closer to Alicia Snow.

So she led him into the caves where passageways grew narrower and more constricted, and Chet's heart rate rose, although he didn't let on. Alicia knew these caves and he found that he liked putting himself in her hands until they reached a short tunnel-like passage so tight that she said, casually, We'll have to remove our clothes to get through this one, the tolerances are critical. She unbuttoned her shirt in a businesslike way while Chet crouched there, stunned at the prospect yet excited by the bizarre setting of her striptease. Later, he recounted this to Anna in detail (why not? no harm), read to her a rapturous passage he'd written about Alicia's nude body in the niggardly light as she squirmed her way into the rocks, and then, naked himself, dizzy, his following her, faint with terror and desire. It was primal, mystical, he confessed (he was prone to confession, he found it liberating), and it sealed something terribly important between them, him and Alicia, and he (as a writer, Anna) was proud he finally had the language to embrace it on the page. I'm not sure that's where you're embracing it, Anna said, and the symbolism is rather strained.

But now, here where she had placed herself at great remove, her sarcasm seemed threadbare, hardly an adequate response to what he'd been clearly telling her: she should have said something straight and honest to him—Chet, admit it, you're helplessly infatuated with this woman, don't make her sound like nothing but a muse. But she hadn't wanted to admit herself how serious the situation was.

Once inside the house, surrounded by her sketches and drawings, her slowly growing montage of this place, the urge passed, if she phoned Chet again, she would sound indeed as he'd predicted—lonely, and over her head. She could not explain the dog to him even if she wanted to, not anymore, it was a story she might share with a lover. Anna and Chet. Even now his name had a tangled resonance. Man and wife so long, too long, if loosely, over twenty years. She could not blame him terribly for falling in love with a young woman. Who wouldn't want to relive that kind of emotion? But he squandered on that affair all the passion and attention he could muster in middle age, and that hurt Anna the most—the extravagant attention, and the memory of receiving it herself. She had been the object of his romance once, of the pleasure he took in them both. And she could never forgive what he'd said to her in the heat of an argument: I wanted to fall in love again, like I did with you, you see, Anna, I wanted that long lovely dive when you can barely catch your breath.

She diverted herself instead by reading the closing paragraph of a Melissa letter she had saved, planning a reply: *There's a new kind of correspondence on the scene now, by the way, called electronic mail, goes through the computer, it's catching on. I'll have to give in soon. Wouldn't touch you where you are, I'm sure. Over at the college now, Roger says students expect him to be on it, you mean you don't have email? they'll say. He grumbles, can't ignore it like a telephone, there it is on his damn screen. Computer stuff coming out so fast, can't keep up, don't want to keep up, here we are, whirling through the last decade of the century. Remember when we saw* 2001: A Space Odyssey *years back? Seemed way way in the future then, didn't it? Maybe you feel closer to older times, being where you are. Anyway, I miss you a lot, so do Emma and Lilli (when is Anna coming back? they're always asking), I think of you there by yourself. I couldn't do it. The tulip trees are blooming, gorgeous.*

Somewhere in her belongings she had stashed, all but forgotten until now, a joint Chet had pressed upon her before she left, There will be a day you'll want this, Anna. She was tempted to dig it out, but it would be one-and-done, a little diversion, a conversation with herself, a possibly amusing high, with engaging but maybe unsettling insights, even, as it sometimes was, aphrodisiacal. She had her fantasies, her teasing memories, and she didn't want to kindle them right now, when afterward the rest of the day would yawn with impossibilities. She hoped there would not be a time when she'd need it more, but there might be.

She bustled about the kitchen stove, clanging pots, a frying pan, the noise beat back any need to hear his voice, to be embraced by the familiar ambience of that town, where her life had touched his life every day—mutual friends, places, figures of comment, politics, benchmarks, allusions, jokes, music. Affairs. Her own were just play.

Weren't they? Maybe there was no such thing as just play, not where love was bound up in it. Had she given him, without realizing it, a license to seek love, opened a door behind which waited Alicia Snow?

But I am here, Anna said, *here*.

Breagh had left her phone number on a scrap of drawing paper but Anna did not recognize her name at first: she'd thought it would be spelled *Bria*. It was like coming upon a little etching on a stone—unexpected, rich with place.

She hauled a bucket of stove ashes to the back porch, then, in a snowy wind, she split kindling with an axe. Standing up, she thought she could make out a boat, a rare sight, no more than a swaying profile in the swirling snow of the strait. To the west, the pond was merging into the whiteness around it, the ice, with its dark stains, veiling over. Anna carried an armload of kindling into her room. Okay, she said, gorging the *Warm Morning* with wood. I'm okay.

VI.

RED MURDOCK SMELLED piss in the room as soon as he opened his eyes. His face burned, like he was a kid again shamed by wet sheets. He lay there without moving but he felt no dampness. Ah, last night he'd dug out an old chamber pot, first time since, Lord, before he took up the old pantry with a toilet and a tub. Something to be said for that china pot handy on the floor, after you'd been drinking, just stand up dreamy, do it, and then back you fell, catching sleep up where you left it. Yes.

But it shouldn't get around, using a pot when he didn't have to. Codgers did that, drinkers. In the old days the smell of your life was here in the bedroom, and you might die here too, laid out on cold boards in the parlor by your own people, the ones who loved you, the nearest, they washed you, after death, readied your body. Who in a house now could do that hard and distasteful act? Waked, and buried you.

He took hold of his sleeping cock, more in confirmation than in lust. He had tried not to think of Rosaire that way, it seemed disrespectful to her those first months she was gone, to his love for her. But yet, yet, the long, lovely curve of her back, her mouth on his, on him, the taste of her in a rumple of bedclothes kept coming into him, this mattered. And why not? She loved the long, deep, naked hug as much as he did, the groan of a kiss. But all this was grief too—joys gone, terribly missed.

"Cloud, you old bugger," Murdock said, his voice rough with sleep. The cat slept at the foot of the bed sometimes, not near the pillow as he had at Rosaire's. Murdock had come to like the weight of him there when he woke in the night, that solid little body at his feet. Sometimes awake in the dark he thought he could hear a faint, comforting purr. The cat swished its tail but didn't move, studying Murdock with owlish yellow eyes. They had grieved together, the cat sitting on its belly for hours with its paws tucked neatly under its chest, not really sleeping, but rather inert, its eyes half-shut in a kind of trance that Murdock understood perfectly—turned into itself tight because it could not be touched by the one who'd loved it most. "I suppose you're hungry, you little bear?"

Murdock emptied the chamber pot in the toilet downstairs, then bent to the little window, his breath coloring a haze in the glass: the strait was thick and silent with fog. What the water was doing he couldn't tell, dark gray, razored with currents.

There'd been just the two of them, really, Rosaire and him, and then the rest of the world. That was so clear this morning, his chest hurt. They had done their daily living in different houses, apart, so they saved the best for each other. How many a man could say that, how many a woman?

Most of the time he had never minded his own company. He'd been led to believe, from way back, that that was a failing, and maybe it was. But his mother's betrayal put marriage out of his mind forever, he didn't need it, she had walked away from him and his father, leaving behind a bitter taste he could not swallow. It hadn't mattered, anyway, for a long time until he met Rosaire Robertson at a dance. Great company right off. Hard to explain that, what went into it. Hers was . . . well, he had liked to be with her, in all situations. He'd never known that feeling.

He thought he knew sorrow before sorrow hit, but he hadn't.

He filled Cloud's bowl with chopped up chicken he hadn't finished and then lay down again in the mussed bedclothes. The Black Rock lighthouse bleated, familiar as a heartbeat. One good day, and then he'd start to unravel again, as if there were a loose thread in him some-where that wanted tugging. He was tired of his own tics and quirks, the repetition of them, saying, this is you and you and you, and you'll never change a hair of it.

The woman down the shore, living there like she was, in Granny's house, he'd spent many days there after his mother went away. Every detail of that bedroom, the old bed was still there, she'd have to be using it. Big, creaking, metal bed. God damn it. What if that woman had knocked on his door? The sight of him would have sent her run-ning, unless, worse, he'd not answered at all, just hid deeper. Some awful hospitality, that. Why was he so plagued by that particular morning? She might have been drawing flowers, something in her head, for all he knew.

A mad flower, a small monster. He'd read about it in Sydney, the doctor hadn't the time or patience to go into it much, after all he was not her husband, not kin, but a nice woman in the library had told him where to look. Rosaire at first had wanted to know what scary thing was happening inside her head, but quickly turned away. What's the point, she said, of knowing that? But Murdock was determined to understand this sinister activity unfolding inside her. Nightmare stuff, blossoming vivid in the brain, blood-nourished, aggressive, piti-less, you could stagger it for a while but you couldn't knock it out, the radiation only winged it, slowed it down, gave her a few weeks more of living the way she had, flat out, good food and drink and to hell with you. And then the chemicals killed all that, her joy turned to a foul taste and nausea she couldn't describe. I'm sick as a dog, worse than seasick, she said, this isn't the boat, Murdock, I want to sail out on. She started to walk badly, with an exaggerated grace at first, like the early drifting stage of drunkenness, later self-consciously, an unsteady actress entering a room. Then one day she fell, just walking along a sidewalk she went face-first to the pavement before he could catch her, bloodied her nose, her cheek, her knees. She cried not then but later, seated on the edge of her bed. It was terrible, Murdock, the humiliation, she said. She was soon in a wheelchair, and he pushed her wherever she needed to go, wanted to go, he would come there to her house, be there, any time of day, he'd have pushed her up the mountain had she asked. He saw the chemo twist her face. She didn't smile much anymore then, her eyes took on the faraway look of treated pain, she was slipping into a place he couldn't come to. She did smile sometimes, quick and warm to remind him the way she used to kid about people, Jesus, Murdock, isn't this too sad by half? Seizures came at random. Her speech went, in patches at first, then just slurring and then the word sounds stopped coming and that embarrassed her, murmuring like an infant, she went mute, only when her feelings welled out of her would she make a sound. . . .

Murdock got out of bed again and pulled on his grubby jeans and a tattered black sweater. Lint. Cat hair. He had to pick himself up. Months of mourning had turned him limp and huddled, and the house he'd let slide, its slovenliness troubled him. Bones and joints still worked, when he got moving. Someday a stumble he would have once caught would carry him to the ground. Hills would steepen, he wouldn't see the hanging branch, the flooded rut, the glib ice.

You had to look into the mirror now and then, see what was rough there. If you had a woman who cared.

He had been difficult at times, he knew that, but he had toned that down after he met her. You're a born bachelor, Granny had told him before she died, you won't want a woman around much. But Rosaire, married once for a short time when very young, liked her own life the way it was, her own place, and so she and Murdock loved somewhere in between. They'd had their quarrels. But he never liked to be angry with her, and they had their own houses to retreat to and cool off in, and they'd come to miss each other quick enough.

Murdock shaved carefully. His ruddy face was florid from weather and wind and, lately, liquor. His hair was gray, but at the temples still a trace of his nickname, and in the grizzled hair of his chest.

He would never let himself be an old man shuffling along the street or playing bingo in the mall, they seemed like aliens sometimes, those fellas. Their limbs were shot of course, God love them, he understood that, the toll of factory and pit, all those wracking years break you down, cripple you. But the first sign he couldn't get through a day by himself, he would disappear like a sick animal, up into the mountain woods where even his bones would be lost.

Wasn't quick better, the sudden unexpected collapse? Too long in decline and people forgot you'd once been an able man, a man to lean on, to pull you up, to be awake for you when you couldn't but sleep.

AT THE FOOT of the ladder steps to his low cellar, cracks of light showed back under the sills and the smell of cold, dug-out earth was strong. He groped for a string cord. A bulb dangling over a crock lit up. The crock sat on a long flat stone like those of the foundation. Willard and all that talk about rum-running and drug-running, as if they had any damn thing in common. Murdock lifted the lid an inch: ouch, last year's pungent mash. He hadn't cooked any liquor since she died, his own good silver, there was no pleasure in it, he drank bought whisky instead. Since he didn't care for hunting, for killing animals, he had bartered a few bottles here and there for a share of venison, a portion of moose, a few partridge or rabbits, a poached salmon.

But here was a bottle he'd forgotten, he held it up to the light bulb: clear in the steam of his breath. I'm surprised, you know, Rosaire had said after the first taste, how smooth it is, and you *made* it. When she was ill and in bed, she'd asked for a shot in her water glass. It set her coughing, tearing up, but she said, Thank you, Murdock, a taste I'll surely remember.

Back upstairs, he set about restoring the neat, clean rooms that had been his way until she died—the home not of a hopeless bachelor but a man who looked after himself. I don't need a woman for my *house,* he'd told Rosaire, holding her in his arms. I just need you for *myself.* Well, dear, she said, I don't every morning need a man in my house either, so maybe we can have fun in the middle somewhere, eh? And there were her ashes in a small canister on his chest of drawers. He had yet to make a beautiful box for them. That had seemed too final, a formal storing away.

Fog hung well up the back field, frozen, the air blank as paper. The walls of his house seemed so thin to him. You could crouch in corners, but it was no cover, something you didn't want would always reach you.

Could anyone describe the kind of absence he felt? It hollowed him out, a cavernous space, every day he teetered on its edge.

The sun, oh, Murdock, it's so low these afternoons, Rosaire said that December, her head turned on the pillow toward the window's brassy light. I won't see it high again, will I?

Why couldn't Rosaire have died on a summer day instead of a night of blowing snow? He had to leave her on a night like that, she loved warmth and light, he drove slowly toward home on the slick highway, flakes floating like crude ash in his headlights. Before he reached the bridge, he pulled into a restaurant where they'd often stopped together for its view of the fjord-like strait and the long mountain running in from the sea. It was deserted and he sat with coffee by a big window, looking out, the dark water obscured, snow whirling like his mind, memories rushing past him, he could not slow them down, they dizzied him until he left suddenly and sped out of the lot. He wondered now which weakening part of his brain made him drive down the wrong lane of the road that night. He sometimes ran it through his mind, what it was like to see headlights coming at him, cursing at first because he thought *they* were at fault, maybe drunk, then glancing to his right where the double line streaked past, disturbingly yellow in the dark, it was all wrong suddenly, there, on his right, and he had to force himself nonetheless to cross it, to sheer into that other lane just before the oncoming car blared past in terror and outrage. He'd picked up speed then, raced, shaking, across the bridge toward home not because he was afraid the fellow might come after him but because he'd call him an old fool whose license should be yanked. He had been proud, until that night, that he could drive anything with wheels. Now, another reason for vigilance lest he die—and worse, take others with him—sooner than he needed to. Did he have a death wish that night?

Did he turn to memories too quickly, did he suck the life out of them?

He wept, it flooded into him, all his anger and sorrow and pity, he couldn't hold it back, alone in his kitchen, his face clasped hard in his hands. When it was over, he sat numb, exhausted but calm, glad for it, that it happened here, in this peaceful room. No one to witness it but Cloud. The cat sat in the chair by the stove, observing him intently, pupils big and black in his owl-yellow eyes. "That's done with, kitty," Murdock said, "you won't see me like that again."

VII.

LATE IN THE night Anna got up, squatted half asleep on the cold toilet, a pale nightlight at her feet, shivering, thinking only, God get me back beneath those quilts quick. But a single, isolated sound crept into her hearing. Howling? Distant, pitched not with menace or alarm but with pain, the slowly waking side of her said, and a coyote wouldn't bark like that, would it, give away its peril? Holding her breath, she allowed the possibility—knowing at the same instant its absurdity—that it was the dog from the bridge, somehow it had survived.

Chilled and frightened, she dressed quickly, pulled on her parka, a red knit hat and heavy boots, stepped out the back door. The night was so still, the wind she'd fallen asleep listening to had spent itself, the cold sharp in her throat. She had not intended to investigate any further than the back steps, but the howling did not waver and it pained her to listen to it. The way it rose to a wail, stopped, then resumed drew her slowly down the steps. It seemed to be coming from the pond as Anna walked into the darkness, every crunching step telling her to go back for a flashlight, but the sound pulled her forward. She found her way along, picking out the familiar path of tramped snow. The dog, a dark form out on the pond ice, did not move but it must have seen her, heard her, because it began a slow, mournful yowl. Anna stopped at the edge, she could feel with her foot where the ice, having thawed a bit and refrozen, was lumpy and rough, beyond it a flat white surface. She started to talk, to herself at first, coaching her way along, then to the dog, urging it soothingly to come, Come here, don't be afraid. She whistled, she made kissing sounds, but after lurching toward her in a rattle of chain, the animal took up again its pitiful call. Of course! Caught in a trap, poor thing, out there in the middle of the ice.

She swore at the man who'd set it. For what, the fox, the coyote, the mink, animals she'd seen and drawn, here, on someone else's land, *her* land for now? She had to stop its suffering, this stupid cruelty. Would the dog see her as the cause of its agony, go for her hand? Why in hell didn't she bring a flashlight. She moved closer, sliding her feet while scarcely aware of them. Of course it wasn't the dog from the bridge, it was bigger, darker, and she knew nothing about traps, could she open the jaws? Okay, it's okay, we'll get you loose, she cooed, barely feeling the ice shiver beneath her.

A trapped smell of pond water hit her nostrils as the ice parted, a clean cracking, a zigzag sound like muted lightning, and the cold iron smell rose as her body dropped, her clothes screening for a moment the shock of water, a convulsion of cold quick to her body, into her fear of depth—Willard told her this pond was crazy deep—her scream brief, more surprise than pain, as her weight took her under, though not far, a deep childhood fear of drowning, from being swept off a winter beach by a rogue Pacific wave, stunned her. Her feet soon pushed into mud, her momentum sinking her into a crouch, silt clouding upward, toward faint light in the ice above, in the broken bobbing pieces, and she uncoiled herself upward, thrashing through the surface, her mouth wide and gasping, her wail in the brittle air weaving wildly into the dog's yowl. Anna flailed, treading water, but her limbs were already stiffening, leaden, ice broke again and again under her clawing hands, she seemed to have no breath. Regrets charged absurdly through her, stunningly irrational, why did I come, why am I not home, there's no ice there, reasons not to die after all, the simple gorgeousness of sun, warmth, of love, of safety. She would remember that it was not searing cold that killed her hope but the slow-motion weight of her body, dense, turning as slow as the primeval pond itself, and not far away the dog's confused barking, the rattle of its trap. But then a beam of light swept the ice and someone clutched her under the arms and she was pulled backwards until her heels dragged bottom and she was set down on the snow. "You took a ducking, girl," he said, his face craggy behind the flashlight. "Let's get you walking quick. I'm your neighbor." He helped her to her feet and held her steady. Her scalp, her hair felt coldly electric as he guided her back up the hill. Her voice came out wobbly and sobbing. "That dog," she said, "he's caught out there."

"I'll free him later from the other side," Red Murdock said. "Ice always bad there, where you went in."

She was shaking too much to talk when they reached her kitchen and she let him sit her on the daybed he called a lounge while he turned the fire up in the oil stove and stoked the *Warm Morning.*

"Can you get out of those clothes?" he said, helping her off with her parka. Her red flannel pajamas were plastered to her skin, her jeans thick with water. "Dry off good and come back to the stove, you don't want a chill now. Put a couple blankets around you."

She fumbled with the laces of her leather boot but her fingers moved like claws.

"Here, let me." He knelt and loosened her boots, tugged them off, shook water from them.

In the cramped bathroom, a former pantry, shedding her sodden clothing was difficult, more like molting she shook so, maybe she should have let him undress her as well. She buried her head in one towel and then another until her hair was merely damp. The old metal smell of pond water rose from the towels she'd tossed into the tub. Her jaw ached from hard shivering but she rubbed and rubbed her body until her limbs, reddened from the towels, calmed. She looked disheveled in the mirror, under the bare light bulb wild, like a madwoman in those nineteenth-century photos from insane asylums. Face flushed, lips pale, eyes glittering. Her cheek was scratched and she remembered Murdock touching it.

On the back of the toilet sat a green kitbag with makeup she hadn't touched for a long while. It could hardly matter now, and the man in the next room was what, maybe fifteen years or so older than she was? But she brushed her hair viciously anyway, put on her heavy robe that hung on the door and the fleece-lined slippers she'd kicked off earlier. She turbaned her hair in the last dry towel and when her shivering subsided to an occasional tremor, she opened the door, self-conscious but too eager for the heat of the kitchen to care that a man she hardly knew was looking at her.

"Here," Red Murdock said, holding up an open wool blanket and wrapping it around her shoulders. He followed it with a patterned quilt and urged her to sit in the rocker he'd pulled up near the stove.

"A lovely old quilt," Anna said, trembling in the cocoon.

"Granny made it. Kept me warm lots of times, when I was a boy." He took in the room as if he hadn't seen it in a long while. "I lived with her for spells. Just me and my dad over there." He nodded in the direction of his house. "Granny was more like a mother."

He'd brewed a pot of strong tea and he took a metal flask from his hip and poured a shot into a mug—"Whisky," he said, glancing at her—before filling it. She gripped the mug's heat tightly in her hands. There was an enamel dishpan on the floor and the big aluminum kettle on top of the oil stove, and he told her it would be good to soak her feet in Epsom, feet warm the whole body toe to top, he said, but Anna said maybe she'd do that later, she had no Epsom, she didn't want to move anything right now, not a toe or a finger.

"Ah," Murdock said, "let's get the blood going anyway." With that he knelt, slid her slipper off and took her foot in his large hands. He began to knead its tendon and muscle, his hands were surely warm from the stove but in the numbness of her foot she could only feel the pressure of his fingers, soothing out tightness, bringing heat slowly to bear. She watched him, bent into this act of massaging, solemn, absorbed, a man who'd been shy and curt at the mailbox that afternoon she'd met him. His steel-gray hair, still thick and tight to his head, had a blush of auburn through it, his eyes deep-set in high, wide cheekbones, their color not obvious at a glance, but they were hazel, flecked with green. And here he was kneading out a stubborn core of ice. She sipped the tea. Her throat felt sore, she'd gagged on pond water, that she remembered, and how the ice opened up sickeningly like a trap door, like an awful trick she'd fallen for, the cold so sudden, like a hard slap.

"There you go," he said, after he'd massaged her other foot and set it gently down.

"Thank you, Mr. MacLennan," she said.

"Murdock will do. I heard the dog, you see. I was coming over."

Steam hissed soft as breath from the kettle spout. Then she heard the dog, more faintly than before, a thin, hopeless yowl and then silence.

"Can you save it? But, oh, it's so late . . ." she said. "And you're cold and wet yourself."

"Have to be sure you're up and running. We don't want a fever. You had two bad choices there, girl, drown or freeze." She didn't see it as any kind of choice, but Murdock was smiling just that much, a flicker in his eyes. Did he say it for a reaction, testing? She didn't understand the setting of his life, not enough, if she ever could, to gauge him: the weeks she'd spent here, the old photos she'd pored over, had given her some feeling about this house, about how they might've lived in it, but tonight told her only a little of that mystery, their calamities and pleasures, the nuances of their life, the words they said to each other, what they expected in response. When Anna stood at the stove it was not to cook a meal as they'd done, the women of his granny's house, Anna's atmosphere was nothing like theirs. What had they thought good and right and appropriate, here, amid family, the sounds and smells? Of this Anna had but a glimmer.

Yet she had drawn, in meticulous, intense detail, objects she had found here, as if the act of re-creating them on paper would reveal them, bring to life a day they'd been put to use, and possibly the user— a small tin grater (for lemon peel, making a pie, a cake?), three thimbles of different sizes, needles and a cloud of tangled threads brown and white (darning socks by oil lamp?), a bottle embossed with a floral design (perfume? medicinal spirits?), a spindled device maybe for peeling apples.

"Do you mind if I light a pipe?" he said. "I'm off cigarettes."

She said no, please, and he put a kitchen match to an old briar bowl, scorched and burnished. She watched him squinting, pulling smoke. Chet had used a pipe for a long time, extracting it from his breast pocket, playing with it, lighting up, gazing thoughtfully through smoke. But he never liked it really, the fussing and tamping and probing with pipe cleaners and the bitter juice on his tongue, the pipe was a prop, part of his dress, like the thick-waled corduroy jackets with elbow leather, and the bulky turtleneck from Ireland he wore next to his bare skin despite its prickly clamminess and woolly smell of sweat. Marijuana came along and he quit tobacco, a small wooden pipe appeared, an implement of transition, shared with others, passing it totemically, after a solemn hit, from one hand to another.

"Do you know the dog out there?" Anna said. "I can't hear it now. I don't want it to die."

"Cottage people leave dogs and cats behind sometimes. Terrible, do that to a dog. I'll get it out when I leave. It's not Willard's dog, his was little."

"Summer. My God, how I'd love to feel it," she said, more to herself than him.

"You'll have a wait yet. Keep your stove wood handy."

He told her they'd be well into April before they got much green, and some years there'd been snow in May, heavy. If you had drift ice, it could linger quite late, way out at sea, so far off it was invisible, but that east wind blowing through it?

"Did you come for summer?" he said. "Killing frosts in June."

"Not just that. But I'll welcome it."

She wanted to be as honest as he seemed to be, to tell him, sometimes I'm not exactly *sure* what I came for, I'm sorting out certain things, but she did come to draw, to turn her work in a new direction, and maybe herself as well. And what would he think about that? She'd already set foot on ice where no one here would have stepped. She rocked the chair gently, it seemed to help, urging warmth into her, and but for Murdock MacLennan, she might be resting on the bottom of a pond. Could she have thrashed her way back to the shallows, found footing, groped her way out of that shattered ice? In her terrible panic, unlikely, she'd been wrenched out of the world. Those moments shuddered through her like a nightmare.

"You're soaked through," she said, "I'm sorry," embarrassed she hadn't noticed his jeans dark with wet, and his workboots, the small puddle at his feet.

"Och, I'm drying, I've been wetter than this in winter. You're looking worn out. A great shock to the body, this, is it not?"

"I only thought about seeing to the dog, not the ice." She smiled. "I *am* lighter than I used to be."

"We had fun on that ice. Skating parties, young and old. A man'd come up to a woman and ask her to skate, like at a dance. A strong fella would lead the whip, we called it, we'd link hands in a line and he'd start us twirling faster and faster until the last one had to let go, fly off. Oh, we chased around, us kids, played hockey with a stone for a puck. Nights like this, hard as glass. A fire on the bank, glowing up to the branches overhead, and the snow red up there and around us."

"I wanted to skate when I was little," she said. "My dad was from Ohio and he would tell me how he missed it, the old pond. We didn't have ice, we lived in California, up north. I went to a college in Ohio, Dad's alma mater, but I guess I was too busy then for skating. I don't think I'll try it now. Not anymore."

"You mustn't fear the pond," he said, "or the ice. I'll show you how to read it. Now I was about to say I will lend you skates, I have a pair, but I really don't, mine are scuffed as an old harness and those feet of yours would swim in them."

Anna's eyes closed, she couldn't stop them. "Sorry," she said.

"Look," he said, "I've got the stove going good, why don't you sleep on the lounge there? I'll fetch more blankets. Warmer here than up there." He pointed to the ceiling.

"I'll vouch for that." Her face felt hot now, her head swimmy, she wanted to lie down, but she'd wait until he left. She didn't want to be tucked in, like a sick child. She heard him upstairs finding blankets, then he was spreading them over the daybed.

"Now," he said, "I've done like my granny did, I found a few splits of hardwood, I put them in the oven and roasted them good and hot. Took a blanket, and rolled them up, put them in the bed there. Keep your feet warm a good while."

"Sounds wonderful."

Red Murdock pulled on his worn peacoat, working its big buttons up. "Greatest wool there is," he said, patting his chest. "Even when it's wet, it's warm. Now, then. I stowed my number on your phone pad there. Call me if you feel worse."

"Murdock, you sound like a doctor."

"Well, I'm the nearest thing you've got to one. Watch you don't take sick, that's the thing. A long drive to the hospital. Damn phones sometimes go out, but . . . anyway. You're okay enough then . . . ?"

She was remembering a story of D. H. Lawrence's where a despairing young woman tried to drown herself in a coal mine pond, the currents of feeling that passed between the woman and the young doctor who pulled her from the dark water and revived her, the almost mystical bond that arose between them, and Anna for a moment wanted to amuse herself by blurting, like the woman had when she woke and saw that the doctor had undressed her and wrapped her nakedness in a blanket, "Do you love me then?" It cheered Anna to think of that, but the joke would be lost on him, flippant and pointless. She'd felt a little giddy, that's all.

But how could she have guessed this man would work in his hands her naked feet?

"I'll be fine," she said. "Thank you."

"Have you met Breagh, the young red woman up the road? I'll ask her to look in on you in the morning."

"Please, no. Don't bother her. So foolish of me, blundering out on that ice."

"How could you know? Who put that damn trap there I can't say. It's legal, you see. They have a right to set traps around water, they don't need permission. Nobody here trapping now. Some fellas must've come by boat, they come ashore. But *that* trap, I'll rip it out. I'm sorry, miss, I forgot your name. . . ."

"Anna. Anna Starling. The dog. Don't forget the dog."

"We'll get him, Anna. Good night then. Give me a shout if . . ."

Would she be fine? She didn't know. He'd laid out on the daybed neatly the quilt and blanket. Oh, hell, it was somehow worse that he'd tended to her this way and then left, her loneliness was sharp and child-like for a few minutes, indulgent, she felt weak with it. But of course the man *had* to leave, in every respect he had to go home, get a hold of yourself, you're a little delirious, Anna. She drank quickly the dark tea, delicious. It swam warmly into her, her head drooped. She listened to her breathing slow. *She is on ice. Snowflakes whirl like reflections from a mirror ball as she spins, in a maelstrom white against a dark sky, skates on her feet, she can feel the laces tight, hear the blades carving arcs in the ice, it is like dancing, flakes melt coolly on her eyelids, she has no partner, she just flows in a kind of wild joy, heightened by fear, pulled this way, that way, a faint wind around her, and through the swirling snow a dim, ambiguous figure watches, she knows it is watching her, she is pleased and troubled by its attention, by the mad grace of her motion, of her spread wings, trapped as she is. The ice flexes like a thin, pulsating floor as she nears something black, a fiery mouth, yawning, hugely out of proportion to its head, this is a dream, she says aloud, but that gives her no comfort. In the dark around her, she senses men, her whirling body stops, solid and still as ice. There is the frantic dog tearing at its chains, why can't she skate away like she wants to, as she once did as a girl, when all she had to do was turn and . . . Murdock leans over her bed in a strange kitchen, she is abashed by her fever, it seems quaint, his hand is warm on her face, slides inside her robe to her breast, she can feel its heat, its touch, she takes a deep breath. Pneumonia's the thing, the old danger, he says gravely, his voice a soft brogue, like a boat being rowed slowly, and he tucks her tighter under blankets of worn and heavy wool, I should take you to the hospital but the road is terrible iced, ah, you're looking better now, I'll carry you to your house, warm as toast there, and she says, No, I want to stay here, my rooms are cold, can't you see my breath . . . ?*

Was it possible to feel more alone than she did now, at this waking? The ceiling light burned. She did not hear the dog. Oh, God, she had to get out of this robe damp with sweat, she forced herself, weeping and shivering, to climb the stairs to the bedroom and find the long flannel underwear in the chest of drawers she could never get the camphor out of, it frightened her now, that smell of illness. But the flannel felt good and she lay down, swathed in bedcovers, the night running in tremors through her body. That patch of open water she'd left behind would be skimming over ever so thinly now, a thickening skin of ice. New snow would conceal it, curious birds would pepper it with tracks, and she, some morning soon, would take her pen and ink to them, and, in her imagination, the dog she hoped was gone.

VIII.

H E WISHED HE could forget about the dog, damn it, he was
chilled to trembling now, wet from the chest down, a wind
was whisking snow into his face. But he'd told her he would go back,
and the dog, poor creature, wouldn't survive the night anyway, coyotes could menace it to death. He pulled his watch cap down tight and
retraced their steps, then veered off to go round the pond to the north
side where the ice would hold him. The dog whimpered, hearing him,
seeing the light. Murdock, shaking and out of breath, kneeled at the
trap, the flashlight throwing the dog's writhing shadow across the ice.
Black Lab mix. He murmured to it as he worked and calmed it, the
animal growled but let him pry the jaws apart. It hopped free, limped
off a ways and set to licking its hind leg, the raw cut Murdock caught
a glimpse of, and though he tried to coax it home with him, the dog
gimped slowly off toward the woods and was gone beyond the flashlight though he could still hear its panting. Had enough of men, have
you, pup, their goddamn steel contraptions?

The flashlight shone in the ragged break where Anna had fractured
the ice, where he'd plowed after her. Maybe he should have stayed with
her longer, sat at the table, watched her in case she took a turn. God
knew he'd done plenty of that with Rosaire, watching over her, but if
he didn't get home he'd be sick himself. He yanked the trap free of the
ice and sank it in the black patch of open water, remembering the night

his father's horse went through, that great neighing animal, and Dad raging in Gaelic in the dark, the thrashing, the splitting ice, and his father without a word tossed a manila noose around that mare's neck, choked her so she reared up like a sea beast and got herself out of that ice and water like it was fire, whipped white by her hooves. Sometimes panic worked, sometimes it didn't. The horse was desperate to live, that was the heart of it, she took wing. . . .

By the time Murdock reached his own kitchen, he was stiff and muttering, he'd have to see to his own self now, God, moving like an old cripple. He stripped with clumsy hands, rubbed himself down with a rough towel until his pale skin was ruddy. He stood naked at the stove he'd stoked before he left, his cock shriveled with cold. Rosaire would have joked about it, but Jesus, right now it just looked sad.

He finished the coffee that had simmered since he left, his clothes steaming on a rope line above the stove. He wouldn't sleep, he felt strangely depleted, wrung out—as if nothing mattered enough, not even saving that woman's life. Get a grip, boy.

Cloud watched him benignly from a cushioned chair, slit-eye dozing, still figuring him out, Rosaire he was not, he did not lift a cat into his arms and nuzzle him, Murdock's turbulent pillow was not a welcome place for a calm animal, where her fragrant hair once spread.

That Anna. She might have died from shock, if not a drowning. The poor dog saved her, really.

Naked. With Rosaire. Oh, my.

He rocked on his heels, rubbed his hands above the stove. The old anger crept into him, how casual she'd been about her health, and he blamed that sometimes, her stubbornness about doctors and medical advice. Jesus, she'd eaten and drunk whatever she fancied and never saw a doctor, not even after the headaches began, and then she col-lapsed in a seizure coming out of a movie in Sydney. Whatever gave her pleasure, she reached for easily, and guilt only seasoned her appetites. Heed what you eat, girl, he'd tell her. Yet she always looked great, that was the trouble. Oh, I can dance all night, can't I? Do I *look* fat? There were mornings with her when, work waiting for him in his shop, he'd jump out of bed, I have to sweat a little now, he'd tell her, and she'd say, sweat with me, darlin', it's good for the two of us.

Who the hell knew the cause of that cancer anyway, what evil speck of something had wormed into her brain?

This need for blame, it came with grief, it dulled the pain, sometimes.

Such a weight it seemed now to dress himself and go on, to wait for first light, boil oatmeal, brew coffee. Wait. For what?

IN DRY CLOTHING, Murdock stood at the long-locked door of the forge shed. His breath smoking in the flashlight beam, he worked a key into the thick stiff padlock. He cracked it open with his fist, then hauled the door aside, forcing a neat quarter-circle in the snow. He inhaled the dark interior: rust, bare iron, its bits and lengths, the car-bon of dead coals. The dry wood of the water barrel, the little brine tub, salt-stained, it had received red iron in crisp hisses, in plumes of steam.

Not a big man, his dad, but he had arms long for his height, they'd seemed to direct his life, in motion even when he talked, like they needed to seize hold of something even at rest. He could quell that at the anvil, hammering out barn hinges, a wagon brace, shoeing a horse. And women. Until he married Red Peggy, Peggy *Ruagh,* he'd taken women tight into those arms, he told Murdock one night when he was drinking, I never made one stay that didn't want to stay, they liked me or they didn't. He stared at his arms held out in front of him like they belonged to someone else. Then he placed a large hand on Murdock's shoulder. Not strong enough to keep your mother though, were they? he said.

His dad had quit it all suddenly, not many months after the bridge went up and the ferry closed down. Shook off his leather apron one afternoon, his face flushed and sweating, closed the door, let the fire go to ashes. Little need for a forge anymore, not here, he said, it's passed us by, I'm tired, the horses are going away for dogfeed, minkfeed, for Christ's sake. Follow your carpentry, Murdock, this is no good to you now.

But he had to do it again, he didn't know why. He would have to work at it to make it come back, and whatever he fashioned had to be good, nothing crude or ill-made.

Murdock hefted a ball-peen hammer. *Òrd.* With the flashlight beam he picked out the anvil, *innean gobha,* blackened and scarred. Remember these at least, his dad had said, our old words for things. Only a few could Murdock call up. *Balg-séididh,* the bellows hanging near the *teallach,* the forge, an old backup for the blower. A dozen kinds of tongs, *teanchair,* nippers, nail moulds, the duck's nest. Punches, there was a heart-shaped one somewhere, he'd have to find it for Rosaire's box. Hammers of various heads, the flatter, the set hammers, the swage blocks and the drifts, the nail-maker's stake anvil, reamers, clippers, shears. Buffers, rasps, hoof parers, fullers. Some were missing, people had tried to talk him out of the tools over the years, and they'd made off with a few before he padlocked it, they were worth money now, that's how it worked. A man from the States had offered him a thousand dollars for the whole works, he wanted to move the shed, the forge, all of it to his summer property, It'll be like a museum, Red Murdock, he'd said. But no, it would stay where it was, as it was, and he didn't want anyone poking around anymore, pricing things in their heads. Leave it in the dark. His father had been here, *bam-bim-bim,* in the small focused roar of fire, bent to the work, fire to anvil to water, iron took shape out of the machinery of his own body, his muscle and brain. . . .

How Rosaire slipped when her time came, oh, Jesus, it was not right. Her hair and her looks, and whenever he came to the hospital in those days he lugged the stone of his sadness with him. To see Rosaire looking beautiful, a joy, always. But the drugs had puffed the features from her face, the face she would die with, rounded and soft like a baby's, a pale mask of illness, of death, not the face he had loved, its moods and glances, its fire. And it disgusted him that he could not feel quite the same way about her as she lay in her last days, her looks so different, he hated himself—*she's not beautiful like she was*—it was selfish, terrible, by any lights it was awful of him to hold such a thought. And so he'd spent every minute possible with her, he had to assure her that she mattered to him desperately, and that was as true as the sun, his love for her, yes, yes. Still, there was that sharp sadness that he could not *have* her beauty anymore, could not daydream about it, wake to it, touch it, take it into his arms, take it, yes, for granted: that face of sickness he saw then would stay with him too, not just the face that had excited him for so long. He grieved over that loss, even as he grieved at her bedside, at her and her leaving, leaving it all.

Back in the kitchen Murdock pokered the stove to life, then sat at the table and drank. He watched the light across the water slide from black to inky blue along the hills of St. Aubin. A lone window lit up near the shore: someone awake for work. Not a Bonner, they had the place at one time, he didn't know who had it now. He needed to *finish* something, complete it. His woodshop sat dark and cold, every piece of work, on the bench or hanging, just as he'd left it the day she died.

The liquor at least he had cooked himself, the last bottle of his last batch. Sweet as good water, hot in the gut. He'd get back to working with wood, soon. Wouldn't he? Livingstone Campbell had pestered him again on the phone, only God knew what he needed with a big desk like that.

This was what Anna Starling needed, a warm swig of this, she'd sleep. Maybe she was sleeping anyway, dreaming of dogs, the stun of water under ice.

IX.

"ANNA?" BREAGH WAS bending over her, smiling, eyebrows high. "Red Murdock asked me to look in on you. So here I am, looking."

Her bright green eyes tempered Anna's irritation, she didn't like this kind of surprise, still shaking off cobwebs, her own face battered by a feverish sleep she'd like to return to. The glaring kitchen windows said full morning, and an unpleasant guilt crept into her, as though she'd been caught out at something or had overslept for work. She pushed her head deeper into the pillow. "I'm not much to look at," she mumbled into the down, funky with her own sweat.

"Well, you're awake anyway. That's a step, Anna. I've got tea going."

"Where's your little girl?"

"With Molly MacKay. They love each other."

At least the child wouldn't see her blowsy and half awake. "Did I leave the door unlocked?"

"The back was open. I got worried when you didn't answer the front." Breagh clapped mugs on the table. "Nobody here used to lock up, but now you don't know who might detour down this road. I'll cook you some breakfast. You're on the pale side."

"Tea's fine. Black. Murdock sent you over?"

"He told me what happened. What a night you had, girl. You feel all right?"

"I'm just tired. I need to clean up."

"What a blow to the body, eh? Still, you're lucky. If Murdock hadn't heard the dog . . ."

"If *I* hadn't heard it, I'd be up long ago and working."

"You and dogs. Can't ignore them though, can we? In distress."

She pulled a chair close to the daybed and Anna sat up on her elbows. "Breagh, there's a brush in the bathroom there . . . please?"

"Sure, dear."

Anna brushed out her tangled hair, then wrapped the quilts around her and sat up. She sipped the tea, wishing for the taste of rum in it. Crows were squabbling outside for the bread and stale cookies she had tossed out yesterday.

"This won't send you back home, will it?" Breagh said, seated with her tea.

That had tracked last night through Anna's wakings, a great excuse to pack up, give it up and go, she was half-sick, wasn't she, who knew what she'd be like in the morning? Yet here she was, sitting on the edge of the daybed, groggy but talking with this young woman from up the road. Did Breagh guess? The woman had a driving energy, you could tell, she'd move ahead regardless, she didn't spend time sifting her past, Anna was sure of that. "When I'm just getting used to things . . . like swimming in March?"

Breagh laughed. "You know what you need in that tea, dear? Some rum."

"Oh, do I. But how?"

"No spirits?"

"Brandy. A little bottle."

"We'll go for that then."

"I should get dressed. I feel worthless."

"Stay there, I'll fetch it."

The Courvoisier Melissa had slipped into her suitcase (You'll need it, honey, take it, it's winter there) Breagh poured generously into their tea and Anna had to admit after two swallows it was worth the lift. Their conversation warmed along with the kitchen. Anna asked about her family.

"I'm adopted," Breagh said quickly, as if to get it out of the way. "I grew up in North Sydney. We used to come out here now and again, summers like. Winter sometimes, if the road was broken. Visit Uncle Murdock. He was good to us, my stepsister and me. I don't know my dad, my mom gave me up and went west somewhere. Must be in the blood or something. Lorna's dad? Don't ask."

"I wouldn't anyway," Anna said.

"More my foolishness than his, really. He looked good, God, I'll say that for him. All flash handsome. Clothes on his back or clothes on the floor, he wouldn't hurt your eyes any. I wasn't after a baby, or a husband either. Blind passion, eh, Anna? It all goes cozy dark for a while and then you stumble out into the daylight and you think, wow, so *that's* what it's like. Happened to you, I suppose."

"Not exactly like that, but close. Hard to remember now."

"My little girl, she comes first. Any man who can't see that, I don't want him in the house."

"I wonder how much they do see sometimes."

"I didn't yearn for a kid, you know? Not like some, you'd think mothering was the grandest thing in the universe. And maybe it is, if you've got nothing else going. But after all, just about any woman can have a baby if she wants, can't she? It's not like some special talent or some kind of genius. Anyway, she's my darling."

"It's hard to want one and not be able," Anna said.

"That's you, is it?"

"I'm past all that."

"You're not that old, girl."

"Oh, but I am. I couldn't have a child in my life now. Not anymore."

"Because you're here, you mean, because you're not home?"

"It's complicated, Breagh."

"Your husband? Sure."

Anna did not want to get into Chet, it was enough to have him dropping in and out of her mind without the prospect of sharing their history with someone else, even Breagh, whom she liked and was inclined to trust. Any details of their troubles seemed only tiresome on this particular morning, and the less they knew around here about her private life, the better, it seemed an advantage she did not want to lose. But she could have told her that in a marriage watch out for things that stop: Chet stopped kissing her good morning, she couldn't remember now precisely when, it just happened, a small thing, really, forgivable if she hadn't known by then just why—there was another woman on his mind so early in the day. Then he stopped discussing with her books he was reading, as if he had talked them out somewhere else. He stopped showing her what he had written unless she asked, a manuscript would lie open on his desk as if for any passerby. He stopped wandering into her studio room to pause at her work and offer a critical frown or a smile or a comment. He stopped taking her to their favorite Indian restaurant once a week, once a month or two seemed enough, and when he did, he often gazed past her face, his conversation dutiful but straying. Then he stopped fitting her into anything that interested him, and his courtesy—he was always courteous—felt patronizing. Chet had always believed that confessing frankly to his sins, the very act of candidness, absolved him in some way, mitigated at least his deceit, but he stopped that too: Alicia was no ordinary lover, no rocket affair, and, after the spelunking chapter, what he did with her was not open for discussion. Anna of course had long ago ceased sharing with him anything intimate, any secrets of her own. She had always been discreet where he was careless, reticent where he was garrulous and self-dramatizing.

So Anna skated over her marital circumstances with a bland summary, almost blushing at the clichés she resorted to in order to close down the subject—they'd each needed "their own space," she and Chet, and felt that this time apart would be good for each other's creativity, his writing, her art.

"I could see that, I suppose," Breagh said with a skeptical smile. "I split from Gordie because he wanted to run my life. No thanks, buddy."

She insisted that Anna needed to eat and she set about making her an omelet. "As a girl I wasn't great for the kitchen," she said over her shoulder, cracking eggs into a bowl. "I learned to cook on my own. I was grown up by then, of course."

"Funny what growing up will get us into," Anna said. "You're a seamstress."

"Clothes designer, I like to think."

"Of course. You're an artist too."

Old Mrs. MacNeil up the hill, she was dead now, had bequeathed Breagh a portable Singer, a machine from the 1930s in perfect condition, all metal and smooth gears smelling lightly of oil, they didn't make them like that now, she said. With little more than the instruction book, she taught herself sewing, baby clothes for Lorna at first, then skirts and blouses for herself and just kept going until she could sew a man's shirt—I like to see a man looking good in something I made for him, why not?—and any dress she had a pattern for. Mistakes? Crooked seams and lopsided collars, cockeyed buttonholes and busted thread? Sure, you learn that way, she said. It all led to the little shop they were opening in May, recycling vintage clothing into original garments, one-of-a-kind, you wouldn't expect a bespoke dress way up in northern Cape Breton.

"Tourist season mainly," she said. "Sew all winter, like women used to here, right in this house they weaved and sewed all the cold months, I bet, on top of everything else. Won't be a grand living. Mostly women's and a few men's things. I'm working on a Byron type shirt, you know, the English poet? Full sleeves and that wide, open collar? It looks sort of Highlander too, you see. Tourists go for that Scotch stuff, hokum and all."

"If you put that on a man, he'd better be handsome," Anna said, "and a good lover, with at least a touch of poetry in him." She didn't want to admit that Chet had sported just such a piece of apparel at one time, or that she'd told him all he needed now was a club foot. That remark seemed bitter to her now, unnecessary, after the chilling hazards of the night before, in this morning light so full of the sea. Yet that's what their exchanges sometimes came to.

"We'll leave the poetry out, I think, Anna. I haven't seen much of that lately."

"It's usually the first to *go* out."

Breagh stayed until Anna had finished eating. "You'll survive the day, I think," she said, and gave her a quick hug. "I should pick up Lorna, get back, I have a new sewing machine and it goes like the devil. You'll be all right?"

"I'll show Lorna my drawings of animals next time she comes. Would she like that?"

"She loves to draw something fierce. She gets those crayons going, that girl."

"I can't thank you enough for coming. And Murdock for sending you. By the way, who is that man in the long black coat I see walking the road?"

"Connie? Walks all day, goes home and drinks. Next day, walks again. He was away in Boston for years. He's harmless, like."

"I wasn't afraid of him."

Anna missed her as soon as she was out the door. She washed and dressed, she'd save the hot bath, too early. She gathered up her damp clothing and hung it on a line she'd strung above the stove: flags of distress. She felt sore and listless, her body strained in odd ways, as if she'd run or swum too far. But she hadn't been idle. Constrained perhaps. Would she see summer and swim in the sheltered lee of the point, from that sandy beach? It asked too much of the imagination right now, sun in her limbs, warm sand, that saltwater smell.

She stood at the kitchen window, pulling herself slowly into the day, staring at the St. Aubin hills across the water, the snow-dusted woods that covered them, the blank fields near the shore. Tide and wind were at odds, the water a dark, dangerous gray where the channel narrowed past the point into a swift, translucent curve, spinning away into currents a fishing boat was rolling through. Fishing for what, now? She'd seen it once before, at dusk, but outbound. Too fancy a cabin maybe for a fisherman? She wasn't sure. Lobster season would open soon, the radio said. She could make out down on the pond the dark, jagged patch where she'd gone through the ice, a wound skinning over, clear of snow. No dog, no trap. Thank you, Murdock. One day, all this would melt. It would seem ages ago, it had that weight already, happening in the night, she might even have dreamed it but for the water's vivid burning, the ice hot now on her skin.

THE NEXT DAY, Anna was beset by a strange hollow ache she knew was not physical. Its cause she could not pinpoint, and she hoped not homesickness for the weakness that implied—the balm of the familiar. Late afternoon she got into her car and headed for town, she needed motion, outward, the day was overcast, the cold air teased with sparse flurries. When she reached the Trans-Canada, she accelerated as if set free, the highway was salted and clear and she drove fast down the winding grade and across the bridge, glancing east toward the sea and the low point behind which her house, from this perspective, was hidden. Although the traffic was thin, she liked the speed of it, the dirty salt-stained cars she passed, the buzz of studded tires, the feel of going somewhere.

She spotted the antique shop near the roadside, she'd noticed it before and assumed it was shut for the winter, but there was an old woman padlocking the door to the little white outbuilding, a big old verandaed house up the hill behind it. When Anna braked and pulled into the driveway, the woman stopped and regarded her and Anna asked if she was open. She said, well, she could be, clasping a thick woolen shawl to her throat, her white bun unraveling in wisps. Mrs. Urquhart her name was and she let Anna into the cold interior lit only by window light. Anna sidled carefully through its packed, dim interior that smelled, as her house often did, of damp wood and metal. Some of its objects she'd come across in her house—testaments to a country life once lived—and maybe gathered here from relatives or friends not sentimental about relics of daily toil. Mrs. Urquhart stood by the door and chatted about the weather and had nothing to say about her wares, maybe she thought they were merely obvious—a churn, a yarn winder, a wooden bread bowl, a pine table holding small items of crockery and utensils, a butter press, patent medicine bottles, two white tureens, old handsaws and hammers and porcelain doorknobs and a thick leather album of studio portraits, a family from the nineteenth century in their best black clothing, all of them, it seemed, a mix of handsome and homely, infants to the toothless old, a bit sad to leaf through, no one had cared about them since how long?

A large photograph was propped on an end table, its thick frame crackly with dark shellac. Behind the dusty glass was a studio portrait of a bewhiskered man in black frock coat and striped cravat, circa eighteen nineties, solemn and without a doubt of his importance. A small brass plate said *Herr Doktor Professor R. Schroeder,* his spectacles, small discs of reflected light, had surely drilled through many a student.

"That's from the mainland," Mrs. Urquhart murmured, "down Lunenburg, and that," pointing underneath the table where an unlidded chamber pot sat, its bottom displaying a fading image of President Wm. McKinley.

"I can think of Republicans who'd fit that even better," Anna said.

She asked about items she didn't recognize—an egg poacher, a blacksmith's tool—but back in the crowded dusk a table lamp caught her eye, its art-glass shade a mosaic of bright colors set here and there with translucent marbles that would surely glow when it was lit, like eyes of animals. She could see its colors beside her reading chair, lifting the winter gloom. Mrs. Urquhart, pondering the lamp as if it had just arrived mysteriously, said, "I think it's from down in Boston." A cousin, long dead, had brought it home. "We had it in the parlor for a spell, but it's a little noisy for me."

Anna said, "Well, it's a cheerful noise." She carried it away for forty dollars but wouldn't let Mrs. Urquhart, pleased with the sale and eager now for background information, learn much about her, she was tempted, just to put the transaction on another plane, to say, I fell in a pond the other night, through the ice. But she did not, she had left that down the winding road to Cape Seal, for now, and saying goodbye to Mrs. Urquhart in the shop that smelled like Anna's attic, clutching the lamp swathed in newspaper, it didn't seem to be true anyway.

She drove all the way to Sydney, where she hadn't been since she leased the car after her arrival, a small city on a big harbor, the only sizable metropolis in Cape Breton, old, but which owed its former prosperity to a steel mill now struggling to survive. In a supermarket's bland fluorescence she was for a while just another person fingering apples and packaged meat. Those around her had homes and families and were not troubled by visions of winter dogs or long spells of stone cold solitude, the only dangerous ice lay probably on their pavement. She did buy a box of chocolates for Breagh and for Lorna a furry white kitten from China. She ate in a licensed restaurant on Charlotte Street, once the main commercial part of town but now a bit threadbare, stores abandoned or on the edge, business having shifted largely to the malls, even the old theatre she'd hoped was open was shut down, for lease. The waitress told her that there was a Cineplex out by a mall, and, after two glasses of red wine, Anna went off to get lost in a movie, a pastime she had shared with Chet since they first met in college. For years they'd enjoyed nights out at an old art theatre back home, it showed classics and the earliest uncensored sex films, most of them mercifully forgettable, and certain rituals could be indulged there like fresh real popcorn, English chocolate, deep seats you could sink into—they revisited old favorites (they both admired British social realism like *Room at the Top* or *Saturday Night and Sunday Morning* or *The Loneliness of the Long Distance Runner,* and Kubrick's anti-war *Paths of Glory,* the dark French thriller *Diabolique,* the black-and-white seemed truer, more honest than color), they were together in pleasure and memory, in cinematic contexts that called up their own early affection, passions, concerns. But Anna ended up in a wide, shallow cinema with no more than a dozen others hunkered among the seats, blasted senseless by the sound system and hyperkinetic action on an enormous, in-your-face screen. She hadn't cared at first how bad the film was, its awfulness was a distraction from herself, an action thriller about a drug gang and their sociopathic boss, full of explosive violence and graphic wounds, she watched it in a daze, how distant and unreal it was from Cape Breton Island, light-years from Cape Seal, where some nights the quiet was so intense it woke her.

She emerged into an evening of wet snowfall, and driving home in the dark, the snow thickened in the further reaches of the Trans-Canada and she had to slow down more, sometimes the car skittered sideways a little, snow tires or not. She encountered few vehicles, and none as she crept tensely toward the bridge, following someone's tread marks, the water below invisible in the snowy air. The dog had been conveyed here, from here it was flung into nothingness. A tractor-trailer loomed and juddered past on the narrow roadway, forcing her to clutch the wheel. The nearer her turnoff, as she strained to make out the road sign, the heavier the dead-end journey grew—I'm going home and no one is there, or will be.

The house seemed desolate as the headlights glared in its dark windows. She stumbled inside, tired, shivering, and set to rousing the slumbering stove. The heat revived her, the crackling, snapping wood, and she remembered the lamp in the trunk. She carried it through falling snow and set it next to the squat armchair she read in. Her mother had never liked old things, Antiques, she said, are for museums, not my house. Anna's taste for them had come from her father, Give me something from way back, he would say, give me a little history at least. She remembered him fondly in his little studio redolent of pot smoke, his chair swiveled toward the big window looking out at misted redwoods, the tall, glistening ferns, his eyes shut as he leaned back into the sounds of an LP from his early days as a man, maybe some Brubeck, Gerry Mulligan, Artie Shaw. What's that burny smell, Dad? Anna had said the first time she walked in on him. He'd answered, That's exhaust from my time machine, sweetheart.

Once lit, the lamp was as she'd hoped, almost ridiculously cheerful, the room blessed with soothing colors, an artful mosaic, from another place.

She would take a long walk tomorrow morning, early, a long way down the shore, beyond Red Murdock's, and then, carrying whatever she found, she would get back to work.

X.

WHEN ANNA FELT strong and steady again, she called Red
Murdock to thank him, tell him she was okay, warm and
normal, as she put it. But he sounded stiff on the phone, distant, as if he
hadn't expected a call or didn't welcome one, not at all as he'd been in
her kitchen that night. Puzzled, a bit hurt, she skipped the ritual about
weather, thanked him for sending Breagh, and wished him a good day,
thinking in the same breath, how California. She wanted to invite him
for a meal, but maybe even rescuing a woman from a frozen pond had
not closed the space between them, now the crisis had cooled.

Anna was released into her work nevertheless, eager for it, she
sorted and refined her sketches, leafed through the animal drawings
she might send to Melissa, a series she could extend if other creatures
came her way. There were tracks of animals she never glimpsed, they
came at night circling the food, trailing away toward the pond or the
woods. She remembered the fox inspecting a plate of stew she'd tossed
out because she had no appetite that day, depressed as she was, sitting
in the kitchen where a single white plate on the table seemed to shout
her loneliness (why was supper, of all meals, so hard on some days to
get through?). *Fox and Meal* she titled it, this animal that had swept
away her self-pity, caught in swift strokes of charcoal, then tones of
its deep red coat so brilliant against the white field, the strewn scraps
of carrot and turnip and beef, dark gravy staining the snow. The fox

sniffed cautiously each piece before it took it in its mouth, chewing with its head turned slightly sidewise, pausing to eye the crows pacing, waiting, planning a grab not far away, and later she'd included them, on wing or scrabbling on the ground, fun to watch anyway, their social antics and play. She'd seen a rabbit nibbling grain she'd sown there for birds until a big gray cat sprang out of a bare thicket and sent it exploding through the soft snow. She did the rabbit in fine pen lines, she had Dürer's hare in mind, that exquisite detail and compression. And the frozen carcass of the beaver, its big teeth, the texture of its fur, the famous flat tail. The coyote had shocked her, she thought it a dog first, how it had regarded her, poised above a tomato-red lump of pasta, its long skinny legs set, its ears back, eyes eerie with intelligence, it knew exactly what little it had to fear from her. Would it have run from a man, from Red Murdock? Surely the coyotes were behind the wild yipping she'd heard late one afternoon, discovering the next morning at the edge of the pond the hind leg of a deer, intact but where it had been ripped from the body, bled out, pink stains in the light snow, bones bit through, crushed, tendons torn, and further out on the snow-covered ice where they had chased the deer, where its hooves would have slipped from under it in its struggle, a large dark patch of something she could not make out, bloodied remains maybe. By lunchtime the leg was gone.

She had material to explore and she bore into it with scarcely a break but for domestic chores and walks to the shore and up into the woods as far as she could venture. Tears came to her eyes at odd times, she couldn't say just why. Some vague sadness kept welling up. Not for losing Chet, that was the end of a long trajectory from what they had years ago—a loss she could feel sometimes in a silent winter forest. No other man had she been close to like that, and she might never again. That only happened when you were young. Didn't it? Chet believed it could come again, and it had, for him. How that gnawed at her, that now she might be kept from that kind of love with another man, that her capacity for passion might be fading.

And yes, she missed friends, certainly, women, men, their company and their mutual points of reference, shared allusions, assumptions, a warm embrace, nearness, the feel of someone she enjoyed, a sometime lover. She hoped this sadness was not rooted in fear, fear that she couldn't hold out, that the choices she'd made were more eccentric than she could accommodate. Still, she had survived her baptismal, she was stronger. After all, back home she'd lived in a terrarium really, a pampered, sheltered city that could smother ambitions that elsewhere might have caught fire. You couldn't always tell ahead of time, could you? Everything here had been a test, and sometimes, yes, it made her feel both solitary and exposed, her aloneness like a feeble beacon above the house—stay away. Those first weeks, doubt, like ice, had threatened her footing.

And yet she had achieved a kind of comfort. Comfort in simply not having to engage with another person, not having to explain herself, her actions, her silence, defend anything she said or did, not having to resist, give in, be judged, gazed at critically, compared, contrasted, receive advice, sought or unsought. No one in this house, on this land, along this foothill road, had anything invested in her or what she did in her private life. An animal's glance or stare was immediate and over with when it turned away, when it fled, there was no history in its brief appraisal—she was what she was. Her work was entirely her own. No one made anything of it, it had no consequences here, she was free.

Sometime later, she would be ready then to send it back to that other world, a long way from Cape Seal Road.

THE PATTERN SHE was used to—a few inches of snow, sometimes pelted into melt by rain, then a veneer of ice, a new layer of snow—was altered by a long, quiet snowfall that began late one morning and continued through the day. She watched thick flakes float dreamily past her bedroom window, a silent spectacle that ushered her into sleep. By morning, features of landscape were lost in one sinuous surface, a fresh sun glittered painfully off deep expanses of white, the pond no more than a sparse stubble of dead cattails. The dramatic shapes of driftwood were gone except for a few gnarled spikes or anonymous humps, and the snow was laced with the sharp, thin shadows of bare bush. Anna was delighted, amazed that March could revert so fast to deep winter, and, after a hurried breakfast and hot coffee at the back window, she dressed for outdoors and shouldered a backpack with sketchpad and pencils, her camera and a thermos of tea.

She waded into powder over her knees, squinting cheerfully into the bright, silent field spreading over the pond all the way to the shore. But not far into it where the path should be, she began to tire: with each step the snow sank deeply and she had to lift her legs high and push down hard to find its depth, which, sometimes uneven, unpredictable, made her stagger. What she'd anticipated as a casual walk turned into a workout, she was struggling clumsily through a drift next to the spruce grove, breathing heavily, sweating, anxious to reach the shore, but she fell headfirst before she got there, snow jamming cold up under her sleeves. The snowfield stopped abruptly in a wave-bitten bank tinged brown with sand. At least no one had witnessed her clumsy, exhausting trek. The beach was narrow now with the tide high, but the bare stones were clear walking at least. She had planned to inspect the fields, the point, see what she could find, but that would be a slog, and she'd have to stay at the shore edge. Looking back up at the house, thick snow layered on the steep roof, she realized that her car was trapped in the driveway and she was almost out of anything sensible to eat.

Over the sensuous contours of the field an animal's tracks snaked toward the pond, the prints clean, it hadn't been running, and she took a photo, then turned and snapped the Black Rock cliffs across the strait, Squatter's Bluff now dusted with snow, and toward the open sea a shoal where waves broke starkly white. There was a fresh wind on her face, colder now that a gray sky had absorbed the sun. Sketching would be difficult, and the places she was after would be a tough haul, there and back, so she wandered the beach, picked up a rusty iron hinge with curlicued design, it might be off a boat. She plunged into a slow retracing of her own steps, uphill, disappointed at how the snow, so beautiful and inviting when she woke, had thwarted her. The crowns of trees were tilting—like me, she thought—meltwater dripping in their branches. How would she drive out of here if she needed? How quickly weather turned simple things difficult.

Tired, her legs stiff, she could not imagine shoveling herself out, so she called Willard. During the night the provincial plow had finished the road, he said, but he'd come round himself and clear her driveway, which he did, a blade affixed to the bumper of his truck, an old four-wheel drive. The new snow had seemed to perk him up, and he accepted Anna's offer of tea when he was done, and talked about the old days here when they had to break their own roads after snow, and, oh, it once come heavy and often, up to the eaves, and a big double sled and chains and a strong horse would break a road, you see, smooth it like the floor here, and he tapped it with his boot. When she mentioned her cold bedroom, he told her about his little brother Andrew sick with pneumonia, they put him in the parlor, see, no stove there, flung the windows open wide for to get his breath, him in just pajamas, but he had a fever, he weren't cold at all, he didn't mind it, that boy was burning, you see, burning, and I sat with him all night until they took him to North Sydney by sled. In the hospital, right away they injected brandy into him, nineteen thirties that's what they did, that's what they had, brandy. He lived though, he lived it out.

She listened and didn't press him about delayed repairs, he'd freed her car, after all, and shoveled, with remarkable speed, a path to the front door.

"Them days," he said, "we had the ferry handy. Not a dead end at all, a lifeblood flowed right through here. People coming and going all winter long. Now you don't know who the hell's around."

"Like me?" she said.

"Och, you're welcome enough, Anna Starling." He reached for a raisin biscuit and chewed on it thoughtfully. "We're all so damned old now, walking wounded. Except Breagh and her little girl, of course."

"Red Murdock?" His name jumped out of her, she was curious about him, though not his age.

"Murdock's got some good years left in him. When my house burned, he took me in till I was on my feet. That's the way his family was, do anything for you." He noticed on the table a clump of dry, gray beard moss Anna had plucked from a tree branch to draw. He clapped it to his chin, grinning. "Halloween," he said. "We pasted it on like whiskers."

"How did your house catch fire, Willard?"

"Old, old house, great-grandfather built it. Stovepipe heated up, too much wood in her. See, they'd used newspapers to stuff the walls with, for insulation. Same here maybe." He rapped the wall with a knuckle.

"If there's old papers in there, I'd like to read them," she said.

"Better news than what you get now." He leaned toward her. "See, it wasn't me that stoked the stove so hot like that. Somebody broke in and did it, make it look accidental."

"Who would do such a thing?"

"Hooligans. Druggies. Them I see at Sandy Morrison's old house."

"Here?"

"Wait till summer."

"Boy, am I waiting, Willard. For summer, I mean."

"Summer will spoil you. You'll see."

IN BREAGH'S FRONT field there was a small, listing snowman topped with a woman's crazy hat. Anna parked at the road, the driveway looked chancy. Breagh seemed pleased to see her at her door. A bit unkempt in a baggy denim shirt and black jeans, but radiant nevertheless, her hair up, a suffusion of red, wisps at her slender neck. Though domestically capable, she never seemed to look domestic. Chet's affair had made Anna doubt her own appeal for a while, she'd lost interest in her looks, hiding in loose and sloppy clothing. Whereas she had once loved to dress up, the pleasure of a flattering outfit, she lapsed into drabness, which only made her feel worse. Stupid of course to make yourself dowdy, but she'd wanted to be free of seeing herself through the eyes of men, to figure out who she was beyond the boundaries of a marriage. Wasn't that one reason she was here? What *did* a woman need from a man, a man from his wife? She had no duty to look sexy or alluring or desirable. So she had told herself.

Anna said, "I like your hair that way," but Breagh scoffed.

"I look like a schoolmarm, it's just for when I sew." Her work lay scattered about the room, swatches of cut cloth in bold textures and patterns and colors spilled over a big table and onto the floor where Lorna sat and assessed, in her busy little hands, the white kitten.

Breagh made them tea and broke open the candy. Lorna got fussy and Anna appeased her with a chocolate. At the sound of an engine Breagh looked out the front window. "Well, if it isn't himself. Snow and all."

Livingstone entered by the kitchen door in a noisy display of stomping boots and clapping hands. "Give us a kiss!"

She offered her cheek perfunctorily. "Lorna heard you, Liv," she said. "She wants to know what you brought her."

"Oh, Jesus, Bree, I forgot. I got things on my mind." He noticed Anna, and stepped back, adjusting his mood. "Who have we here?"

"My neighbor down the road, Anna Starling."

He appealed to Anna with mock helplessness. "I always bring my little girl something. We're trapped in a habit."

"You've been trapped in worse ones," said Breagh.

"Bree, here. Give Lorna these, three shiny loonies. She'll have to learn money sooner or later."

"Later the better, I think."

"Next time, Bree, I'll bring her something grand. I've been busy, a little project on the side."

"I hope it's the right side."

"There's money in it. Is there any other side?"

"What kind of scheme is this?"

"Not for discussion. Don't want to jinx it."

"Fine. Excuse me, Anna, I have to put Lorna down for a nap."

"Is there any tea for this man?" he called after her but she didn't answer. He looked at Anna and shrugged. "Poor hospitality. I hope she's treating you better."

"She's treated me fine. There's tea in the pot there."

"She can be unpredictable, that girl. So you're living down at the old MacLennan place?"

"I am. How did you know?"

"Things get around. You like our winter?"

"I like this beautiful snow."

"I'm surprised." She dreaded the predictable questions, the nosy skepticism about her circumstances, the undertone of bafflement she'd encountered before, much of which had to do with her being a woman on her own here, and married yet. But all he said was, "How could you give up California for this?" gesturing at the lines of fog now flowing above the cliff-edge behind the house. He was more interested in the pond incident Breagh had mentioned to him. "Red Murdock heard you and hauled you out?"

"Not me. A dog caught in a trap got his attention."

"Ah, dogs. Dogs in traps." He shrugged. "Women in traps."

"I don't think so."

Livingstone raised his hand. "I'm just kidding. I'd like to know the whole story, the details."

"I'd like to put it behind me."

"That? No, Anna. Can't be done." There was something presump-
tuous about him she didn't like. He had a handsome head, one that,
in an actor, might make up for deficiencies of stature—you'd always
be looking at his face, his profile would hold you, a strong chin and
nose. His black hair fell over his brow, and his eyes were a deep, irisless
brown, seemingly intense. He was tall but slight, with long restless
hands, his fingers riffing silently on the tabletop as if it were a piano.

"Are you a musician?" Anna said.

He nodded, rooting inside his leather jacket until he fished out
a cigarette and lit it with a kitchen match, squinting. "Guitar, key-
boards. It's not a living." He smiled, blowing smoke. "I drove a truck
too, down the province." He did a steering motion with his hands.
"But I've quit that. Better money to be made. You, Anna, what do you
do besides fall through the ice on cold nights?"

"That keeps me pretty busy."

"Ah." His smile was charming, seemingly disingenuous, but without it his face took on a flat, appraising look that yielded little.

Breagh returned, she'd taken her hair down, it fell golden red to
her shoulders. Anna could see her easily in a Rossetti painting.

"Liv," she said, "you know I don't want cigarette smoke in the
house. Okay?"

"She prefers weed," he said to Anna.

"My preferences go through changes, so watch out."

"Where does she get her ideas for all these funny clothes? You seen
the hats in there, Anna? Wild."

"Is this what we have to listen to?" Breagh said. "I haven't seen
you for two weeks."

"Been looking into a couple things. And I had gigs. Eddie's Pub, and a wedding."

"Must've been a long wedding."

"Days. You know Cape Bretoners."

"I know you."

"You know, Anna, when she's pissed at me, she always puts her hair up."

"Nothing at all to do with you. Don't flatter yourself. We don't always do what's expected of us," she said to Anna. "Do we?"

"Never."

Livingstone nodded toward Breagh. "Unless we expect the same thing. Eh?"

"That's all that's on your mind."

"Not really. Only when I'm around you. . . ."

"You wouldn't have a little money to spare, I suppose? I'm behind on the electric."

As he was reaching for his wallet, he said to her almost in a whisper, "I'll have a hell of a lot more before too long."

"I believe it. Hundreds wouldn't."

"Don't sell me short, Bree." He glanced at Anna as he handed Breagh a few bills. "Stick with old Liv."

"Haven't I? Anna, please, more tea? That cake's from the store but it's tasty."

Livingstone steered away into a story about two bachelor brothers who'd lived back up the mountain, long dead, and when they finally got a television set, they would dress up in coat and tie to watch it because they thought the people on the screen could see them. Anna could tell he was deft at diverting Breagh when she pushed at him. He was a good mimic and had Breagh laughing despite herself. Anna was glad not to be Exhibit A, to be included like a local on the road who'd stopped by, not a woman from California whose presence altered the tenor of conversation, turned people guarded and wary. For the first time she felt like a person with some small stake in the place, she was wintering like everyone else, not a tourist, an object of curiosity, possibly derision, for all she knew, the woman who almost died in the pond (what was she *doing* out there, wee hours of the morning?). When Livingstone looped back to her night on the ice, she had to fall in, she simply started at the beginning, pleased enough it wasn't a resumé or a defense of her current life but a discrete incident. She gave them details, but not of Red Murdock, of how he cradled her foot and the feel of his hands, or her almost shattering loneliness when he left, or even of missing her husband who, regardless, would have tended to her as he once had, or the whirling delirium that visited her in that rocking chair. She did try to call up, as strongly as language would permit, the sensations of being plunged suddenly into that killing water. Speaking of it, she imagined it again, one depthless second of bone-cold nowhere. She told them how glad she was that Murdock had freed the dog, how difficult that must have been, he already chilled and wet, the dog frightened and suffering. When she finished, she smiled and took a sip of warm tea.

"Jesus," Livingstone said. "You might've stepped in that trap yourself, girl."

"You'd have heard me howling."

He smiled. "I'd like that."

"Livingstone," Breagh said, "give it a rest."

He took binoculars off the windowsill and aimed them toward the sea. "Billy been by?"

"Looking for you. He said they got the boat, whoever 'they' are."

"Guys I know. They fish."

"What kind of fishing can you do? Never heard of Billy fishing except for beer."

"All kinds," Livingstone said. "Any kind going. Then we'll have some fun."

"You won't get me on it."

He smiled at Anna. "We don't *want* you on it. There's others around."

"Not here, there isn't," Breagh said.

"Summer, girl. Summer is different."

Anna, uncomfortable in the middle of their conversation, looked to the window. Not far behind the house a patch of snow was enclosed by a high fence of thin, bleached spruce poles, varying heights driven into the ground like rough spears. Old Dougal's deer fence, Breagh had told her, a whimsical form against the gray sea, artfully assembled in a ragged but tight line, high enough to hinder deer from leaping into an old man's garden. Seven feet high now, he'd made it only five the first time, he'd said, then he looked out the window and saw a big buck soaring over it like a show-jumping horse. Anna tried to imagine vegetables leafing in that blank white spot but couldn't. Summer seemed impossible, almost a fantasy.

"I think you're crazy, getting involved in a fishing boat," Breagh said.

Livingstone panned the glasses slowly back and forth, fixing them for a few seconds toward the sea before he set them back on the sill.

"There's fish, and there's *fish*," he said.

XI.

RED MURDOCK HAD felt glum since the morning she'd called, he couldn't forget it. So unexpected to hear Anna Starling's voice on the phone, he got few calls anyway now, and the morning liquor had knocked him into a nap that left him muddled and grumpy when the phone rings rattled him. After he'd hung up, he stood there dumb: God, he must have sounded the wooden man he was.

He wandered down to the forge, avoiding the woodshop, he was not ready to face it, Livingstone's desk sitting there half-done, a big slab of oak. What the hell did he want with secret drawers? What secrets for a drawer could you have at his age? I'll need good money for that, Murdock told him, and Livingstone answered, I'll have good money for you when you're done, don't you worry.

But Murdock was mulling not wood but a pair of skates, the old-style stock skate his dad had fashioned. He'd once promised a set to Rosaire, way back, she was keen to skate the pond on them, What fun, she'd said, I'd love it, but then . . . You love me, don't you, Murdock? she asked him often in those last days. Yes, yes, he said, in every tone of voice, desperate that his love was not enough to save her, dismayed that his love had changed, just a little, love for the dying was different, for a woman he'd loved as hard as he could imagine, it was not quite the same.

Losing his mother as a boy was some like this ache, sure. She went off and left us, his dad said, without rancor by then, years later, like old news he'd just remembered. That was painful to me, Murdock, I hurt for, oh, a long time, don't ever get like that, so tight to a woman. But Murdock got over his mother, there was so much time out ahead of him then, endless, he grew, he healed up, he moved on, he learned what a woman felt like with his arms around her, and he could always release her and let her go.

Now he felt on certain mornings paralyzed, like his heart had ripped.

But, yes, for being cold and stupid on the phone, he was going to make skates and give them to Anna Starling. You see, it's like getting back on a horse, he would tell her, strap these on and take to that ice, just once, and the fear will leave you.

Could he make them, could he remember enough? He wanted something that had weight, had consequences. All the ordinary things wanted power, it could still amaze him: the hammer striking red iron, clangs sparking from the anvil—what took shape there wasn't just anything, you *made* it. He would dig out some of that Swedish steel, must be a piece or two left, get him started. They had to be well made, the skates, handsome enough she'd like even the looks. His dad had said, If your work is flawed, do it over, you're wasting good steel, do it right this time or that's the end of it, I'll give you something easy instead. But Murdock, if far more slowly than his dad, had made his first blades out of an old rasp, and that winter his little cousin Kay skated on them over the pond, wobbly but happy.

The air dropped suddenly in the afternoon, into that cold zone he'd hoped was past but knew better, and what might have been rain came snow, fluff dancing to the thick crust remaining from the last heavy fall. Flurries tickled his face as he stood at the shed door, looking out, remembering horses. Shaking them loose in a barn late at night, a bit drunk, hot from the kitchen and rum. His father could never get up the enthusiasm for cars that he had for horses, Where's the life in them? he said. The used Meteor he finally bought, he drove, battered and muddied, with a look of monotony, Give me a horse, he said, farts and all, she'll love you and she'll take you home, drunk or sober. His father's final driver horse, *Sìoda,* Silken, a beautiful black, sleek mare, like a racehorse, she did it all, plow, dump cart, buggy, sleigh. When Murdock came into her stall, he felt her heft and presence, the low rumble in her throat, she was like a great animal engine idling there. The leather stink of harness, and droppings, the nervous clapper of hooves on planks. That night coming home through black woods, half-cut happy in a borrowed horse and sleigh, he and Rosaire, what a ride up through a logging road in moon-bright snow where he stopped so they could work their hands inside each other's clothing, her lovely warm skin, her delicious mouth, she there in the seat with him under that buffalo robe that belonged to his grandfather, how warmer did a man need to be anyhow, on a night like that? To snap the reins now, glide away over snow, Rosaire beside him, how that would settle his heart, like rising into the air. . . .

When he saw footprints disappearing into his back field, Murdock cut across it in the stinging cold, his boots crunching softly, through a few wind-beaten spruce and the wiry tuckamore all the way to the far east bank where he could see MacDermid's Cove below. Soft, hazy snow hung like gauze over the afternoon, everything cast in gray shades, darker, lighter. The sea was no more violent than the silent fields, and just as still, a driftwood gray, ice white and startling along the shore, fixed in a slack tide. Whoever had tracked to the cliff edge had retraced their way out.

Squinting in the wind, Red Murdock picked out tire tracks, growing faint. They came out of the woods below almost to the shore, intersected in two dark loops, and wove back into the little road there. He didn't know who that would be this time of year, not an easy spot to get to without a four-wheel drive, the narrow road was runnelled and rock cut, tear the bottom out of a car anyway. He kept an eye on that property, for trespassers, vandals, a favor to Donny MacDermid, a saltwater captain who lived in Boston but intended to fix up his mother and dad's old house for retirement summers. It had a good roof and Donny didn't want people from town roaming around there like they owned it, as they would, had. His father, Robbie, had looked the other way when rum-runners ran booze into that cove, he got his cut of it. Nowadays, a few drinks and mischief, then broken windows and anything else they could smash, and, sooner or later, a fire.

Up at the road he had built a stout gate out of thick poplar poles and padlocked it, of course you could walk around it, but you sure as hell couldn't drive around it. So he had believed. Whoever it was, they hadn't stayed. He would go have a look down there.

But when he reached the house, someone was waiting, hunched out of the wind at the back door: Connie, hatless, in his long coat, his hair shiny with melted snow. There was a clotted cut along his eyebrow, on his cheekbone a nasty bruise. Had he fallen? Murdock had never known him to, not since they ran together as kids. Murdock stood with him when they took on the bigger boys who'd ragged him. They had coasted on homemade sleds, bullied cows out of the woods and scolded them home, wandered the reaches of the mountain. They drank their first, stolen, liquor up in Murdock's clearing, a bottle of rum he'd found stashed in the forge shed, not full but enough to get

them silly and stumbling, dancing around trees and baying into the
sky until they reeled with sickness. When they could vomit no more,
they staggered back, pale and shaking. Only much later did Murdock
know that was a day of divergence, that his pal's thirst would grow
far greater than his own, pull him into corners Murdock did not want
to go.

"Who you been tangling with, Connie?"

He waved his hand dismissively. "Little shits." His eyes were raw,
the collar of his white shirt soiled and wild.

"You're a little worse for the wear, boy."

"Murdock. . . ." Connie struggled to focus his eyes, his lips shifting wordlessly. He pulled a hand from his coat pocket to show skinned
knuckles. He grinned foolishly, blood pink on his teeth.

"Just a d-drink, Murdo. Eh?"

"Come inside."

At the kitchen table he downed two fingers of rum, then watched
glumly as Murdock placed the bottle back in the cupboard.

"I know you're tough, Con, but you've got to quit mixing it up
with people. We're slower now."

"Fucking B-Billy." He flexed his battered hand, laid it on the table.
"Hated that d-dog."

All his life Connie had wrung words out of himself, you could see
the strain in his looks, the taut cords of his throat, his lean cheekbones,
the tight line of his lips, as if to say, don't make me speak unless you
have to, and the dark, warning eyes, primed for slights, for mimicry,
his hand already in a fist. He fought often, from boyhood to manhood,
sometimes winning apology or regret, sometimes not. Asked his name,
he'd say only Sinclair because he could hiss it smoothly through his

teeth, whereas Connie, trapped deep in the cave of his mouth, choked him, flared up in his face. He discovered that alcohol could, though not always, sweeten the bitterness that troubled his life. But once out of school, he veered off deeper into drinking, became too much of what Murdock did not want to be—a man without mornings, a man sick in the middle of his work, everything a back seat to drink, drink his sole ambition. Murdock met up with him less and less, then he moved to Boston where he married and ruined the lives of two different women, and little of what he'd been before he went there was left when he came back home to the old family house, run down but habitable, alone under its leaky roof, visited for a while by drinking pals who, except for Peter Ingraham, gave out along with the last of his money.

But Murdock remained loyal toward him, he knew his tempers. Even if liquor had burned away the best in him, there was still a husk of his old good self, if you were patient enough to wait for it, to see it. He trekked Cape Seal Road every day, working off his thirst, searching out old haunts and ruined houses. If we weren't lucky, Murdock thought, or put together the right way, we might wander like Connie all our lives, fit for nothing special, happy nowhere. This was the only help he could give him now, a little booze, a little money, a willing ear. The man stuttered less with Murdock, always had.

"Doing a little work for Billy? For Livingstone?"

"Of course the dog b-barks, t-told them, just a d-dog, for Jesus sake."

"Liked you, that dog. Used to follow you down the road."

"N-not like it was a stray, M-Murdock. Not far. Willard's. Known him all my g-goddamn life."

"Take this," Murdock said, pushing a twenty-dollar bill across the table. "There's fresh tracks going into the tuckamore. You at the cliff this afternoon?"

"I t-told Willard, for fuck sake, let g-go of that d-dog, I can't stand your sorrow anymore."

"He'll get over it."

Connie looked out the window at a thin fall of snow. "Drunk as l-lords, Murdock," he said, his voice low and raspy. "Whole g-god-damn bunch."

MURDOCK DROVE HIM to the bottom of his long unplowed drive-way on the high side of the road and let him out.

"Take a rest, Con," he said, knowing the man would sleep awhile and then resume his walking. Connie stood swaying while he stared at his own tracks in the snow, wind-softened and dark, marking the way up, he had lost his driver's license long ago. He bent to the open door, trying to fix Murdock in his eyes. "I'm in up to me ass, Murdock," he said.

With high, careful steps, the noble gait of the very drunk, he set off toward his house.

Murdock turned back in the direction of the wharf, he'd have a look at Sandy's house, see who was there. In the front yard sat Billy Buchanan's gaudy pickup, surrounded by tire burn down to mud and crazy swerves in the snow as if cars had made a hasty, disorganized exit. The cottage, gray and peeling but sporting a new stark white door, was dark and quiet, no heavy music pounding from its windows. Funny, but years ago the Morrisons, childless, had been known for throwing parties and kitchen rackets, if there was a fiddler handy at any time they would pull him in, and sometimes when the waiting line for the ferry was backed up along the road, Sandy and Kate would fling open their door and hail inside waiting drivers and passengers. Good souls, they were, generous, hospitable. Who this current crowd was, Murdock could not say. There was Livingstone's pal watching him from a side window. Billy. No one had a bead on him, he was from New Waterford, somewhere over there.

But now, for the first time in a long while, Murdock knew exactly what he wanted to do in the morning, and that's where he put his mind. Skates for Anna Starling. He looked up at the mountain ridge where a single, smoke-blue cloud took hold of the hot red sun and, like a fist, closed it away.

He spent some time rehearsing, recalling the steps, jotting them down, sketching a little with a rough pencil on a piece of paper bag. Had to be sure he didn't leave one out or have to backtrack. Chaff and dust filmed the tools, all the tongs his dad had made, for different uses, they hung on a rack on the wooden bin beside the forge, the cutters hot and cold, the chisels, punches, he made them himself out of bars of tool steel. Years of use still latent in wood and steel. There were the tin cans of rusty bolts, nuts, screws, nails, hinges, brackets, scavenged, saved. He could still hear his dad rummaging in one of these tins or a salt cod box, the dull rattle of iron bits as his fingers dug for just the fastening he needed. Murdock too would leave his own woodworking hoard behind, a legacy of thrift and necessity that he had nobody of his own to care about.

He'd need coal for the fire, it wouldn't heat the air but just be good to see going. Even when his dad had the forge roaring and was banging

iron on the anvil, the room in winter never warmed, the tight little fire
fiercely hot from the blowered draft, focused, and the heat went up the
chimney fast, the gases and smoke, though in summer yes it could be
suffering hot. The old blower switch was dead. His father had gladly
given up the hand-crank blower late in his life when power came to
the road. That and the grindstone were the only things electrical, and
there was a blown fuse in the little wall box. He rummaged through
ruined fuses in a dirty wooden drawer until he located one good fifteen
amper.

Under dusty burlap, frayed into tufts by mice, he found soft coal,
old coal waiting for fire. In the spent ashes of the forge Murdock spread
shavings from the ash stocks he'd been since yesterday carving roughly
with an axe, then whittling them into a shoe shape.

He remembered her foot in his hands, narrow, fine-boned. He
formed the ash to suit it. He'd finish them smoothly, sand them to a
sheen.

But now the shavings flared from his match and he gently brought
up the blower, building the coal until the draft was strong. In the stream
of air soon the coal burned red. Into its heart he set one end of the steel
bar and left it. This would be a blade. He took up a ball-peen and a
hole punch and when the bar end glowed red like the nest of coals, he
pulled it out and on the anvil hammered that red tip flat. Punching the
screw hole, where the blade would be fixed to the wooden stock, was
awkward, he had to balance the bar in his lap and it took a reheating
and another try before he placed it over the hardy hole in the anvil
and punched it through. Then the feathering, sharpening the top edge
of the blade where it would set into the grooved ash, this was difficult, he remembered it, but would his hand follow? Maybe it was like

swimming or playing ball, you never forgot how, you just weren't so good at it anymore, and you had to concentrate like hell. And that was good.

Murdock had to heat it again and again as he drew out both sides of the top edge with the hammer, but the lower edge would curl up, and then it came back to him how to beat it flat, heating a few inches at a time he beat his way toward the toe, feathering first one side, then the other, then flattening the bar. Then the little hump that went up deeper into the groove, he had to draw that out beyond the feathered edge and punch a hole clean.

You've got the knack, I think, his dad said after a while, you got a feel for iron.

He heated the blade once more and using the horn of the anvil pounded the front into the graceful curve that would thrust forward over the ice when Anna Starling pushed it. On the grindstone he squared off the bottom edge, then ground a slight groove the whole length of it. He went back to the blocks, they were like graceful little boats, the blade a keel, the hull narrower than the feet that would ride them so it would never touch ice when Anna Starling leaned.

He drilled holes for three strap slots, then chiseled them out and ran a hot bar of metal through, cleaning the slots. He clamped the stock in the vise and started the long bottom groove with a saw, finishing it clean with a chisel to receive the feathered edge of the blade that he fixed in with wire pulled up tight and twisted. The straps, which he planned to fashion out of old reins soaking now in neat's-foot oil, needed through-rings, and he cut two lengths of thin metal rod, rounding them hot over the horn, then scarfing the ends for a smooth weld, and put borax at the scarfing and the rings back into the fire.

Welding is like bread, his dad had told him, it's no good if you burn it. Leave it raw and it won't stick, you need accurate heat at both ends. Watch your metal. When it's just starting to melt, it's ready.

Murdock put an open ring on the anvil, worked the ends together, and with light taps of the hammer at first, then heavier, he welded the ring, then did the other one. If you looked close, the circles were not perfect, but they would do, he wouldn't do them over.

The air was still cold but he wiped sweat from his eyes, such had been his concentration, calling up memory, in head and limb, the muscles of his jaw felt clamped. He stood back and worked his stiff fingers, his forearm had tensed up, tightened. Jesus, this was only small steel, he hadn't been banging big iron all day like his dad.

He flipped off the blower and the flame withered into flickering coal and ash. He lowered his hands, dirty with dust, into the cold water of the brine tub, then rubbed them over the coals. He could hear the wind now, moaning softly in the chimney, amplified in the forge hood. The skates lay on the workbench still strewn with tools and dies as his father had left them. He'd sand their wood tomorrow, find small buckles for the straps, there was more old harness in the corner. A coat of varnish on the ash would brighten them. He wasn't sure of the time but he knew he had pressed on through the afternoon, in the flow of memory, he'd had to keep moving through it, seizing the next step and the next before it was garbled or lost. He was tired, so hungry his knees were weak. I'm out of shape for this, he said, but he liked what he had done. Rosaire, God love her, she did not skate. But she danced, she danced.

You know, I can still dance, she told him, I can step out. How is that? said Murdock, taking her hand as she lay there. He didn't want to concede her any pipe dreams, not then, not anymore, much as he'd loved them, indulged them. Up here, she said, tapping her temple. I'm light on the floor, light as a shadow, she said. But nice, fast, would you dance with me, Murdock? Now? The way I look? Quick, before they burn me up, you can't dance with ashes. Sure, dear, I'll dance with you, he said easily, you're a feather, I'll whisk you along. You'll have to paste your wig on, but it's a pretty wig, you're right fine in it. Yes, and not a hair of gray either, she said. Why am I crying? For the love of God look at me, the tears. She closed her eyes and tears welled in her lashes. From the hall a nurse's scolding voice rose and subsided. Through a haze of curtain Murdock saw in the parking lot below a woman hobbling to a car, a man shielding her with a black umbrella. God damn it, she was going home, on her own feet, what fortune. The asphalt was black with rain, puddles flickered under the street lamp. In the hallway a gurney hustled past, a clatter of equipment and murmuring attendants. I'm not sleeping, Rosaire said. Well, your eyes are shut anyway, Murdock said gently, sleep if you want. Pay no mind, Murdock. I'm still here. Her voice was soft, precise. I don't want sleep while you are here, while you're in the room with me. I hate to wake up alone. I'm not going anywhere, he said. Can I give you some water? She nodded and raised her head enough so he could slip his hand behind it. He put the plastic cup to her lips. He watched her pillow as she sipped, the shallow dent her head had made, oh so light now, in his cupped hand the thin, feverish hair. He eased her back. He knew she'd sleep, her face had relaxed, her lips parted as if for a kiss, and he kissed them. He wondered how deep she went then, how close she ventured to the edge you couldn't come back from. Would she know it, would something change suddenly that said, this is a different dream entirely, girl? Or were you just out, unknowing and forever, if forever meant anything at all?

Red Murdock leaned close to the dusty window above the workbench. In the waning afternoon light a chain of footprints paid out in the snow, coming up from the shore they formed an angle, its tip just beneath the window, one side from the east, the other fading off west, dark and fresh. Who would be at the shore? Anyone he knew would have tapped at the window, but cost him his momentum at the same time, the rhythm of memory.

Couldn't have been Anna Starling. Why would she come to this window anyway, much as he'd have liked to see her there?

XII.

ANNA HAD GIVEN up on a genuine spring, like ones she remembered from the Midwest. Her dad's wish was that she attend his alma mater, a small liberal arts college in Ohio. Why so far away? her mother argued, there are good schools here, she could go to San Francisco, but her father said, No, she needs a different space, somewhere new, and he prevailed. She remembered winter giving over to warm rains in April and then the fragrant heat of May, the blossoms and ground flowers, and men soon in short sleeves, women in shorts, legs, flesh, muscle out there again, light clothing at a party, everything warm again, out in somebody's backyard, the night, the air, the man next to you, the spice of shaving lotion and liquor, the old lilac beside the garage, the plain good humor of fine weather.

Winter here still crouched off the coast waiting for an east wind, then the temperature would fall, all her easy expectations of summer would again recede. Off the coast of northern California where Anna grew up, gray whales would be migrating south, from shore cliffs she and her friends had vied to spot them, their erupting spouts.

Now it was April and snow had just fallen after what seemed a slight thaw. Patches of pond melt had, this Saturday afternoon, frozen again and flurries had dusted its surface. Anna took two bold steps onto the pond and stopped: in the bottle-gray ice a smudge of dull scarlet, just under the surface. She uttered a soft, short cry. Someone's . . .? No!

Her woolen cap! She backed slowly away, her heart quick, as if she'd seen her own face, trapped in that dark water, waiting for spring.

The strait was empty but for an ice floe here and there like a small white boat adrift—drift ice is a *sign* of spring, Willard said, encouragingly. On the St. Aubin shore, through a gray dusk, the few, sparsely placed houses were already lost, and night was coming down. She had worked hard all week, a series of drawings in pen and ink, found objects mostly, sometimes with landscape or seascape as background—a striking piece of driftwood, a battered black pontoon from a hatchery float, a huge ball of manila rope so intricately tangled she could imagine the violence of the seas that had whipped it, wrung it into this deep, unravelable knot. She liked what such things could say, or be made to say, without words, their latent moods. Melissa had asked to try a few pen-and-inks in her gallery but Anna was still fussing over them, she lacked the will to pack them up and send them away. Not yet. Melissa's garden would be abloom with azaleas and orchids, gorgeous hybrids of iris and lily, luscious globes of hydrangea. How lovely to inhale it, to float in its scents, a warm Santa Ana wind gusting through her yard.

After that afternoon at Breagh's, the possibility of a purely social occasion, which she had all but abandoned, pulled at her hard tonight, that old Saturday anticipation of conviviality and license, of kicking loose.

Breagh, however, was not at home, no answer on her phone, and doubtless in her own circle of fun, somewhere in town.

After a supper of smoked haddock in white sauce, a now-favorite recipe she found penciled in a kitchen notebook, Anna filled the bathtub with the entire capacity of the electric tank. She submerged up to her neck in hot water and steam, dozy, dreamy, unwilling to rise out of this bliss until the temperature grew tepid and forced her back into the cooler house. She quickly added wood to the *Warm Morning* and sat toweling her hair near the caressing heat. Flames crackled in the firebox.

How long since she'd seen Red Murdock through the dirty window of that blacksmith shed, drawn there by a smoking chimney? His fierce gaze as he worked, how intense it was, at that different fire, his jaw set, his eyes in shadow under the bare bulb, and then turning toward that core of coals that seemed to mirror his own burning focus. She'd stayed so still at the dusty glass, watching him, the beat of the hammer, a sound from another time. She had wanted to go inside, but she didn't know how to break into that contained little world of his, to ask would he part with any of that array of marvelous iron hanging and in bins. That strange intimacy of the pond night had passed, frozen over. But how she would love to do a junk sculpture, though she wouldn't call it that, the iron odds and ends, the tools in his hands, were not junk.

What was *he* doing this Saturday night poised somewhere between winter and spring?

Anna poked listlessly around her workroom, picking up sketches, setting them down. She'd done a quick study of Murdock at his anvil when she got home that day, a strong play of light and shadow, the outsized hammer raised high above his head, his brow darkened in a scowl. She would fill it out in oil pastels later, reds, deep yellows, all that glow and energy, power and noise. Sometime, if she got to know him better, she'd do a quiet portrait, just his interesting face, in ink.

She thumbed a book about rocks from Melissa (*I heard they have a lot of them there,* her friend had written inside), then read over her letter: *I've been stopping by to check on your garden, like you asked. Looks nice, could use a bit more watering, Chet says he's been on top of it, but maybe not every day, he's not here much. The azaleas and rhododendrons are lovely as usual, the orchids are coming out, lemon trees have lots of blossoms. I miss seeing you at the pool on campus, so do the girls, you got them and me into swimming, you were our incentive, but we're sticking with it. I did my hair blonde last week, wanted a radical change (don't we all?). Mort is indifferent, but Chet took one look and said, Melissa, that color is not you. I felt like asking what is me, but I was afraid he'd give me a detailed answer (!). A handsome flock of cedar waxwings blew through for a couple days, all over the holly tree and the ivy, then they moved on. Moving on is the slogan of the day (?). Chet asked what I knew about you, I said you were doing good work. That's still true isn't it?*

"Yes," Anna said out loud. "It is."

She poured a glass of white wine and sipped at it. She supposed she would get comfortable in the scuffed but meaty arms of the easy chair, as she had so often under the lively colors of her lamp, and put on music—what sort didn't matter much at the moment—read a copy of *Art World* she had saved like a treat. Tightening her robe, she was aware suddenly of her skin beneath it, of warm flannel on her breasts, and that took her back somewhere nice for a few seconds, called up the last man who'd touched her there and brought his lips to hers, until the windows rattled with wind. Wake up, Anna! Chet would be enjoying himself, that was a given, hardly a Saturday passed that he didn't. *I could be a Saturday night man every damn night of the week,* he said once, *I can't help it.* Many times she had joined him, but that had stopped even before his wooing of Alicia Snow. Anna had her work, her own friends, she didn't need him to help entertain herself, and, God knew, Chet didn't need her anymore, as participant or observer, to enjoy himself, he had his woman.

Anna had been a bit plump growing up, but she learned that it didn't matter much to the boys and later the men who wanted her. She would never be lean and lithe like Alicia Snow, but she had toned her limbs swimming, and she was comfortable with her body. You're deliciously curvaceous, Chet had told her, in the days when he loved to nuzzle her and define her shape with his hands, you have a lovely ass. My legs are strong, she might have said to give the assessment a different slant, even my arms, but she didn't. The night she beat him arm wrestling was still some years away.

Maybe it was a fluke, the strength in her arm on that particular Saturday night. They'd lain bellies-down on the hardwood floor of his study, gazing hard into each other's eyes, dark with too much wine and some kind of passion that had moved on from physical love, from adoration, from the simple delight of each other's taste and warmth, to an unspoken competition neither of them was clearly sure about, only that it sometimes filled them with a brief, intense hatred of each other, as if one of them was at fault for all the unnamed grievances that ground at them, like sand in sweat. Her modest but growing repu- tation as an artist of talent? She could guess what Chet's were—his literary mediocrity, the truth of which he had feared for a long time but which youth could always excuse, there was time to get better, to get good, for some writers it came late, the mastery, the vision, and of course he was trapped, he knew that, there was nowhere upward he would go, and nothing else he could do. But how was she at fault for that? She wasn't, he knew she wasn't, but his resentments still flared up too often, she was right there in front of him after all, she was the one who had fallen in love with him with all the hope that implied, and only her could he truly hurt enough to regret it deeply afterward, basking in the pain. Anna herself, well, if he wasn't getting anywhere, how could she presume to? Yet eventually she did, her artistry grew and flourished even though she knew he had narrowed down her life, put a fence around it, trapped her too inside his own limitations.

But that night on the frayed oriental rug beside his desk she had slowly pushed his arm to the floor, there was no way he could have beaten her that night, and she never forgot the look on his face, inches away, no intimacy in his eyes, blazing as they were with confusion and shame. Of course they both laughed about it the next morning, in the languor of hangover, a spontaneous absurdity they wouldn't visit again, drunken hijinks, Chet had been weakened by wine, hadn't he? We're going to hit the bars, Anna, he said, I'll take bets, Who dares to arm wrestle my wife? She can beat any man in the house, I'll say, slap your money on the table, boys, and then your elbows! But it was as if he were relating someone else's story, she laughed along with him, quietly, watching his face. They'd clutched the heat of their coffee at the back door and watched stars fading like ice bits in the black sky, their whispers shivering white in the open door, winter, there, on a safe street in a safe town. He never mentioned to anyone the story of how Anna'd put his arm straight to the floor, and neither did she, because where that strength came from she did not know. Nor what she might do with it.

What she craved right now, terribly, as she hadn't since a long time, was a cigarette, what it might conjure. She could taste the acrid burst of a struck match, the unfiltered smoke of a Pall Mall, the lift and buzz, the vigorous talk that had gone with it drinking in bars, huddled with friends in old, dark, high-backed booths batting opinions back and forth, so much was new then, exciting to discuss, especially what they hated (sexual hypocrisy, the gray dreariness of the Cold War, real and ugly racial injustice, the Vietnam War). They embraced the changing mores eagerly, the emerging liberties in words and images and deeds, the fading taboos, they tried out drugs (Anna rejected the hallucinogens, something unsavory and unhinging about LSD), she and Chet flirted with Beatnik poses for a little while, it was fun.

Yet although they cohabited almost by principle, it seemed natural that they would eventually marry: they were children of an earlier time, marriage still had weight, it signified mutual respect, it testified that their love was singular, and for the long haul. It was, at least to Anna, a kind of protection, though just how was never specified, never spoken. But perhaps its erosion had been inevitable from the start: you couldn't "mess around," as Chet liked to call it—divesting it of all harm—and keep that particular kind of love intact. They'd lived on together, barely aware of their own easily rationalized infidelities, barely acknowledging the shredded marriages around them. Until Chet's fascination with Alicia Snow turned into, as Anna saw it, a blinding and sappy love. At first, he had wanted both: to keep what he had with Anna, the comfortable old clothes of their marriage, while dressing up for another life with Alicia Snow, and he had been deluded enough to believe Anna would go along with it. The Swinging Sixties.

Alicia Snow. Anna couldn't utter her name without feeling that it carried a kind of spell.

INSTEAD OF BUTTONING up in flannel underwear and jeans and a wool shirt suitable for a lumberjack, Anna on a whim pulled out of the little upstairs closet the dress in the old garment bag. She expected something plain or worse, but no: whose special dress was this? Nineteen forties clearly, with the squared shoulders, a soft, light, draping wool, deep burgundy. Full gypsy sleeves gathered at the wrist. There in the cold room Anna dropped her robe and, in panties, shivered into the dress that fastened like a coat. Soft pleats flowed from beneath the bust to the hem, the right side wrapping over and fastening snugly at the waist where a large sequined oval showed like a delicate buckle. The buttons were hidden under the drape so nothing disturbed its comely lines, the hem falling just above the knee. She wouldn't bother with a bra. Pity she didn't have a scarf for the vee of the neck, maybe cream or a rich yellow, but she turned in front of the dresser mirror and even in its mottled glass and the poor light, she thought it stunning, the fit of it perfect. It smelled of the wood shavings in the bottom of the bag but she felt so good in it she didn't care.

In her bedroom she dug out first a pair of black leather shoes she'd tossed in a suitcase at the last minute almost as a joke, narrow two-inch heels and an open toe, party shoes. She hooked into her lobes a favorite set of earrings, silver hoops encircling small moonstones, a long-ago gift from her dad, he liked to see women in striking earrings. And then Anna plucked out the flattened joint Chet had pressed tightly into the binding of a book he'd given her, *Poems of Departure,* with a note in tiny script—*Some night you'll want what these have to say, and this.* She hadn't, mainly because in its smoke she would yearn for places she could not be, and its pleasures would be quickly over—this little stash was it. But this once, she would slip back into that old high, let go, do what she wanted. Who was here to judge her? She had not yet allowed herself even one night to get good and tipsy on wine and sink into the music of her past: too hard to come back from it, to hear the house silent when she climbed the creaking stairs to bed.

Downstairs on her small boom box she put in a cassette of B. B. King. She lit the joint with a kitchen match and closed her eyes as she took a deep hit, held it, then another before pinching it out. Chet, he was four hours behind her, yet, knowing him, probably way ahead. Anyway. The grass set her shivering, oh, if she had one of those short mink coats of the forties, how fine that would look with this dress, but she had to settle for hugging herself in a yellow wool shawl she found upstairs. In her room she cranked the music up and began to dance slowly into the kitchen, smiling as she moved, circling the table, clinging to herself. How long since she'd *been* in a dress, felt the air on her bare legs? Not here. The music evoked old parties, flirtations, dancing, fun, she didn't know at the time why she'd dropped them in her suitcase, these tapes, but maybe she knew there'd be a day when she'd need them, her beloved blues—Etta James, John Lee Hooker, Buddy Guy, Keb' Mo'—she'd had to create her own space for them, they were not the music of here.

She smoked a bit more, sang along with B. B. King's "Never Make Your Move Too Soon," though moves like that she had no worries about, then took a break in the fat armchair, crossing her legs, showing her knees, she lifted her feet up to check out the shoes. Yes! She laid her head back, let her mind go. That tall, lanky Aussie at a party a couple years back, a geologist, gentlemanly, leaning his tanned face toward hers as they talked, how she'd loved getting close to him when things warmed up, he wore a soft suede shirt, his muscles moved slowly under it as they danced. Something good might have come of that but he had to return to Perth suddenly, and she found out later that he was married as well. Just another empty shirt on the back of a chair, Melissa said, you didn't miss much.

The cassette was winding out its final number and Anna was thinking of the next tape that might sustain her mood, what other fantasy she might entertain, she didn't want the silence to flood back, when she heard the knocking. Oh, hell! She jumped to shut off the music, but whoever it was would have heard it already. And the pot fumes? Unmistakable. She felt almost heartsick at this interruption, she was *enjoying* herself, she had needed this evening so damn *long,* she'd paid her dues. What were they doing here? She had to shift herself to another place, and quickly, she swiped angrily at the smoke. Who would understand this private little party anyway, the only guests her and her memories? She hid the chardonnay in the fridge, enough remained for another time. She wrapped the shawl to her chin and tried to reel her mind back somewhere close to normal.

THERE ON THE porch, smiling in the light from the hallway, was Livingstone, hoisting a bottle by the neck, dancing from foot to foot, hooing breath smoke to exaggerate the cold. "Breagh's not home! She was supposed to be! But hey, I see Anna's lights, and then I hear that good music, so . . ."

Heat rushed into her face: glad it was *him* and not someone else, yet she didn't really know him, he had intruded after all, yanked her back, and he'd have had to come almost the full length of her driveway to see her lights. She could not help but believe that letting him in would be a mistake. But what was she to do, send him away as if she were the local schoolteacher? She sighed and opened the storm door.

He seemed to sense her coolness and stood just inside as if waiting
for instructions or a sign he was not unwelcome. Anna thought of seat-
ing him in the parlor but it was ridiculously chilly, and a room where
people had probably sat up straight, the couch smelled of mice and the
ceiling light was a gray globe, about as welcoming as a funeral home.
Unrealistic to think he might leave soon enough to save her evening, its
prospects were rapidly vanishing.

Livingstone proffered the wine, a bottle of Chilean red, and she
thanked him and led him into the kitchen, that's where social life
occurred here anyway, wasn't it. She didn't know what he expected—
maybe that, absent Breagh, Anna would do in a pinch? For what?
Amusement? But people did drop in on each other here uninvited, if
not often on her, and never at night.

She found herself talking faster than she should, just to get him
greeted and seated, not in the true, warm, private heart of the house—
her workroom—but at the kitchen table, with its cloth checkered
red and white you could clean with a sponge. She sat near the stove,
opened the shawl. He reached for the corkscrew, sniffing the cork it
held before he unscrewed it.

"You having a séance in there, Anna?" He nodded toward her
room. She'd left a candle burning on the little end table with her tapes
and her books. Oh, that was bright of her, yes.

"No . . . maybe I was, sort of."

"Must be a few spirits roaming around this place, I'd think. Old-
timers thought so."

"Benign ones. So far."

He stood at the back window, hooded his eyes. "They like the
blues, do they?"

"Do you?"

"You bet. I play mainly Celtic stuff, but I can do some mean licks of that kind." He kept peering out. "Nice spot here. Good view of the water, up and down." He turned around and stared at her. "That's a dynamite dress."

"It's borrowed. Would look great on Breagh, don't you think?"

"Better on you. Not her color."

"Any color is hers, I think."

"What's the occasion?"

"Saturday evening."

"It is, so."

He popped the cork and Anna wanted to let him drink alone, it might cut his visit short, but where would such hospitality get her? She was coming down anyway, her nervous system falling into more familiar paths, pulse rate dwindling. She fetched two water glasses.

"Sorry," she said. "No stemmed crystal."

Livingstone filled the small tumblers and raised a toast. Anna drank quickly, she didn't care, the evening was out to sea. Then he sniffed the air, tilted his head. "Wouldn't happen to have a bit of that lying around, would you?"

"A bit is *all* I've got, believe me." There was no point in denying it, she wasn't fooling him, he had taken in the whole ambience.

"I'll pay you back, and then some," he said. "I'm just not holding tonight. Breagh doesn't want it in the house. Her little girl and all."

"I don't need any payment, thanks. This was just a souvenir, you might say. Just that, that's the end of it, finis."

"It's not exactly unknown even on *this* road. Don't worry about it. I don't."

"It's not the worry. . . ." She had tried hard to avoid the California stereotypes, striven to be taken on her own terms. So, the matter of discretion, of giving in, of consequences. She did not want Livingstone to provide her with anything, she was on her own.

"I'll keep your secret," he said.

There was a cool, subtle draft on her legs, she should have put on tights.

"I'm sure you've kept a few, Livingstone."

"Can't live without secrets, Anna. They heat up our lives. Look, save the roach. I feel like I'm bumming your last cigarette."

"It *is* my last," she said, "don't forget that." She took the half-smoked joint from a kitchen drawer as if it were money soon to be squandered. A small piece of her past done with. Would that temper his gossip?

"Cool," he said, reaching for it with the broad smile that softened his face. "I was right about you."

"I'm afraid to ask." She didn't care right now what he meant, she hadn't much control of what he thought about her.

They passed the roach back and forth until Livingstone pinched it out in a teacup saucer she'd used as an ashtray. "Good stuff," he said. "I always like to try something new. California? Mexico? Maui Zowie?"

"I don't know, it was a gift."

Then he began to talk, there was no theme or thread, local or worldwide, it didn't seem to matter,

"You know, Anna, this farmer in South Africa, he had a good vine-yard, but it got raided over and over by a pack of baboons. Man, they loved those grapes. So what the farmer does, he plants this different kind of grape, see, real juicy, dark red, all along the border of the vineyard. The baboons they start eating these grapes first, they ripen early, but when the juice stains the baboons' hands, it looks like blood, and that scares the hell out of them. They run away, they don't come back." He raised his hands and turned them slowly, backs to palms.

"No baboons here," she said.

He laughed. "Have to know where to look. Follow the grapes."

He kept glancing into her room, so she gave in and showed him her drawings, and his questions about them, even if they were just talk, were not flippant—what attracted her to a subject, why the pond under a harsh moon instead of a day with sun and snow, why a composition of fractured pieces of an old barn instead of how the barn really looked? She told him that "really" was a key word, that there were different sorts of reallys, ways of seeing, and this was how she tried to get at them, get into them. It was wearisome to be forced to explain, she did not want to sound pedantic or superior or artsy, and she'd had to come down from a totally private high that had little to do with her work, and nothing to do with him.

He paused before a big sketch of the dog and the bridge, still holding his empty wine glass as if he were at a gallery reception, then took a step back, frowning. "And what kind of really is *this?*"

She didn't want to tell him about the dog, her instinct was to pass it off as dream or surrealism, but maybe, possibly, he might say something useful. She told him what she'd seen.

"Jesus," he whispered. "You sure? Might've been a bag of trash, people do that. People get shitfaced and do anything. Could I have more of that wine?"

"It was a dog."

"Maybe it was dead anyway."

"I heard it yip. The moon was bright. I saw its little legs going as it fell."

"You saw it *all?*" He narrowed his eyes at her, then filled his glass from the bottle she handed him.

"All what?" she said.

"The guys up on top, on the bridge . . ."

"Too far, too dark. A guy, yes. A woman would never do that."

"Wouldn't put it past a couple I know."

"I've wondered was it Willard Munro's dog."

"No loss if it was. Somebody burned Willard out a while back. He ought to remember that."

"He'll never forget it, I'm sure. Who would?"

Willard had told her, Nothing I could do, I couldn't watch it, no. Every God blessed thing in it. They didn't even put shoes there to try to save it.

"Breagh thinks it was the wharf rats."

"The who? How the hell would *she* know?"

"Guys from town, they hang around that little house by the wharf."

"Billy stays there. Well, I know those fellas, a few. He has a habit of phoning up the Mounties, old Willard does. Not a way to get popular."

"I doubt that he cares. Why would he call them?"

"He's a nosy old woman, that's why." Livingstone nodded curtly at the sketch before turning toward her stack of cassettes. "You dreamed that, I think."

"Maybe I did, maybe I am. And go easy on Willard, he's my handyman. He might even drop by."

Livingstone gave her a look. "Way past his bedtime, he's snoozing up there where the pulpit used to be. Good place for him. Anyway, I'm your handyman now."

"Nothing needs fixing. Sorry."

"Around here, something *always* needs fixing. Even music."

He shuffled through the cassettes, squinting at titles, murmuring or grinning according to what he liked. He approved of the Celtic tapes she'd picked up in Sydney, Capercaillie, the Bothy Band, Planxty.

"You need some Cape Breton stuff here," he said, "I'll drop a couple by."

She felt she should usher him back to the kitchen, out of this private space, but she hadn't the will to orchestrate what they did now, how they arranged themselves. Let it go.

"You mind putting this on, Anna?" holding up Creedence Clearwater's *Bayou Country*. "This flies at my altitude."

Anna almost said no, such were the good times packed into that album. She'd first heard it on the jukebox in a college bar. Chet bought a copy later, a staple of many parties, no one could resist dancing to it whether they could dance or not, and in those days it didn't matter, you just got up and did your thing. But she took it from his hand and slipped it into the cassette player.

"Yeah," Livingstone said, brushing her breast as he reached to turn up the volume.

At first she just watched him slowly spin and shuffle in the small area by the door, his eyes shut, smiling, snapping his fingers softly, his scuffed side-zip boots sliding on the bare floor, he'd already kicked the throw rug aside. She tried a few easy steps and turns, she didn't want to get dizzy. Feeling flushed, she tossed aside the yellow shawl. But soon they were both into it, swapping smiles when they bumped each other, lightly, and at the song breaks. "Oh, I love 'Proud Mary,'" she said, tugging at the neckline of her dress, how could she have broken a sweat? But she had, and Livingstone said, "Let's keep on chooglin'." Her azaleas at home, their stunning white blossoms rushed into her mind, so fragrant. She inhaled the memory, then brought in the rest of the wine and they both drank while he slapped in another tape.

"Change of pace," he said. These blues were slow, a tape she'd put together herself, selections from here and there and the radio back home, "Slow Stuff," the label read, and in the first strains of "Thinking of You," Livingstone, his eyes just slits, his smile lazy and fixed, reached out to her, she knew that moment when dancing closes in, when you're not apart and lost in the rhythm of your own body anymore but suddenly joined to another's, and all points of touching speak—that was when she might have said, No, Livingstone, you're Breagh's, let's cool down, but she didn't, that kind of dispassion was not available to her then, there was no time for the burden of consequences, of loyalty, she was floating and light and she liked the feeling, of him, of a man in her arms, his hands sliding over her back, warm through the fabric of the dress. He whispered something she couldn't make out, his breath in her hair, his arms tightening around her, the dress seemed so thin now, insubstantial, she could feel him harden against her, and she thought, this feels like home, this could happen there, but you're in a very different place, you have no history, no connection, you don't know this man who feels so good, who is he? What are the rules, the lines, the limits? And why think of them now, why *must* she? She had to recognize she was pleased that Livingstone desired her, lost in the mood and the moment as she was. She'd made herself attractive for no expected man, yet she *was* appealing to him, like beautiful Breagh—a small, mean triumph she instantly rejected, real as it was—another ingredient in the complex, intoxicating mix she and this man were engaged in. He was humming to a song, swaying her gently side to side, she could feel the vibrations of his voice, and then he kissed her neck and she didn't need to hear what he was murmuring there, it was flowing through them both. He danced her slowly into the kitchen, toward the daybed, but she said no, not here, and she led him up the stairs as if some voice were calling to her up there, she had to laugh, the room felt so cold. He pulled her to him and kissed her hard, he took the shape of her into his hands, moved them under the skirt of the dress, up her legs, the cheeks of her ass, oh, how might it have gone had she encased herself in her winter clothing, protective, frumpy, chaste, but she unfastened the dress and slid it away and he drew her panties down, kneeling to help her step out of them. He grasped her hips and pressed his tongue in little circles over the soft, taut skin inside her thighs (did she taste of that salty dancing?), pushed it hot and insistent into her bush, the wet lips there. She took his hair in her fists and pulled him up and kissed him, their tongues entwining. The bed groaned as he sat on the edge and yanked viciously at his boots, his jeans, his curses muffled in the bulky black sweater that caught in his wristwatch. She whipped the quilts open and fell back with a yelp onto the chilled sheet. She waited there shivering until he rolled next to her and they plunged under the quilts, shouting with the cold, "Jesus!" he said, "as bad as the pond, this!" But there was nothing of ice in the feel of his hands, the heat of his mouth, and when his cock slid inside her, all was pared down to sheer, blind pleasure, beyond guilt or care or censure, it was all now, now, now.

SHE DIDN'T REMEMBER Livingstone leaving, they'd lain there under the quilts amusing each other over what they could make out in the room's weathered ceiling, with just a nightlight in the hall. She last remembered his insisting a stain was a huge insect, which he described in minute detail. Anna dozed beside his warmth, slept, but he was gone when she woke needing to pee and groped for her robe. Then she remembered what he'd said after a long silence, in a different voice: What were you doing at the bridge that night? She'd replied lightly, not catching his tone, Sightseeing, I guess.

Downstairs a lamp was on in her workroom where their empty glasses sat on the big table. The kitchen was cold, and would remain so until she got up for good. She lifted the saucer on whose pale blue forget-me-nots the roach lay, a black stub of congealed ash: he must have singed his lips before he went out the door. She put on a down vest and took up a pen.

Dear Melissa, you asked how was I doing. I've been doing charcoal, it's a charcoal kind of weather anyway, the shades I'm seeing out the window now wouldn't challenge a palette much. I prefer drawing anyway, I never took to paints. I will send along a few inks, I'm pleased with them. How are the kids? I miss having them tumble into my studio and be charming pests. They'd get a kick out of some things here. I had a weasel in my bathroom one evening, came up along the pipe, took a long weaselly look at me while I was poised to step into the tub and then disappeared below the floor. I hear noises at night in the walls, which doesn't thrill me, even if they're only weasels or mice or something. Cold drives them inside, can we blame them? I'm not into that lately. We waste so much of ourselves with blame, I hate to think of the time I've devoted to it. The cold is good for that (this is a cold house, believe me, you've never known a real draft, one seems to find me wherever I'm at), shivering has a way of focusing my attention, my inclination to dwell on all the ways I've been wounded tends to fade. Chet is Chet, it's not like we were in the middle of a romance. Everything here heightens my sense of myself—not always good, of course. I can't take much for granted anymore, and isn't that how we get along, how we make it easy on ourselves? A man did visit me here. Yes, here, in my house. Intense, and over. Not in the mood today to talk about it, or probably any day. Going for a walk. Tell me about a good movie you've seen, or a book, or a face, anyone, anything we both enjoyed, I want to hear.

After three cups of coffee, Anna negotiated the slippery stones of the shore. Swells, mushy with gray ice, washed lazily near her feet. Maybe a rogue wave would come quietly out of the fog and sweep her away, she didn't care. Too much wine, too much everything. And the high ride stopped and thumped you to the ground, that was the payback, in this wet and chilling wind. The pain of regret was far more acute than a headache, the nausea of remorse no pills or seltzers could relieve. She'd lost her distance, like a reputation, that saving perk of maturity that had been hers, and much of her privacy too, as casually as if she were twenty. She'd tossed away intimacy on Livingstone because . . . he was an attractive man, and that's what she'd wanted last night, to lose herself in the physical, simple as that. Yet things he said came back to her now, bits of talk she could barely recall, but unsettling, suggesting a side to him other than music and dancing and sex.

But wasn't she free to take a man upstairs if she liked? Of course, but, oh . . . something to be said for remaining the solitary woman from away. She lingered over a lobster trap the tides had shoved high up the shore, its netting gorged with sand and seaweed and bits of shell: like her mind.

His body was lean and warm, his tongue was all over her. What mood did he take out the door with him? What sense of *her?* And if he talked around about her, about *this?* To Breagh? Anna would never get back to where she'd been, her footing would be as wobbly as walking these stones.

My deceptions, Chet had told her, are only sexual, all of them. I don't expect, of course, to be thus forgiven.

She was good and cold by the time she reached Murdock's shore-bank. No smoke in the forge chimney high up the back field, but there was a light in his woodshop window. Working. Unavailable. She wouldn't break in on him, not with last night still on her skin. Why his opinion of her should matter so much she couldn't say. Would he ever know?

All right. She had opted for escape. What after all was more timeless, placeless, than the intimacies of sex, when there was no world beyond the one that enwrapped you? What, during its illusions, more uncomplicated, intense, direct? And for a short while that evening she'd left everything gladly behind but desire, and she spent it with a man who felt good in her arms. Was that terrible? Familiar complications, followed by new ones. But the act itself—all the whispers and breathing and lips and tongues and hands—was what it was.

She would have liked to go to Breagh's, just talk with her about anything mundane and ordinary, but she couldn't, not yet. Too fresh, too exposed. What would she do but sit there feeling sick and rather tawdry, Lorna on the floor at her feet, drawing pictures with her, soothing in her innocence?

That afternoon, after fog closed nearer to the house, Anna began a nude study of herself, carrying into her room the wide mirror from above the parlor bureau and setting it vertically against her table. A study of what? She looked over her naked self, at a brutal angle, catching some window, foreshortening her torso, she was all legs, and then upward, goosefleshed, startlingly pale. As honest as Dürer in those ruthless nudes of himself? Could this contrapposto arouse Livingstone again, in this quiet, gray, unforgiving light? Just what he'd thought of her body she wasn't sure, the room had been dim, perhaps her breasts were not as firm as he was used to, her belly had more flesh now. She seemed incredibly bare in this room where, surely, no woman had stood unclothed sketching her intimate parts with scrupulous detail, her hardening nipples, the curls of her dark bush that Chet had once loved (was it thinning, just a bit?), the vague triangle of hair she scribbled in, the locus of all the fuss. And her breasts of course, more pendulous now, she was standing, not lying on her back. That Livingstone had wanted to fuck her was not much consolation after all. She was filling in too many blanks, or creating them, and she had to quit that, even though she wondered what responses she might elicit from him, what kind of play his talk would take, what he might notice, remark on, remember, dislike the day after, posed here as she was: that mattered, she knew, more than it should. She had no understanding of how he felt about her *now*, what respect remained, and the pleasure of the night itself was seeping away. Maybe mystery, fantasy, was preferable to the real thing, you could feel then as you wished.

Later, she pressed her cheek to the window's darkness, she wanted to hear a voice from home, where taking a lover for the night would, among her friends, be forgiven, understood—as long as he didn't belong to one of them. And after all, she was an artist.

XIII.

RED MURDOCK WAS working wood again, the skates had got
him going, pulled him out of that dark pit. He stood amidst a
jumble of stopped work—chairs awaiting varnish, a corner cupboard
without doors, a long block of pine just beginning to turn into a leg in
the lathe. He had walked out of here after Rosaire's funeral, locked the
door behind him.

Frowning, he slid his palm slowly along the smooth oak grain of
Livingstone's unfinished desk. Did he know Anna Starling? Good God,
it couldn't have been him in her window.

Murdock got up a good fire in the small wood stove, a smell of
resin rose out of the shavings and sawdust. On the cluttered workbench he cleared space for two boards, their lush, flowing grain deep
reds and yellowy browns. Long ago his Uncle Hugh, a saltwater seaman, brought them back from Africa, he loved wood, and he'd passed
these on to Murdock. Make a lasting thing out of them, Murdo, he'd
said, I never got around to it. Murdock had so often caressed their
surfaces, the oil of his fingers had darkened them some, polished them.
But their beauty had paralyzed him too: what object was worthy of
them? He could never imagine wasting a centimeter, and anticipating
that first cut always tightened him up as if it were a surgical incision,
and then he hesitated, postponed. But at last, a box for Rosaire. Not
for jewelry—oh, how he wished to see her in the broad silver bracelets,

the amber pendant, amber earrings, topaz ring, the necklace of dark pearls upon her comely skin—but for her ashes.

She'd said, You build me a box, Murdock, please. Flushed with fever, half out of her head at times. Handsome boards, she said, maybe hard maple, I like maple. You'd do the best job, Murdo, I'd love that. Brass fittings maybe, shiny. That's all, I don't want anything fancy. You'll do it up nice, I know, the wood would be pretty. Sand it so smooth, like a mirror. You'll see yourself in the lid, when it's closed. Murdo, don't frown, dear. I mean it, I mean all of it. The love. Lovely, lasting hardwood. Holding my ashes. You love me, don't you? Come here, sit by me, sit. Let me touch your hands. . . .

Very hard was this wood, exotic, from a forest in Africa. Murdock inhaled the oily, spicy scent.

By early afternoon, working slowly, the strange, bitter aroma of their dust in his nostrils, he had the boards sawn, planed, the joints dovetailed. The ice skates sat on a wall shelf. The pond ice was all but gone, a thin rim at the edges, gray among the broken cattails. She wouldn't skate this season, and who knew where she'd be come winter again? Even so, they were hers.

He wouldn't tell her he had come near enough her window that Saturday night, just visiting, just stopping by, to catch her dancing in her workroom. Alone, at first. And then with a man.

On his way to the house to eat, there she was, coming up from the shore, Anna in her parka bright red against the wan spring turf of the field. She hailed him, some object in her hand, approaching quickly as if he might rush inside. She seemed not at ease, uncertain of him, as well she might be, given that cold morning she'd phoned him up. Last Saturday night, following the shore to her house, he'd hoped to make up for that, but he'd had to settle for a window look, unclear and troubling.

"How are you today, Anna?" he said, offering his hand. She grasped it, returned his smile.

"A little out of breath, Murdock, is how I am." The wind had ruffled her rich black hair, rouged her cheeks.

"What have you there?" he said.

"Look. A wooden wine goblet from the beach. You'd think it'd be beaten up but it's not even cracked or scarred."

Murdock turned the stemmed goblet in his hands. "Teak." He sniffed the rim. "Odd item to wash up here. We drink more plain than that. Tipped off of a yacht, I suppose."

"Let's hope he didn't fall overboard along with it," Anna said.

"Or she," Murdock said. "You collect things off the beach, do you?"

"I'm afraid so."

"Come inside, I'll show you mine."

Red Murdock conducted her through his collection of beach-combed objects. Bottles, some from the shore, others from ash pits, he had blended along a wide windowsill, shades from a bitters molasses brown rising to an old golden beer bottle, an aqua cough syrup beginning a run of blue that concluded in a cobalt jar.

"My grandfather was great for the patent medicines," he said. "Any with alcohol." Rosaire had laughed, surveying the glassware arranged to catch the sun, and flowers in season in the now-empty vases, columbine and lady's mantle and early lilies, Oh, Murdock, aren't you the bowerbird! In her own house, she'd have candles lit when he came in the evening, such a comfortable light around her.

Anna aimed at the sea a pair of German binoculars, the lenses clouded with mist. There was also a seized-up clock, its face gone but revealing a rich collection of brass gears and wheels. A carbide miner's lamp, its brass polished, sat in the bight of a small harpoon. She picked up a large white conch.

"That's my granny's. She'd blow that when she wanted us. It carries a long way, if you know how, we had our signals."

"Your things are far more interesting than mine," she said.

"These are culled. Not long since you've been at it, wait till summer."

"Wait is the word, I guess. Where's the spring, Murdock?"

"You're in it, but once it turns, it turns quickly. Buds on the trees, if you look close. New grass just poking up in the old."

He couldn't remember when he'd last had a woman in. Breagh probably. "You're in good trim again? I should have doubled back on you after your accident, but Breagh told me you were coming along and . . ."

"I'm fine, Murdock. You got me through the worst of it."

She said she'd like to see his forge but he said they'd have tea first, and he laid out bannock and tinned salmon and blueberry jam from last summer, a pot of tea. She had questions, once they warmed up with each other, about the old house and its idiosyncrasies (yes, when the wind is sou'west, you get that kind of howl in the chimney, scared the hell out of me when I was a boy), about his work (I did all kinds of carpentry once, but mostly finish now, cabinets and furniture and the like), about living since birth, as he had, with the sea to his back (oh, I was cradled here, when I woke up, when I lay down, it shaped my mind, no doubt about that. Funny though how we all like the water).

He was enjoying her there, across his table, her lively smile, her interest in what was his, in him. But Anna Starling was not a solitary woman anymore, she'd had a man in her house. Beyond this friendly acquaintance, he did not want to feel anything more for a woman. The way Rosaire died had exhausted him, she could not even speak at the end. Anna glanced at a framed picture on the wall—displayed there because in this room he did most of his living—Rosaire hugging his neck, both of them laughing. He could remember every little thing they had done that day and into the night, and what she wore, the smell of her perfume, the way she felt in his arms, the whisper of her voice.

But he only said, "She was my woman."

"Ah," Anna said, "she's pretty."

"She was," he said, looking away. "She was, yes."

"Breagh is very pretty, isn't she?" Anna said, sensing his unease.

"I'm not keen on some of her men. I've said so and I guess I shouldn't."

"Livingstone Campbell I know a little," Anna said, carefully, wanting another take on him besides her own. "I haven't met any others."

"Aren't many others." Murdock frowned. "He's from a good family, across the water there, St. Aubin. Related to David Livingstone, through his mother's side."

"The famous missionary? Stanley and all that?"

"I don't know if that matters to him. Oh, he can play music all right, good guitar. She'll tire of him." Yesterday Livingstone had showed up in a new car, mud-splashed, powerful. When he stepped out of it, setting his polished cowboy boots down carefully, holding his black cowboy hat against the wind, he looked, gazing through dark sunglasses,

like a man dressed for a part in a movie, and Murdock didn't like the
role. They talked, as they usually did now, coolly. Tension had grown
between them, he knew Murdock didn't think him fit for Breagh.
When will that damn desk be done, Murdock, supposed to be months
ago? he'd said. Fancy drawers take time, Murdock told him, they're
tricky. And why so damn big? You could sleep on that. You just finish
it, Murdock, I'll worry about what to do with it, and what I sleep on.
Murdock wondered how Anna knew him, in what way.

"You've seen him perform?" she said.

"At a dance, he's got a little band. He was younger then, easier to
like. Well, it was okay, I wasn't struck by it. Not enough fiddle for my
fancy. Little Lorna, she needs a dad, and it won't be him. A man who
can play music, you see, a woman can't help but like him, eh? That
music coming out of him, knowing it's inside him? She thinks it might
be there all the time. But no man can put music out there all the time,
they forget that. No, it wears, like everything else, in the light of day.
You know, she's a smart girl altogether, but headstrong, stubborn.
Not always smart about men, a little careless that way, our Breagh."

"She'd have her choice of them, I would think."

"Wouldn't you? But who knows what goes into it."

"I don't know myself sometimes."

"We can have a look at the forge, Anna, if that's what you'd like.
Not much to see."

"You mean for a woman to see?"

He laughed. "I suppose I did."

"Well, Murdock, I happen to love old iron things, how they're
made, how they look, what they're used for. Even scrap. I do metal
sculptures."

"Don't know as I've seen that."

"Then I'll show you. Some wonderful old stuff in my tumbledown barn. And there are pieces of an old sleigh, I think, runners with a beautiful flourish to them, parts of a seat."

"A shame it went to ruin, I'd have saved it. My uncle raced that sleigh on the ice. His children let it rot."

"I'll give what's left of it another life, if your cousins don't mind."

"My blessing. Who cares if they do?"

WHATEVER SHE TOUCHED or pointed to in the forge, Murdock explained its use. She held up a large horseshoe. "Could you spare one of these?"

"Sure, take it. There's more in that basket. Draft horse. We always had horses, horses were the means for us, always. Even when my dad got a second-hand car finally, we still had a horse. He never used a tractor, tractors came late here if you had one at all, seems a lot of things came late to Cape Breton. The sound of horses never leaves you, you know? Horses aren't dumb either, people say so but it isn't true. Oh, you can make them dumb, but give them a chance. Horses, yes."

He told Anna she could pick out other odds and ends for sculptures, most of it wouldn't be used anymore and better it go for that. Pleased, she gathered a pile together, put what she could carry into her backpack.

"I'll drop those heavier pieces by as soon as I can."

He took her to his workshop, where she quickly noticed the big desk.

"That's Livingstone's," he said. "Look at this." He twisted a brass drawer pull in two directions, the hinged front dropped open and revealed a hidden compartment extending deep under the bottom. "I guess I shouldn't have done that, it's not a secret anymore," but it satisfied him anyway that she knew.

"Secrets in a drawer," Anna said. "Those are the easy ones to keep."

"And these are for you," he said, reaching for the skates.

"Oh, how beautiful!" she said, running her finger along a blade, the oiled stocks. "You made them?"

"For the pond, so you wouldn't fear it anymore. Skating goes way back in time, did you know? A few thousand years ago people made skates from the bones of animals. No blades, just flat on the bottom. Skaters pushed themselves over the ice, with sticks."

"I'd love to wear these, I would."

"Maybe next winter. On new ice."

She touched his hand and for a moment he thought she was going to kiss him but she stepped back. "I hope I can find a way to thank you, so thoughtful of you."

"Don't forget your goblet," he said.

"You keep it, Murdock. You like wood."

"I don't drink wine."

"You never know, there might be an occasion."

"There used to be lots of them."

Tracing absently the smooth teak contours of the goblet, Red Murdock watched her from the workshop doorway. She leaned forward against the weight of her pack, into the swirling fog that closed around her before she reached the shore.

She would never know that he'd stood in snow to his ankles, outside her window, his bare hands deep in his peacoat pockets, fingering a tear he'd meant to sew. The skates, wrapped in a paper bag, were tucked under his arm. The wind was sharp in his hair, he'd come without a hat because he thought he'd be inside her kitchen by then. But how could he knock on her door? He had heard the music—not his kind of music but a sort that might get you dancing anyway, he could understand that—and there she was, a shadow swaying, and he took a step toward the window to watch her, just for a minute, the pane dewed with the inside heat, Anna moving in candlelight, twirling in a yellow shawl that had belonged to his grandmother, she'd been into a drawer upstairs, but he didn't care about that either. The wind had played across the field behind him, a zephyr of snow dusted his face and he tasted it on his tongue. She was dancing with herself, in a place of her own, he didn't belong there. He wasn't the man to disturb a spell like that. He'd pulled the seaman's collar up near his ears and was about to turn for home when he saw someone moving slowly toward her and back, a man dancing too. Who the hell was that? Not enough light to tell. A confusion of anger and envy rose in Murdock, but he'd turned away, that wasn't his business, he had no right to feel as he did.

part two

WHATEVER'S
OUT THERE

XIV.

B Y THE TIME the odd rains began, Anna had made it through
a sort of spring. After she'd called on Murdock and lugged
home, like booty, the iron gifts, she had joined a few—the tongs,
closed into a heart shape, and hooks and rings and chains—into a
sculpture, and set it on her back porch announcing, she liked to think,
a connection, a shared totem, a mysterious effigy no one could ignore:
Anna Starling lives here.

The last of the shaded snow, granular and sallow beneath trees
and brush, shrank away into the black duff and the soaked, purplish
carpet of last year's leaves, nothing left of their autumn blaze. Shoots
of hay, fine and wind-fanned like flames, began to green the dun fields,
and although it seemed late and slow, the hardwoods lost their gray
filigree of winter and joined the conifers in darkening the woods of the
mountain and the hills of St. Aubin across the water, emboldening deer
to come down from higher ground. A doe had peered at her out of the
trees one morning, still as a tree herself, and they exchanged appraisals
through the curling mist until Anna reached for her camera: a buck
she could not see snorted and the doe bolted away with him, crashing
out of sight. She found violets both purple and white, so pleased to see
their fragile blossoms she took a bouquet to her room but they quickly
wilted in a canning-jar vase.

Red Murdock she did not see after he dropped off the hardware from his forge—I'm terrible busy just now, he said, I'm catching up— just his van on the highway one day. The muddy road out was pocked with teeth-jarring potholes that kept her off it as much as possible. She saw chimney smoke from his workshop when she walked the shore where she sometimes fled to evade, in its breezes, the vicious little blackflies hatching from the full brooks and streams, digging into her clothing, her hat, her hair, raising welts. In the forest of her youth, there'd been few insects, the bug-resistant redwoods were dominant and decomposed slowly, the huge old stumps sprouted ferns, their root stock sending up rings of saplings around them, the heart of new groves whose trees would never, like their unlogged forebears, reach one or two or even three millenniums.

She was absorbed one afternoon in a soft, windless forest rain that reminded her of her early home, the feel of it. There was a moist eva- nescence in the mosses, the rotted red marrow of a stump, a patch of black bog leaves. To add to her still lifes, she sketched the texture of aged bark and dead wood, the gnarly encrustations on windfalls.

The skates she hung from a hall tree in her workroom as if she might, summoned by another skater, sling them over her shoulder and fly out the door. The night with Livingstone had faded, whatever risks it ignited seemed to have guttered out: it was like one of the old photo negatives she'd found in a drawer—the faces dark and unrecognizable in a livid but indefinite landscape. At certain times, especially during the moody rains, she'd wonder about him—there was nothing vague, in the chilly damp of her house, about his body pressed to hers, the heat of his mouth, his hands. She did one self-portrait after another in charcoals, in graphite, lacerating in their frankness, refractions of herself day by day. Some she lit morning fires with in the wood stove, holding the door open while the crushed paper blackened and curled. Others she kept like entries in a daybook.

It was afternoon, she wanted a walk.

The dark pond was bordered with green spears of cattail shooting up through the rough tan mat of last year's reeds, an animal skeleton woven into them, skull and spine and bits of hide, some winter victim. She was surprised to hear the thrumming engines of what turned out to be a big black-and-white freighter passing down the strait, inbound, Willard had told her, for a gypsum mine in the Island's interior. She watched the ship, its deck full of machinery, until its wake sent a succession of swells hissing up the shore. A wooden fisherman's buoy bobbed toward her, painted green and yellow. She picked it up by its frayed rope. So much to sketch, to collect, to gather into something new, she felt as if she were striding again, not crawling, not standing still. She wanted to work, and she was—when she pushed clutter from her mind.

Was Alicia Snow mainly a matter of *degree?* Dalliances, affairs, flings that always flamed out had been *okay?* She was the woman you feared all along but didn't know it, the one who would show up at the wrong time and against whom, at your age, you had little defense. Anna's mother had delivered warnings—Don't let men have their way with you, or Don't make yourself more attractive than you need to be—as if they were ancient wisdom, not clichés. No man in her life now. Livingstone, the one-night flame, was not there at all. Good. She could not even contemplate a relationship of any duration or depth, it made her listless, irritable, impatient—the effort that went into learning about another man, his idiosyncrasies, and making room for him. *Living* with him? Tiresome to think of.

The sky went heavy and dark and she turned back to her path. Sometimes the weather arrived high along the mountain ridge behind the house, as if the roiling convolutions of cloud, swelling and black and veined with light, would play out their drama there, but soon rain charged down the mountainside or in from the sea, lashing her as she staggered home.

But this was a different rain and Anna watched it from her room, she couldn't turn her back to it, the sudden gusts, the trees seething, rocking madly, and after dark, heat lightning started up in the west, great white flares, and the wind soon drove pelting rain and thunder. It beat mayflowers to the ground, muddying their petals flat, and cut sharp little gullies down the driveway, so intense at times it felt apocalyptic, as if something as common as rain had gone suddenly wrong, become thick and vengeful. Any patch of blue was quickly chased and overtaken, the slow, rolling, rain-laden clouds releasing a dense and steady downpour. When that ceased, a mist took over, or a relentless drizzle filled the windless air, the woods trembling with wet, mosses luminescent in the gloom, light seemed to rush from them. In the black pools, raindrop rings shimmered outward, intersecting, disturbing the light there, then moved on to the mad brooks that before had seemed tame, now one little vigorous falls after another, foaming in the darkness.

The next day the sky was a blank foggy white out of which rain drummed. Anna walked out in it anyway, half-blinded, squinting through the streams, rain crackling on her rubber hood. She wandered the glistening, soggy landscape, stooping to slip some object into her pocket—a long eagle feather pasted to the earth, black fading into white, a small burl of wood hard as a rock—every day, she'd not let this diabolical weather shut her inside the house, waiting for it to break. She could see the shadowy form of a fishing boat pitching in the slow swells, tending a lobster trap before it blanked out in mist. She swiped rain from her eyes and moved on down the shore, bent over, searching, evading the waves reaching for her feet.

When she glanced up, she had gone as far as Red Murdock's beach, his house lay up the field, two rectangles of light in the rain. Kitchen. She ached for company. She was tempted to knock, sit with him in that hospitable room, listening to his calm voice, she would show him what she'd found, a small, unspectacular stone that had cracked open to reveal its cluster of crystals. What a bedraggled sight she would be, he'd think her crazy for scouring the beach in a punishing rain like this.

He had pulled her from the winter pond, she had not forgotten the gentle feel of his hands. But she hoped never to need rescuing again.

THAT NIGHT THE storms rose, pounding into her sleep, and she kept to her bed, clear of windows. When everything else went quiet, none of her activities could fill the dangerous spaces or distract her from them, and she was left to listen against the incessant dripping of the eaves. Through her slightly raised window the brooks were like heavy rain behind rain, unleashed, scoring the mud of the mountainside.

The rooms were damp, the wall plaster, her sheets cool with it. The power clapped out into a sudden, aggressive darkness as blinding, as she stood there flicking a switch, as a dream. There seemed a rush of fragrance from the mayflowers she'd found off a woods path, pink, delicate blossoms hidden beneath heart-shaped leaves. . . . She hadn't heard from Breagh, and that wormed around inside her, that she might know about her madness with Livingstone. How senseless and unnecessary that would be. Anna admired her, and she had not intended to interfere in her life, not *intended* . . . anything.

Downstairs, the window in her workroom leaked. It wasn't as if a dam would burst or her ceiling cave in, but this nagged at her, this responsibility for the house. The outdoors was creeping indoors. Willard had not showed up lately, he seemed to get into funks and disappear, then return suddenly to the back door full of talk and a thirst for tea. Of course Red Murdock would help, if she asked. She wanted to depend for a little while on someone *else,* a man, for repairs at least. But no, she wouldn't call on Murdock for a nettlesome leak, for puddles along the wall, though once she would have turned, without a thought, to her husband. Chet, could you see to that, please? Anna, I will, give me a little time. Oh, how much time she had given him.

WHEN SHE MET Chet, he was a jazz-loving writer, editor of the campus literary magazine, his dark brown hair long and shaggy, wearing tight jeans and rumpled corduroy jackets, declaiming about literature and politics late into the night, in bars, at parties. They were both undergraduates then, and they soon moved in with each other, enjoying the fresh, guiltless passion of that life, free of responsibilities, the pleasures of throwing their own parties and drinking and smoking and sleeping late and, on the heels of the night before, making love again as soon as they opened their eyes and sometimes before. They had an unabashed physical fascination with each other, in lying open and naked any time of day. They were Chet and Anna, or Anna and Chet, depending on which friends or acquaintances were referring to them, which end of the scale a man or woman might place their weight. They both went on to the same university for graduate degrees, she an

MFA, he a PhD, but the closer they got to marriage, the more Anna felt his career overwhelming hers, not in any overt way—he did not demand that his take primacy or even that she adopt his name—but the assumption was there, and she failed to challenge it until years later, she'd felt perhaps that they could work it out once Chet got his doctorate and was hired at a decent university, she might be able to resume her own studies, finish her art degree, at least, be her own person, an artist. Then an unplanned pregnancy, a miscarriage. Chet was honest about his relief, she realized he had no wish for fatherhood (neither had her own dad, but he loved her deeply, and showed her in every way he could), and her desire for a child faded away. Her art filled that vacuum, or so she believed.

But Chet did not finish his doctorate, he saw himself as a writer, not a scholar, he hoped to be another Chekhov (she might have asked him whether another Chekhov was called for, but she didn't say things like that to him, not then), and he said one day, Let's go to California, things are happening there. He took a job at a small college in central California where the pay was not good, but Anna was glad to return, she felt it some consolation for her interrupted career. She got work as a secretary in the art department of his school, continued her artwork on her own, at home, at night courses. Since Chet's career as a short story writer seemed, to him at least, always on the verge of rising into some kind of literary notice without actually taking off, his faculty advancement, in the absence of a PhD and notable publications, was on hold. He resented this quietly and his belief in his creative abilities seemed to grow in proportion to the lack of stories in print: you had to know the right people, he said, you had to get into an influential clique and get blessed by the right critics and stroked by the right editors or you didn't have a chance, and he wouldn't take that route, his work spoke for itself, he wasn't going to go down on his knees to anyone.

Anna continued her employment so she'd have money for herself, for travel, a second car, they were stuck in this college town for whatever future they cared to imagine. We could be in worse places, Chet said, who wouldn't want to live here? Who indeed? she said. I ought to know.

He published in small literary quarterlies, the ones that came in a flush of enthusiasm, manifestos, and obscure titles and were gone as soon as their grants ran out. She began to feel sorry for him, and tried her best to hide it. He was not a bad writer, and now and then he turned out a story she genuinely liked, it had power and something fresh, and she felt it *should* appear in a good magazine or compete for a prize. But Chet could not break free of the academic pack, not set himself significantly apart from other competent, mediocre, able fiction writers. The ground was laid for his discontents, his boredom, the diversions of sexual pursuits. I like pretty women, he said. What can I say? Hang me.

Anna pulled away on her own, nurtured a reputation for skillful and original drawings and she demanded eventually the time and means to explore them full-time. Chet complied, thinking it, she did not doubt now, a fair trade-off: so long as he saw to their livelihood, and gave her room, there would remain a part of his life he need not answer for. He said to her, You know, it's not bad to be a nobody? I've come to like being ignored. It frees a man up.

ANNA COILED BATH towels on the floor beneath the windows and in the morning tried to work at her table, but water streaking down the wall distracted her almost to tears. Like a leaking boat, and how could she ignore that, in the one room she *worked* in? It had the southern light, and a good feeling about it—women had sewn here, by this light, they had spun wool, the spokes of their spinning wheels flickering through the rays of a winter sun—except when the walls wept and cried for her attention. She changed the towels, she wrung them out in the sink. Okay, was she bailing or was she not? She couldn't finish a letter, even to Melissa: *I spotted tiny flowers close to the ground yesterday, blossoms are scarce here yet—I think they're wild strawberries and it gave me joy on an overcast day. One day Willard brought me two early lobsters, his cousin has a boat, they were cooked, glad for that, I could never drop them in boiling water. I watched crows carry away the heads full of that green and red stuff (roe?), I wouldn't eat it but Willard said it is "some good" mashed on bread, tomalley he calls it. Saw a snake when we had a snatch of sun, bathing in the field. It didn't want to move, but did. I knew how it felt.* She didn't care to talk to anyone else right now, and letters were talking, that's what she always liked about them, their special conversation, deliberate, thought-through, not like gabbing on a telephone. How important had become her walks to the beat-up and rust-stained mailbox, she could feel, defensively, its empty, chilled interior before she lowered the lid, but when an actual letter lay inside, one with cancelled stamps on a clearly personal envelope, she would save it until after supper and her room was good and warm, it was like receiving a guest.

The grumblings of thunder passed away and the last squall blew through, followed by a washed, leaden silence. Everything was waterlogged, smothered, even birdsong. It took all her will to rouse herself, to lift the night off her chest. Dangerous days, she might have packed her things in a frenzied, unexamined joy and driven away, stayed at the wheel until nightfall and gotten deep into New Brunswick, closeted herself in a motel like a fugitive, closed the drapes, watched TV numbly, drunk wine, eaten takeout food to country-and-western music.

But here she was, the house draped with damp clothes and strewn with belongings like a ship battered by a long storm. Sheets of drawings lay about, curled into loose tubes. And there on the big clipboard was the dog drawing in which two animals had merged into one, into some entity she was trying to understand. The dog in the trap was a dark, howling figure here, but what the work needed she had not yet fully realized: into the energy of her lines, her strokes, there had to be the shock of her own falling, the burning surprise of the water, the dog tortured in different shadings of that frosted pond, its agony in the icy light.

The dog in the air was another matter, clawing at her consciousness, and the instrument of his suffering was not a thoughtless trapper but someone worse. What she wanted was that one moment when the dog grasped its own helplessness, its yelp of recognition and despair. The trust of an animal in a human being, that was heartbreaking, wasn't it, to see it so awfully trashed? The beaver who'd diligently built its house in the pond, oblivious that its life was not ordered only by itself and its perceivable world, was not betrayed, only hunted. It had no master to defer to, its loyalty to be shattered by.

She put the drawing aside, not in the mood for its difficulties, the complexities of its composition, it would come together, sometime. She would concentrate instead on the yellowed skull she'd found in woods moss, possibly a feral cat's, with its long incisors, rendering it in meticulous detail, the fine lines of bone, of teeth, stained like an old teacup. How had it died?

A breeze trembled through the crow quill jammed into her pencil jar. She rushed to the open window: just the field and its new grasses, sweeping to the shorebank, the stones, the blue currents. The long hill of St. Aubin like thick, uneven hedgerow, a house tucked into it here and there like a nest. The sea was empty. No one. The pond below meandered into the woods, its dark surface barely riffled, new cattails bristling at its margins. No one, just three gulls dozing, nudged in lazy circles by the wind, out where the ice had opened underfoot.

High above the sea a bald eagle soared in slow circles, until it dropped suddenly, gliding low over the water, legs down, claws yawning before, with a sharp splash, they clamped a fish, the bird's broad wings laboring for a few strokes as it climbed toward the tall pine near the shore, a long-used nest of sticks secured on the treetop's half-dead branches. Anna watched it through her binoculars as it landed, storing the images in her mind. She had begun a collage of eagle sketches, in flight, at rest, and, like now, tearing scales and flesh.

She would phone Willard about the leaky window. In the kitchen mirror: sleeplessness darkened her eyes, a swipe of charcoal on her cheek.

After a supper of cold salmon and cold potatoes, Anna took the party dress from the clothes tree in her room, as if it were evidence, and carefully hung it back in the garment bag, zipping it shut. She closed the closet door. It wasn't fair her sweat was in it, whoever it belonged to, but hadn't it hung there all these years, waiting for someone? The woman from here who'd owned it, worn it, would surely not approve of Anna, how she wore it, how she took it off, but the dress still looked fine. Another woman might dance in it yet.

Red Murdock was not far, she would talk to him, if he was at home, after she pulled the frayed ends of herself together. She would go with an errand, bring him biscuits still warm from the oven. That was what she wanted to do.

On the back porch she sipped coffee. Clouds like train smoke were moving away over the sea. The apple trees in the old orchard, in fits of wind, shook loose little showers from their leaves. At the pond, above the new stalks of bulrushes, red-winged blackbirds harried a crow, like tiny planes in a dogfight. The brooks were running loud.

XV.

ANNA TUGGED OFF her boots inside the door and stood in her stocking feet. Breagh sat in a turmoil of sewing, scraps of material scattered on every surface and the floor, bits of black velvet, strips of a glistening chocolate satin, crimson cotton bands, and torn tissue, a spool of red thread Lorna was twirling like a top, strands entwining her hair, the sewing machine humming in bursts, pausing while Breagh manipulated a hem under its needle, telling her daughter through teeth gritted against two common pins, "Lorna, honey, play with the *empty* spools, okay?" She told Anna to clear off a chair and sit down, she'd be done in a sec, just had to finish this waist.

ANNA PICKED UP a whimsical tam, a rainbow of dark pinks and lavenders spiraling out from a black pom, it flopped alluringly to one side when she put it on.

"Looks terrific," Breagh said, glancing at her. "I've been at this most of the night, have to get more stock finished before next Monday, and Molly's dropping by a few sweaters. Isobel hates a lot of forlorn space on the racks, empty hangers and the like. So I'm stitching fast as a witch. Eh, Lorna? Oh, Anna, would you take that red thread off her? Hard enough keeping her away from pins."

Anna talked to Lorna as she unwound the thread from her hair, Lorna shut her eyes and hummed, and Anna hummed with her,

159

listening for her song. She could see no trace of Livingstone, a full ashtray, a tossed hat, a toy for Lorna. She had almost hoped he might be here, together with her and Breagh, to know what he'd say, what he would do with himself among all three of them, and what *she* herself would do, say.

"What do you hear from Mr. Campbell?" she said lightly.

"Not much. *About* him."

"Gossip?"

"Not exactly. Molly saw him over at MacDermid's old place, on foot, disappearing down the driveway, what's left of it. I was down north then anyway."

So he'd been on the road, he'd driven past Anna's house in the rain. "Awful rain, wasn't it, tearing through everything? Potholes and mud now."

Breagh stopped her machine, raised the needle. "Lorna wants to get outside, and so do I."

Anna had Lorna coloring a figure she'd penciled for her on a big sheet of paper, a galloping horse, its rider in a flowing baroque cape, a hat with a swooping feather Lorna was intensely turning green.

"What was Livingstone doing over there?" Anna said.

"That house? It's completely shut up. Who knows? It drops down to a nice beach, a cove, people used to come out from town and treat it like a public park. Nothing new there. Tea with rum?"

Breagh clapped the kettle on the stove. Lorna wandered after her asking for juice.

The view out the windows was simple and exhilarating—just the back field sloping toward the cliff, beyond it a wide and breathless sea, as if you were airborne.

"Do you know about this Coastal Watch Program?" Anna called to her. "I heard it on the radio."

"Liv had his own watch program, I think. He used to go down to the cliff there, have a cigarette and look out for a while."

"Likes the sea, does he . . . ?"

"Oh, he was curious about old Dougal's shore down below, that broken-down boat skid there. I told him, you wouldn't haul a boat up that thing, not anymore, you'd be far better off at MacDermid's Cove further up. I said ask Red Murdock, but I don't think he ever did. They've got a good-sized fishing boat, him and his buddies, you'd need a wharf for that anyway. Whatever he and Billy are up to, I don't care to know. Schemes, big plans. Talk. That's Livingstone."

Breagh served tea at the kitchen table and two cups seemed to put Livingstone on the periphery. Anna relaxed. Had Breagh cooled toward him?

"You're busy, I know," Anna said. "But if you could take a break, would you pose for me? A figure study? Just for a while."

Breagh took a slow, thoughtful sip of tea, her eyes on Anna. "No clothes, you mean? Whoa."

"Yes. Nude."

"Nude. That's a shivery word, Anna. I'd have to think about it. Couldn't you just do me . . . ?"

"Clothed? It's a figure study, Breagh. Artists have drawn nudes for ages."

"I know that."

"An elemental subject, really, the human form. Nice light today. But of course, if you're not comfortable. . . ."

"It's a cool room."

"Without a stitch on. Never done that, I have to say."

"Of course. Why would you?"

"Why me?"

"You'd make an appealing model. And there's your pre-Raphaelite hair."

"*What* kind of hair?"

"Brilliant, full of color. The Pre-Raphaelite painters in the nineteenth century loved vibrant hues. A famous model, Rossetti's muse and lover, had such coppery hair. I only have my black charcoal with me, but I'll touch it up at home."

Breagh fetched a small bottle of rum from the cupboard and poured some in her tea. "Why not Lorna? She loves to run around in the buff."

"Her figure is not rich like yours, and she'd never sit still. I need a mature form."

"Rich? I'll have to remember that when I'm fat and ugly. I'm not a prude, by the way."

"I'm sure you're not."

"I'll put Lorna down for her nap. You need rum in your cup?"

"No thanks." Anna smiled. "Maybe you do."

"Yeah, half a bottle."

Anna listened to her gather Lorna up in the next room, their soft talk back and forth, Lorna resisting but by rote, then their slow steps up the stairway, their murmurs in a bedroom. Anna reached across the table for the bottle and took a quick nip of rum, coughing as it went down. Maybe she should not have asked. There was a long silence upstairs before Breagh came down. She had brushed her hair.

"Okay, Anna. All in the name of art, right?"

"Thanks, Breagh."

She undressed, tossing her clothes among her sewing with an air of nonchalance belied by a blush high on her cheekbones. She stood awkwardly hugging her breasts while Anna suggested a pose. "Sit on this throw cushion, it's less tiring." On the floor she tucked her long legs under her, one hand in her lap, leaning on her other arm, her unbound hair falling over her shoulders.

"I hope that's not a strain," Anna said. "Tell me if you need a rest."

"I'm not used to just sitting, naked as a baby at that."

Sketching her gave Anna an odd feeling, seeing her outline emerge slowly on the sheet of paper, the graceful lines of her body, she didn't need to diet or work out, she took her beauty for granted, as the young could do, at least for a while. Why did she seem so much more naked somehow than any life model Anna had drawn?

"You never posed for anyone?" Anna said.

"Oh . . . I let Livingstone take snapshots once, at that rocky shore back there, down the cliff. Nobody around. Nothing trashy. I just hoped he didn't develop them at the supermarket. All he wanted was a tumble anyway."

"Did you?"

"Want it? Do it? Well, yes, it was a beautiful, warm day. Wouldn't you, Anna?"

She felt her cheeks heat up. "I wouldn't be above it, no."

"With Livingstone, I mean."

"He's a lot younger than me, Breagh."

"Age has nothing to do with it, girl. You're attractive enough."

"Thank you. I'll take that to heart." Was Breagh teasing something out of her? Did she know after all? Gossip could touch anyone, even a woman from away. "I can't imagine I'm Livingstone's type."

"What type is *he?*"

"I don't know him well enough to say, Breagh. He's just young, and I'm a middle-aged woman."

"You're new. You're different. Men like that."

"Not different enough, I think." A flash of anger rose in Anna. Discrepancy in ages must have crossed Chet's mind more than once, an issue, no doubt, he had dealt with successfully. He was, after all, a man, and Alicia Snow had been right there in front of his eyes. Anna could, if so moved, render Breagh's face, those breasts, those limbs, any way her inner eye might choose, distort, exaggerate those maybe too-long thighs, the brown mole on her ribs, the incipient fat of her belly, imbue her body with something not visible in this room, do a Lucian Freud, for instance, she had the artistic license. But she kept it straight and representational, seeking the currents that had passed between Breagh and Livingstone, Livingstone and Anna. She had asked Breagh out of her clothes, she was there as he had seen her, and so she owned a little of what they'd had—not enough to claim anything much, but enough to take the edge off her guilt, and her own feelings about that man. What was more selfish anyway than sex, more consumingly personal? Did she and Breagh even know each other well enough to think of that night as betrayal? It had turned into a certain kind of evening during which any sensible moral perspective seemed irrelevant, not in the emotional mix. Nothing shocking in that. Would Breagh, in Anna's place, have done differently?

The drawing went smoothly, Breagh's figure a rhythm of sure lines, of shadow and light. The soft scrape of charcoal lulled them both, the wind playing about the house. Anna glanced out at the ocean where a dingy white fishing boat was sheltering in the lee of Bird Island, no gulls swirling and diving above its stern as they usually did.

They talked softly back and forth, as if the enterprise were solemn. Anna didn't want to keep her much longer from her sewing and the room felt cooler.

"Your shop all fixed up, Breagh?"

"Nearly. Isobel is up there now painting the inside. Lorna will like it. There's kids close by and she can nap in the back."

"I'm all but done," Anna said when she noticed her shiver. "I'll touch it up at home."

Breagh pulled on a green sweater long as a short dress and stood over Anna's shoulder. "So. There I am." Anna could feel her staring at it as if making up her mind. "That's classy, though. Too good for the likes of Livingstone."

"It's yours when I'm finished. If you like."

"Really? I'll show my friends when I'm old and gray, tell them, hey, that's me, I used to look like that. If anyone cares."

"Anyone who looks at it will," Anna said.

Breagh smiled, shook her head. "Just don't pin it to your wall, okay?"

"It's between you and me, if that's how you want it."

She pressed upon Anna a whimsical hat, cloche-like, in three shades of purple and trimmed with black velvet. For the drawing, she said. Anna said no, you needn't, but she rather liked herself in the hat—Breagh said she looked slightly wicked, possibly dangerous. Anna didn't want to think, as she cocked her head in the full-length mirror, what would Chet say about it, but she did, hearing at the same time his sarcasm, which of course she would deserve. As for Livingstone, she could not guess. . . . If the hat had an occasion, it would be a private one.

Lorna had awakened and was calling for her mother.

"No need to run," Breagh said.

"I won't. I love seeing Lorna. But I might walk out back while you get her up."

Behind the house the turf was a saturated mat under her boots, but the wind raced through the grass newly green. She did a quick sketch of old Dougal's deer fence, the singing line of its poles corralling only weeds now. The ocean opened to the eye here, the field ended abruptly at a cliff. Bird Island's bleak plateaus seemed nearer, and birds were there, bits of white and dark circling the cliffs, diving. What a place for a little farm. Did that ever lighten the labor here, the sea always near? Island and sea. The weather must have hit them full-on, and oh how they'd be *in* it. Anna tried to steady her sketchpad but the wind buffeted her about and she had to quit with only the vertical lines of the fence. A steep path nearby zigzagged down the cliff face of clay and rock to a beach mostly stones where the swells swarmed and whitened. Was that where Breagh had undressed for Livingstone? Near the path a stream cut a narrow valley in the cliff, and at its mouth where the rocks were scattered flat lay an old boat cradle fashioned out of heavy poles, bits of bark still clinging to them. A rusty winch was affixed to the head of it to haul a boat up clear of the sea. Old Dougal's rig, for when he'd fished. He was a tough old man until the rest home got him, Breagh had said, and that depressed him to death.

Anna looked back to the house and Lorna waved to her from a bedroom window, the curtain parted by her mother's hand.

XVI.

RED MURDOCK, AFTER rains he couldn't remember heavier finally broke, headed up into the mountainside woods, into their drizzling leaves and needles, the soft path shining with puddles. He'd been awake since the wee-hour dark when the rain fell so straight and thick he couldn't but listen to it, hard as it was, it could have beaten a man to the ground, that gray water sheeting his windowpane. And when it stopped suddenly, as if a long wave had just receded, everything was noisy with water, the trickle of roof and eaves, an attic leak pinging in a pail, restless bushes shivering, dripping, rivulets snaking through the fields. The brooks were soft roaring torrents, worse than spring, than snowmelt. Sometime in the night they'd climbed their banks and rampaged down through the forest floor, gouging tree roots, flattening brush and saplings like grass, silting the glistening green moss brown, clotting recklessly with jammed rocks, plowed out by the force of the water and dammed against windfalls that had crashed across the streams. The light was peculiar, as if the woods were shocked, still shimmering with what had swept through them.

Murdock was soon lost in a pale mist, feeling out with his feet the rhythm of the ground, then the little clearing emerged that he'd cut out as a boy, to play in, to gaze out from, to be high up in alone. But he was going gray by the time he'd built a bench here, and from this nick in the mountainside he could see a long way in three directions, and not far behind him the mountain turned steep, bare, unclimbable.

Rosaire, on a fine autumn afternoon, crisp and bright, had come here with him. Tired that day, a little breathless, she was, her illness unknown then but eating politely into her. She was a strong girl anyway, her legs could stop his breath.

The look on her face when a kiss was coming, when she wanted a taste of him, her lips parting. Good God, what he would give. . . . The pain of impossibility, he could never have guessed how strong and real it could be.

He had hiked up here often since he and his father had hauled firewood down, twitched trees, they would fell a big one and leave two limbs for runners so the horse could drag it home.

He pushed on, breathing hard, he'd sprawled on his back in the kitchen too many days, on the keg, how could he have stamina? Proud of it once, he could work like a demon, daylight or lamplight. Oh, the grieving had drained him like a sickness, slowed him to a crawl. Rosaire was gone, for God's sake, where was the will to be fit? Now he might snap like an old rope.

Before Rosaire took sick, he'd felt sharp enough and his body did, for the most part, what he asked of it. He could lift a day over his head if he had to, and his mind was clear as clear as that. Age hadn't mattered so long as she was in it with him.

Nothing big, nothing shattering. Maybe a name came slow, a place, a year. Of course there was the boredom, the lack of will. Yet other times his mind fairly stormed with memory, with the lived and living. Anyway, he was a man all alone, *duine 'na aonar*. How many times, in how many voices, had that message whispered through his head, Gaelic or English? Might as well have tattooed it on his bum.

The bench sat in the dappled shade of old maples and birches, the mist had cleared. Out of the canopy burst a cold shower of drops. Far below, the strait lay leaden against the rain-brightened greens of St. Aubin's hills. To the west the last of the fog streamed slowly through the bridge. A Cape Islander, a chalky, weather-beaten white he'd never seen, was making its way outward, in no hurry, a rolling wake. He knew all the boats from around, there weren't so many now anyway. Had a big V8 rumbling in her. Maybe a pleasure boat, though it didn't look fitted out for that, and not much pleasure to be found in this fickle weather. She wouldn't be lobstering here, these grounds were taken. The boat veered suddenly toward shore, just off MacDermid's Cove, they cut the engine. Someone in a black ball cap stepped out of the cabin and leaned over the gunnel like he was checking the depth. She was too big to beach at MacDermid's, he'd need a dinghy or a rubber raft if he wanted a landing there. He yelled back something to the cabin and then ducked back in. Hard to keep people away, they sought out that cove for parties, though not likely in May.

Too far to pick up her name, but he watched the boat head out, turn southeast toward Cranberry Head, bouncing into a swell. Out of North Sydney maybe. He'd have a look down at the cove later on, he'd forgotten to do that, still getting back, as he was, to ordinary things.

On the bench, Murdock eased into that August afternoon some years ago he had built it out of driftwood, grayed in ocean salt, he'd toted here piece by board. Plain with a couple flourishes, suitable for two, maybe three if you weren't too broad. A simple structure, but most of the afternoon he'd crafted it slowly—a backrest of lobster trap lattice, a wharf timber, smelling of creosote, sectioned for legs, wide bleached boards from a beach shack somewhere made a good seat, two-by-fours washed from a dock, a piece of a lifeboat gunnel he hoped to God had been scrapped. A saw, a hammer, a square, an assortment of nails, that's all he had. Something about that day, working alone so high, all that world of his own out there and below him, a west wind weaving through the trees, white scars of current with the tide, two sailboats an hour apart gliding briskly past the point where the ebbing water curved darkly, into the sweep of the sea widening out toward Bird Island that a lone coyote had reached once across the winter ice but who, well fed on its birds, had to be shot in nesting season, how contented that solitary animal must have been for a while. Murdock would stop his work and gaze out, isolated, timeless, the sun warm as it moved up the mountain. Every act felt good that afternoon. How often could you say that? Sawing a clean yellow line, joining two pieces, feeling the seat grow level and solid, planning the armrests, the seatback with a relaxing lean so it wouldn't feel like a pew, that's what Rosaire would like. How he felt that day he could not explain. Impossibly rich? He'd closed his eyes, under the sway of the trees, he didn't need to be anywhere else just then or be any more than he was, no one on earth knew his location, no one was expecting him anywhere. It was like being carried up in the first long swoop of a tree swing, and stopped still at the moment you peak, just there, squeezing the rope. Peace beyond words. He knew he'd never have that joy here again, so tight in his heart, when he'd been alone in a certain, unrepeatable way. And so it troubled him, uselessly, that even with Rosaire he had never found that same afternoon, though with her he had found others just as good.

He had liked his privacy, yes. How odd was that? To be on his own time, that's all, without others' opinions. But he'd had to take Rosaire into all that, hadn't he? What she thought of him, what she saw in him began to matter, and so he was not really alone anymore, he'd just lived alone. On his own, still, but not entirely, not as he'd been. Some of himself he'd had to give up, offer it to her. A risky gift, Here I am. She didn't ask him to, at some point he just knew he must, was ready to, maybe. The feeling was new, a little troubling. But hell, he'd been waking up in the wee hours, thinking of her already, she was in his head so much he'd taken up cigarettes again, and it had little to do with privacy.

Murdock stood up. The roofpeak of Anna's house lay far below, mossed and maybe leaking now, marked with a few dark squares of flown shingles. Anna Starling. How had she fared off in this crazy weather? He didn't want to nose in, she had her own life going there, a woman life. But he would stop and ask, see what she'd done with the iron things he'd given her. He was shy to show up at her door without a mission, but maybe that was mission enough.

XVII.

WHEN RED MURDOCK appeared around the spit that hid his shore from hers, Anna rose from the tangle of flotsam she'd been poking through and hailed him with a hearty wave. He picked his way toward her over the stones. The long rains surely had not depressed him as they had her, used as he was to this weather, but her work was going well, she'd mailed Melissa a series of pen-and-ink drawings of what now seemed a distant winter.

"What are you finding then?" he called as he drew near.

She held up a long tin box, the lid flapping, its label dented and scratched. "Malt whisky," she said, tapping wet sand from it. "High-end."

"Where would this be arriving from?" Murdock said, peering into the brassed insides. "Can't think of anyone here who'd stow that on his boat."

"I'll keep it for pencils," Anna said. "The bottle is long gone, unfortunately."

They discussed the unusual rains, she told him about her leaky window waiting for Willard.

"He's that way," Murdock said, "since he lost his dog. I'll have a look at the window, if you like."

Anna was pleased to lead them up the path along the eastern leg of the pond, the water turbid from the rains, toward the house he hadn't been inside since the night he half-carried her home. She felt strong, proprietary now from just the turn in weather, a warm breeze in her curtains, sun hot in her hair, it gave you confidence somehow, illuminated possibilities. They passed her seedling pots of fresh green sprouts, "Things grow fast here once they're under way," Murdock said, "if we don't see a killing frost." He suggested Anna trim back the bushes near the back door, they were shading iris bulbs, all blades and no blooms now, he said. When his granny lived here, out the kitchen window in the morning sun they flowered yellow and red. He touched his nose to the first blossoms on the high lilac bush and smiled. Anna mentioned the high-pitched birdsong she heard even after dark, "They sing like lights blinking randomly."

"Peepers," Murdock said, "little frogs calling for mates, you won't hear them in July."

They paused at her new sculpture on the back porch and Murdock knelt to look at it. She'd rooted around under the collapsed carriage shed and in the barn ruins and pulled out bits and pieces of hardware. Even the old ash pile she'd discovered down the brook bank offered doorknobs and stove parts and holed pots, a lid from a kitchen stove and an old crank handle and a small blade from a plow, piled there in the yard awaiting artistic attention.

"Funny, we'd never give a look to it, chucked-away junk like that. But you bound it together, all of a piece like."

Anna wanted to serve him tea, as the custom was, and the oatcakes she had baked from a found recipe in faded pencil, so she put the kettle on the stove while he examined the window in her workroom. Now she could use the pale green teapot trimmed in gold and the matching cups and saucers from the downstairs bureau.

When she joined him there, his attention had stopped on the nude study of herself, forgotten on a clipboard. Back home, she wouldn't care, she was an artist, everyone knew that, but when he turned away, his face reddening, she didn't know what to say, so she made light of it. "I was the only model on call that day," she said. "And was it chilly."

"I bet it was," Murdock said, moving back to the window. "This needs new flashing. Wind drives the rain under the shingles there."

Anna had also forgotten the shaggy black bundle on a chair, Livingstone's sweater he was so proud of, knit in the Hebrides, he'd told her. She had tossed it in a closet corner the day after, but later, on a damp, cold night, she'd yanked it out and pulled it and its woolly smells over her. A faint odor of pot, of harsh tobacco, the funky alcohol smoke of a bar. Almost undetectable, but there too, a tint of that sweat they'd shared? Anna wore it sometimes while working, over a baggy denim shirt, but one evening she slipped it on after a bath, like a floppy wool dress barely touching her thighs. She'd walked through the house that way, through the rooms, the air cool on her legs, before she put on underpants and jeans, and dressed herself for weather unkind to fantasies. Murdock would make nothing of a sweater limp in a chair, never link it to Livingstone, but she wished it hadn't been there.

"Should I tell Willard then?" she said.

"It seems somebody might've done his dog in, back in the winter there. Connie Sinclair hinted as much, but he was steering a little wide when he told me. He seemed awful bothered about it, not even his animal."

"Who would do that? Why?"

"Connie had naught to say on that. He picks up things he hears, some true, some not. I'll fix your window, before the next storm, if we're lucky."

"I'm sorry about Willard. His poor dog." Should she tell him what she'd seen? She didn't want to revisit that cold recollection, not on a day like this.

"Bad year for dogs, Anna," Red Murdock said, smiling.

She was glad he glanced at her drawings and sketches but didn't ask about them. They soon relaxed at the kitchen table with strong black tea and the oatcakes. She recalled the night on the ice and how ungodly cold the water had been, and the luck of his coming.

"Did you ever see that dog again?" she said.

"Hightailed it, if the coyotes didn't get him." They sipped quietly. Voices from the point drifted in on the wind, summer people, she had seen a few on weekends, rarely during the week.

"What brought *you* here, Anna?"

"Cape Seal? Well . . . do you have an hour or two? Oh, I needed to get away on my own for a while. I won't bore you with reasons. Let's say I had to put myself in a new place, and draw what I saw and felt there."

The battered whisky box sat on the table, open.

"You're finding what you wanted then?" Murdock said.

"I'm working on it." Anna smiled. "I was hoping to swim at that nice beach around the point. Before too long?"

"You know what cold water's like, Anna, you could swim there now," Murdock said.

"Thanks a lot, Murdock, I'll wait a while. One rescue is enough. You can't rush things here. But I like that. Excuse me a minute."

Anna slipped into her workroom and quietly moved the nude behind a chair. She rummaged through rolled-up drawings, among them the one of Breagh, she'd almost forgotten it. She turned it toward the light: she had tried not to dwell on the contrasts with herself when she'd put the last touches to it, the downcast eyes, the light on her breasts. The fussing had more to do with Breagh than with the drawing, as if the more perfect the portrait, the better Anna herself might appear. She set it aside underneath the table and then found what she was after.

"This is for you, Murdock," she said, unscrolling it on the table in front of him.

"Well, then," he said, "what's this?"

There was his forge in oil pastels, as she'd approached it from the snowfield, but the shed dominant, the mountain dark and high as a rogue wave behind it, chimney smoke torn in the wind, somewhere deep inside the glow of fire, and against a wall the shadow of an arm, a hammer raised powerfully. She knew its distortions were dramatic, exaggerated, but suddenly she so wanted him to like it, knowing at the same moment that sometimes art was not enough, no matter how serious its beauty, its vision, or what it told us about ourselves, about our worlds. Murdock held it at arm's length.

"Yes," he said. "The forge, right enough. That's what goes on in there, something like this. I see it myself . . . a little different, but that's good, isn't it? We don't have the same eyes for everything."

He wondered why she hadn't put him in it.

"But you *are*. Very much so."

"No," he said, "it's finished and it's fine, I'm pulling your leg." He nodded at the drawing. "I'll make it a nice frame. Thank you very much, Anna."

Outside they strolled the soggy fields while he told her where pasture had been, now wooded with scrub spruce and poplar, open spaces of rose brambles, early goldenrod and bull thistle, and some of the things he'd done here as a boy, happy to be with his granny, helping her tend two cows that sometimes fought, one butted the other over the bank and she broke her neck on the rocks. His granddad had died early on, he barely remembered him. He regretted the old saltbox barn had been so neglected, they let the roof go, his cousins, he had no say in its fate, and the carriage shed collapsed after they were good and away and not likely to come back. But if it was iron and broken things she wanted, there'd be plenty under those heaps of gray boards.

"Just be careful there, a snake might surprise you. They're harmless."

"Oh, they're small," she said, "I picked one up. I'd like to plant a little garden, herbs and green onions, ordinary things."

Murdock showed her a fertile spot where they'd piled manure, he'd break the sod there for her, wouldn't take long, if Willard didn't show, he would fix the leaky window too, she couldn't have rain in the room where she worked. Nights were still cold, eight Celsius yesterday, did she have enough wood? The apple trees, scarred and bent, shook down flurries of white petals in the wind.

"They've done that over a hundred years," he said, "the apples will come and the deer will come for them, green or ripe, hunters will be around, you'll hear their guns."

The same question seemed to hang between them: would she?

They stood looking out on the strait, the pond below a blue not like the sea but tinged dark with iron. From behind bulrushes, a heron rose in great lazy wingbeats and headed downwind toward another marsh. Two lobster boats, done for the day, were passing inward not yards apart, their hulls a vivid red, a vivid blue, the throaty rumble of their engines muted seemingly by the misty air. With Murdock beside her, talking in that slow brogue, saying he would be back, and her saying, I hope you will be, and not just to fix something, Anna felt for the first time like a genuine neighbor, sharing a place, she had woven a few threads of herself into the pattern of its life, and that itself was a kind of shield, she would not be easily shaken. The worst of winter seemed to fall away that afternoon, its cold, lingering threat, and the gloom of rains.

XVIII.

GUSTY DAYS TOOK Anna into July, a heady mix of sun and sudden rain, mist that moved in stately lines through the strait, lit silver by the hidden sun. They'd been well into June before summer took hold of the land and she basked in the salty air. On bright afternoons the white, bulging clouds swept enormous shadows over the landscape as if it were the floor of an utterly transparent sea. The shore was reconfigured often in tides and winds, shifting sand and rock. She had a fondness for her garden scarecrow—a favorite, baggy, paint-speckled shirt she'd used at home, a pair of torn jeans, and a pummeled, limp-brimmed fedora she'd found on a nail hook inside the door—whose windy antics she could watch from her room. Its crazy flailing seemed to unnerve none of the birds, but she liked it anyway.

Above the point, looking down at the cove through a fence of spruce, was a small cemetery, and Anna wandered through it for old gravestones on whose faces she might do a rubbing. A few had lines in Gaelic and she wished to know what they said, but she settled on one for its texture and inscription: instead of doggerel sentiments, it said simply, *Some day we shall understand.* That seemed like the best that faith could offer, it covered everything. She had not grown up with religion, but her father had urged her to respect the spiritual, You're in a kind of cathedral right here, he'd said, gesturing to the shafts of light falling through redwoods above their house, and his yoga meditation, still and serene in his room, seemed a kind of praying.

Anna taped a long sheet of paper to the stone and set to rubbing it firmly with a hard wax crayon, blackening the surface until the incised letters showed clear, *Lionel MacLennan drowned Cape Seal 18 July 1881 aged 47 years.* She worked patiently in the warm breeze, hoping that Lionel did sooner or later understand. Out past the point, terns and gulls were feeding at a white, jagged shoal, circling and crying before they dove. How had Lionel, the same age as she, drowned? Somewhere out there, fishing? Swimming? In a storm?

On her way back, she sketched a boneyard of driftwood snarled into a wide heap, and, where the last finger of the pond went dry in sand, an ossuary of sticks thin as bird bones. The wind had risen, buffeting across the point, cool out of the east, and it had weather with it, a darkening sky, she could read it now.

She didn't remember leaving the back door open but it was wide to the wind and a note on a torn sheet of paper fluttered on the floor. *Anna, stopped in to see how you're doing, try you later. Like your new drawings. Liv.*

Her face heated with anger and disappointment. He had walked in, maybe poked around in her room? What new drawings? She couldn't care less if he liked them or not. Weeks since she'd seen him.

She sorted impatiently through old sketches on the kitchen table, whispering curses, trying to concentrate on what to send back home, what to revisit. Why did he have to show up *today?* She was doing just fine, thank you very much.

She had rolled up several drawings into a mailing tube when she sensed someone outside: a man, his back to the house, was standing at the head of the shore path scanning the strait through large binoculars. She held her breath until she recognized the long dark hair, the hat, the leather jacket, the lanky slouch. Her bras and faded jeans and cotton shirts streamed out on the clothesline, like flags of distress. She waited before opening the door.

"You just walk into people's houses?" she called to him. "Go over their things?"

"Only people I know," Livingstone said, without turning to her.

After he came in, she closed the door to her workroom. No more of that. This was a kitchen visit, as far as she was concerned. His face looked gaunt behind a new beard, giving it a thin, dark seriousness Anna was unsure of. Whiskers could turn a face, and falsely. Had Breagh bestowed upon him the Byronic shirt, or was it hanging in her shop? He spread the kitchen curtain and put the binoculars to his eyes.

"You planning a naval maneuver?" Anna said.

"How did you know?"

"I hope you had a good look around in here. We don't do that where I come from."

"We're not scared of each other here."

"I doubt that."

"You have a little garden out there, I see," he said.

"Carrots, lettuce. Good old zucchini."

"No weed?"

"Oh, there's lots of weeds, I can't keep up with them."

"Must grow like mad where you come from. Weed."

"People don't generally put it in their gardens. Is something on your mind, Livingstone?"

"Just you, Anna."

"I don't think so. I really don't."

Livingstone peered east, then west along the strait. "They used to bring schooners up here, into the nineteen thirties," he said, his voice low. "Bootlegging too, boy. Speedboats."

"Before your time. Mine even."

"My time is now. I think you know that."

"Oh, I do."

He glanced back at her. "Done any beachcombing lately?"

"Odds and ends."

"Like what?"

"They wouldn't interest you."

"You'd be surprised." He dropped the glasses to his chest.

"A rusty padlock? An old tobacco can?"

"No, nothing I'd drag home. But you're an artist and all." He rubbed his breath off the glass. "You've got a lot of shore there all to yourself, eh?"

"Not so much anymore. That beach around the point, I hear swimmers there some days. Or someone fishing or . . ."

"Or what?"

"Red Murdock walks the beach now and then."

"How often?"

"You'll have to ask him. I don't stare out the window all day." That Murdock had been here was no affair of his. She was not offering details of her life to Livingstone, any corner of it.

"How about at night?"

"Night? I doubt it. Who'd be out there at night? I'm at the front door so often checking to see who might show up, I don't have much time for the back. Sorry."

Anna sat down at the table and he let go the curtain and pulled out a chair across from her. He aimed the wrong end of the binoculars at her face for a few moments, then grinned and set them down. "Anna at a distance. I've been one side the Island to the next. Late-nighters. No zees."

"You look it."

"I didn't mean women." He touched his cheeks, his eyes.

"You need some sleep. Are you coming from Breagh's, or going?"

"Neither. My buddies are waiting out front. Got to get back to our boat. Anyway, she's been on my back some, Breagh."

"With good reason probably. Do you want tea?"

"That's the liquid of the day, is it, Anna?"

"I'm afraid so." She filled the teakettle with a slow, thin stream from the tap. Flower shoots on the outside sill trembled in their pot. The pane creaked. "Windy," she said. "Your friends want tea?"

"They can wait. Southeast," he said. "Tide's on the ebb, it's rough at the point."

"White water there, I can see it." The sun had disappeared, the sky was darkening.

"Yeah, she's a little dirty out there. We spent the night over Englishtown, tied up to the wharf, me and Billy and fellas you don't know. Took a beating bucking out of that bay, five-foot swells when we hit the open water."

"Fishing?"

"We none of us fish. Bores the shit out of me. Billy got seasick. We picked up a skiff in North Sydney, towed her back here."

"What's that, your lifeboat?"

He smiled wearily. "You could say that, Anna, and not be lying."

They had their tea as if they had never danced in a hot embrace, or climbed her stairs together. But her small talk—Breagh's clothing shop, the terrible rains, her plans for flowers in the ground—soon washed up against Livingstone's reticence and she stopped talking. He stirred more sugar into his tea, the spoon clattering in the quiet kitchen.

"I meant to stop around, Anna," he said. "Been so goddamn busy."

She had not wanted that business to open up, she'd hoped to get him smoothly out the door without a word of it. Yet it was on her mind too, where an apology might take them, the measure of his sincerity. Would she learn anything new? What particulars of that night was he still remembering? Were they like her own? Probably not.

"Busy with what?" she said.

"A little enterprise in the works. . . . Performing some, a gig or two here and there."

"I never expected you anyway, Livingstone. And there was Breagh to consider, wasn't there?"

"Do you keep secrets, Anna?"

"If I make them."

"Say, if somebody was to ask, was Livingstone Campbell around today, could you answer, yeah, after dark for a couple hours, say between nine and eleven or so? Would you do that?"

"It depends why you're asking, Livingstone."

"Can't tell you. Not now anyway. You want some weed?" He took a rolled baggie from an inside pocket and held it up. "Free. I owe you."

"No, Livingstone. You don't owe me anything. What do you owe Breagh?"

"Breagh." He stared into his tea as if weighing her name. "Drives me nuts sometimes. She's pretty as hell, but a big distraction."

"From what?"

"My music. Projects."

"None of your music comes *from* distractions?"

"Some of it, I suppose. Yeah."

"I don't see what you're complaining about."

"She gets in moods, she wants to be on the move somewhere, our Breagh. I don't know what she wants."

"Ordinary things, I suppose. Attention. Love."

"Too much attention. She does what she likes."

"Like you, you mean. You left your sweater here," she said, instantly sorry: it touched on everything.

"That all I left?"

"Yes. It is."

He pulled out a cigarette, waved the packet at her, but she said no, go ahead. She watched him wince into the match, inhale deeply. His dark eyes were bloodshot, his forehead scored with fine lines she'd never noticed. "I haven't forgotten that night in April, Anna, you and me. I didn't forget it."

"Hard to believe that."

"I liked you in that dress. The wine-colored one. A knockout."

"It isn't mine."

"Oh, I think it is. I like you, Anna, you know."

"Thank you, Livingstone. That's comforting. And I like you," she said.

"Oh?" He gave her a tired grin. "Maybe I should leave. You're jerking my chain."

"I didn't know you had a chain, Livingstone. Finish your tea. I have biscuits. Made them myself."

"I'll take one with me. That's all I'm likely to get here anyway, this afternoon."

"Likely," she said. That was not what she wanted to say, but she had to play out the dialogue she'd begun.

He leaned toward her on his elbows. "You ever see a Mountie boat out there? In the channel?"

"A police boat? I don't even know what one looks like."

"Doesn't say *RCMP* on it. Just an outboard boat, red. Little cabin. You might not notice it."

"There's not much I don't notice, if I'm looking."

"How about today, this afternoon?"

"Just fishing boats."

"Breagh said she saw them out there when she was home a few days ago. I don't always trust what she sees."

"Nothing wrong with those beautiful eyes, Livingstone. She wouldn't make it up."

"They patrol here every once in a while, that's all."

"That worries you?"

"I got busted myself, good while back."

"On the water?"

"No, no. Mainland. Down in Truro. After a show."

"Cost you some time, did it?"

"Jail? You're in Canada now, girl. You can do some nasty things here before you get serious prison time, and even then it isn't much for what you did. Look, we're just setting a couple of bootleg traps out there, Billy and me. You had lobster yet?"

"A couple."

"We'll bring you a good hefty one."

"An illegal lobster."

"Tastes the same, Anna."

"Where's your boat?"

"Off MacDermid's Cove, up there. Anchored. We bought the skiff to row back and forth. Billy's not too hot on the oars yet, but he's got a good back on him. We have life jackets."

Outside, trees were bending in the shore woods, crowns swaying, clouds crowding above the water. At the point, where the channel narrowed to half a mile, the ebbing currents roiled white against the wind.

"You aren't setting traps in this, I hope," she said.

"After dark, yeah. Weather's building but slow, we'll squeeze it in. If you see lights out there, might be us."

"Might not, too, is what you're saying."

"You're close to the water here."

"Yes?"

"If you should see a boat like that this afternoon, red, put the glasses on it. That's all I'm asking. If Mounties are nosing around. Stick a rag or a hanky or something on your mailbox flag. Billy'll drive by."

"Actually, Livingstone, the RCMP wants all of us along here to watch out for drug smugglers, suspicious activity. You probably heard about that."

"What do you mean?" His voice went thin and hard. "You being funny?"

"I'm just telling you what they told us. Out in your boat, you might . . ."

"I wouldn't tell them a damn thing. And I'd appreciate it if you wouldn't either."

"You've been up all night."

"Jesus, is it that plain?" he said angrily. "So what?" He got up and snatched his cigarettes from the table, mashed down his black brimmed hat. She would have had him stay longer, just for their give-and-take that made the day different, tense, anxious. Were it evening instead of morning, were they a little way along a certain path she missed, she might have said, Nap there on the daybed if you like. But it was afternoon, there was no background music, just themselves, mutually opaque. They'd had not so much as a drink, and Livingstone was annoyed with her and she was not sure exactly why, what, today, pale with sleeplessness, he had expected of her, or she of him. He stood at the door window and checked his wristwatch.

"I'll crash up at Breagh's," he said. "She and Lorna still up at the shop, are they?"

Anna nodded. "Billy too?"

"What's the difference? A nap and we'll be out of there."

"I guess you're seamen now."

"We're getting there."

Anna followed him out to a mud-spattered car, salt-stained and scabbed with rust, Billy at the wheel grinning.

"Hey, Anna," he said.

"Where's your resplendent pickup, Billy?"

"My what? Oh. Not far." A man sat behind him, his face obscured under the long bill of a ball cap, and next to him, looking glum, was Connie in his black coat. He raised a hand to her like he did when she drove by him, then turned his face away.

She held her hair against the wind, thanked Livingstone for stopping by, but he halted and looked sharply at her before he got into the
passenger side.

"You're just a visitor here, Anna. Don't forget that."

"I can't," she said. "You keep reminding me."

"Hang on to that sweater. I'll be back for it."

Billy waved amiably as he pulled away, the car bouncing on bad
shocks up the driveway, out of sight through the trees.

How had she handled him? Not exactly the way she'd intended—
to be cold, give him nothing, cut him, at least. But he had other things
on his mind besides her. Just a visitor. And she was not a cold person,
that didn't come to her naturally, even Chet told her, Anna, you were
never cold, that has nothing to do with what's happening between me
and Alicia. Well, she had kept a distance at least, salvaged some pride.
That was better, had to be, him still entangled with Breagh in whatever
way, and Anna didn't want any of that for herself, whatever Breagh
still had with him. Maybe one more evening alone with him sometime
would have been nice. Was that terrible, to want that? One night?
Risks, of course. Murdock could find out, it might get around to him.
Where would that leave her in his eyes? Did the men in that car know
what she was doing with Livingstone's sweater? How much did he
care about her anyway? Just sex. Why not—as long as it was mutually
enjoyable, singular, private, discreet, not a pale imitation of something
else. But what did she know about him? Even less than she had, it
seemed. One intimate night, little more. He wasn't fishing lobster, for
her or anyone else. Sorry, Livingstone. No rags on the mailbox.

She stayed outside in the swirling, electrical air, the wind swept
coolly through her clothing. She braced herself in it at the top of the

path. She had taken to daily swims, unless it was storming, and now clouds blackened over the sea, whites in them like the wild, rolling eyes of horses, charged, a little mad. Tiny waves moved over the pond like echoes, its gulls were gone. The shore stones would be restless, shifting under foam. She felt tremendously alive, anonymous, given over to this weather growing huge, until stinging rain drove her indoors.

THAT NIGHT THE tail of a hurricane swept through, she woke in her bed to slashing, window-rattling rain. Shingles flapped away like wings. She stiffened at times under the storm's eerie, cooling wind, wailing through the trees, not from the sound itself but the force it was announcing, a breadth of ocean so suddenly near, arriving from far away, hurling its gray and breaking weight against the land. She imagined, in the smothering dark, waves swelling from her shore, an angry spume surging over the bank and up her hill.

The storm's thrilling racket did not unnerve her as it might have once, gasps of lightning lighting her room, sounds from old movies, from country-house terror in the rain—groaning woodwork, flailing curtains, moans in the eaves: her fear lay in her isolation, lightning-lit. She might even have turned it into fun were someone sharing it, a warm and humorous man perhaps, lying against her. At its height, she felt her way to the kitchen and picked up the telephone, just to hear that homely, leveling tone in the receiver, nothing more. But the line was only a loud silence in the windy noise.

XIX.

THE PADLOCK ON the road gate looked secure until Red Murdock yanked it. The shackle slipped free and dangled open from the thick chain. A corner of the brass had been dented by a hammer strike, it looked like. Beyond the gate, the soft treadway, scored with tire tracks, curved into the woods.

He drove slowly through the trees that all but hid the old house now. So much forest, silence, it had pushed out the former life here. The shutters he'd made were still in place and the gray of the spruce shingles showed through what was left of the white paint. He'd kept the roof patched but it would need a new one soon. He left his truck idling while he checked the doors. Nothing forced, he'd put in new deadbolts after a break-in that cost Donny a few family heirlooms, but they shouldn't have been left there anyway, not in a house now so hard to see from the road. Robbie and Rowena would be saddened at that, God love them, to see their home blinded by forest, good people, they'd do anything for you, even if they did boil the same teabags over and over and not light a lamp until the room went dark. Robbie over ninety and still hauling eelgrass from the beach with his horse and cart. Worked right up to his death, a pipe in his mouth all day long till he got so he couldn't pull it anymore and he'd ask Rowena to light it and blow the smoke in his face. He'd have killed for tobacco, old Robbie, he'd have smoked in his sleep. And sleep he did when the rum-runners were here, Murdock's dad included, Robbie had looked the other way when a boat slipped into his cove after dark, and the crew made sure a case of liquor found its way to his barn.

Some vehicle had come into the weeds and poplar saplings behind the house, flattening them, then continued toward the cove. Murdock followed in his truck, the late sun filtered through the closely packed trees, until he emerged into a small, grassy, treeless field. Near the short path that dropped quickly to the shore, the turf had tire gouges deep enough to hold water from a recent rain. Had to be a truck, a van or pickup, and it got good and stuck here, rim-deep before they freed it, the site congested with the busy slide of boots where they had slipped and strained pushing it out. Mud-smeared pieces of board had given purchase. Scavenged from the barn ruins and scorched with rubber burn, they lay where flung. Up above ran the border of his own field: a lip of turf and wind-beaten spruce along the cliff edge, the clay face studded with rocks waiting to work loose in storm and surf. At the foot some were scattered among boulders still carrying wet clay from the hard rain a few days ago. Murdock couldn't have heard much from the house, if anything, not when a wind like that was on, and he slept on the west side anyway, deeply.

A night operation, whatever it was, but after several tides anything left behind had been cleansed from the rocks and sand. Not a party. No burned-out bonfire or litter, apart from cigarette butts in the grass. But there'd been action nevertheless, frantic maybe, at some point. They'd wanted to get in here, and they'd wanted like hell to get back out.

Would they return? He couldn't think why, not after miring themselves like this, and there was more heavy weather working its way up the coast. But he would make that gate a tougher barrier, more chain, heavier padlocks. If they came here for a good time, they could just walk in, he might never know or care, but these folks were not revelers. He couldn't keep a vigil up, he had a trestle table to finish and book-shelves for a doctor, that damned pretentious desk for Livingstone. And now that swamped skiff he'd salvaged just off his beach. He was keen to make her seaworthy.

But he'd ask Donald John and Molly to keep an eye on the road once in a while, if they'd leave their picture window for a bit, and Willard was always watching of course, suspicious of everything. But none of them, you could be sure, would be up late. Maybe Connie? No telling what end of the road he'd be on at night or what shape he'd be in. Even so, he knew what went on here and who was in it, didn't he?

Murdock plucked out of the mud a cheap yellow flashlight. *Click.* Batteries dead. Tossed. He was too late anyway. That's the way it was now—things passed and you didn't notice, you didn't see them because memories were always coming at you clear, strong, seizing your atten-tion. Like his father's suitcase that he had called a grip. Why? Good God, he could feel its pebbled hide, could see it lying open on the bed, Dad carefully layering in his unpressed clothes, he didn't have many and he was going to the hospital in Halifax for an operation he never came back from. You fold a shirt like this, Murdock, he said, crossing the arms into an X like a knight's on a tombstone, your mother showed me once, and then years later Murdock himself laying Rosaire's cloth-ing into her red luggage, pressing a blouse of hers to his face for a few seconds of her scent.

IN SWIMSUIT AND sandals, a white canvas hat, Anna made her way along the high-tide line where rocks had diked against the deep strip of sea oats, green as hay. Clumps of sand grass whispered like taffeta. The oats ran to the higher, darker bulrushes, vigorous as a cornfield now, their new tufts coppery, iridescent, yielding gradually to the green, velvety catkins forming beneath them. She broke one off to draw at home. A red dragonfly chased a frantic moth, its jerky, evasive flight no match for the smooth bull's-eye strike of the dragonfly—moth in mouth. Just under the pond's surface lurked a thick feathery plant whose touch she would not care for. A bleached tree trunk was pushed into the cattails like the keel of a boat. Beach pea was in bloom at the edge of the grasses, and a red-winged blackbird hovered over the rushes before perching on the tip of a reed, trilling its warning.

The high surf had shifted stones of all sizes, and Anna stretched her stride from one big one to the next. Everything had an edge to it today, charged somehow with what she'd found yesterday, shoved ashore in storm-swelled waves. The sea's cleansing hiss had been a constant sound in her morning window.

She looked back at the spit near Red Murdock's, casting a high bank shadow where spruce trees clung to the sod at dangerous angles like the masts of a careened ship. She'd hoped Murdock might be out here this morning, but the weekday beach was deserted. Good. It gave her more time. Would she tell him what she had in her kitchen? Not yet.

After he'd fixed the leaking window, he showed up to attend to a balky water pump, a loose door latch, a moody lamp socket. Anna would watch him work, asking questions so she might fix it herself the next time. He seemed to like her looking over his shoulder, appreciate that she wanted to learn such things, No reason why you can't, he said, be glad to show you.

Would he be glad to know what she'd found after the storm, that it was likely more than innocent flotsam? Probably not. Couldn't she put her situation within the pale of his understanding, his sympathy? Or was that only a fantasy of him, like others she'd had?

THE BEACH OF fine buff sand, cradled in the arm of the point, protected from tidal currents, was littered with rope and eelgrass and small crabs flipped on their backs, their innards plucked clean by gulls or crows. Crows, Willard told her, had keen sight because they liked to eat eyes, even humans'.

In the distance a semi truck was crossing the bridge, a pale blue box moving between girders. The night of the dog and the bridge swept into Anna's mind sometimes, she would turn around suddenly, hot and dozy at the shore, and feel winter gust through her, a blank chill, a door flung wide and slammed shut in the same instant when that sight came back brilliantly, searingly cold and clear, the dog tumbling through the air, trying to right itself. Or at the kitchen window in a glance at the bridge's shape inked in the mist, glimpses of the dog flickered and froze. Why did it seem worse somehow, more persistent, than her own terrifying moments plunging through the ice? The ice had held her, and it had let her go.

That night and its aftermath had strengthened her, that long, cold bridge. She was sure of that now. She unfurled her towel on the sand, hot from the high sun, and sat, hugging her knees, absorbing the summer fullness. How long she'd waited for this, the sun in her hair, on her skin! She bought a new swimsuit in Sydney, a sleek black one-piece in a sporting goods shop, she'd lost weight in those cold weeks, so much walking, driven to get outdoors and move, some days she barely cooked. Now the swimming, the sudden chill charging into her, the long, calming strokes as the water warmed, it pumped her, cleared her mind.

But today she waited, lazy in the midday heat, somehow excited but fearful too, uncertain, pondering a next step. Cut open the plastic bale still damp on the kitchen floor? No. She'd wait.

The day felt so good, uncomplicated, sensuous, here on the sand alone, she let herself muse on Livingstone, no harm in that, a little fun, luring him back—if his mood had mellowed. She lay down and shut her eyes, smiling into the bright heat. Her Riviera. If her own alluring self were not sufficient, maybe what was now sitting in her kitchen might be. Ah, such foolishness. Were he to reappear, she could never let him know about the bale, for any reason. Murdock, on the other hand. . . . Why did it seem so necessary to involve him before she acted? He might, troubled by the illegality, insist immediately they turn it over to the Mounties, and she'd be on her own again, the woman from away. Yet, she *wanted* him to know, or she couldn't move ahead.

Anna turned onto her belly and amused herself with possibilities, as if she had great wealth to dispense, to indulge in, and that was all she needed to think about.

It had arrived on the evening tide, on slow swells crashing up through the stones, stirring them into a dull clatter, and there, something slowly tossing in the surf. A flash of rain gear? Any moment skin, a face, limbs skewing as the waves pushed it clear? She was afraid of its touch, of what she'd have to attest to, of responsibility.

But it had turned out to be a large bundle, bound in the dark green plastic of garbage bags, smaller than a hay bale. She had kicked it as if it were faking, then pulled it higher up where the stones were dry. She'd walked off a ways before returning, hoping somehow it might be gone, swept magically out into the tidal currents to a further beach, turned up by someone more innocent than she. The light had been in that strange bright zone of a passed storm. There were no boats in the channel or heading in from the sea, no one along the shore but herself.

So she'd dragged it home, assessing the heft and feel of it along the way, her heart beating so fast she laughed: my kill. She did not want to admit she knew what it might contain, that she was in fact probably certain. She'd never have towed it all the way up the path were it anything but, would she?

When she felt sleepy in the heat, she shook it off and waded into the water, moaning as her hot skin clashed with the chill. A long, flowing school of minnows shimmered away. She dove into the clear, sandy shallows, swimming hard until her body warmed. It was an exhilarating swim, and when she tired, she floated on her back for a while before walking slowly to shore, the sand so fine under her feet a crab scuttled away in a silty cloud.

IN THE SPARE bedroom Anna sat refreshed and dry in the old rocker, placed as it had been near the window when she'd first arrived. She liked the soft bowl of the seat, compressed into haunches. She could look easily toward the sea where Bird Island lay low and flat, and then south to the cliffs of Black Rock Head, the distant lighthouse tiny and white above the bluff. If she leaned a little forward, she could make out, just above an eastern tree line, the mossy ridge of Red Murdock's roof—a comforting detail somehow. And she could see the beach, the soft afternoon waves, the water deep blue but greening near the shore.

And had there been a figure on the shingle there, at the rocks, Anna could have seen him too.

She stood up near the window: running slowly and close to her shore, where she'd never seen the lobstermen haul traps, was the white fishing boat, its hull scarred and dirty. She couldn't make out who was at the wheel, but the crewman on deck, leaning over the rail and studying the shallows, the beach, looked like Billy Buchanan, that head of curly hair. He raised his arm, the engine reversed with a roar, stopping the boat while he probed the water with a long boathook. Was Livingstone steering? Billy motioned ahead and the boat crept on seaward, swaying in the light swells until it disappeared behind the shore woods. They wouldn't be looking for a bootleg trap in daylight, would they? What then? A sunken bundle? Waterlogged, it wouldn't be worth much.

Might someone have seen her trundle that bale up the path? Push it with her foot, winded? Someone on the other shore, along St. Aubin? Not without binoculars, and they could have made little of it, nothing illegal.

Her eyes shifted sidewise to the dresser mirror. Its old glass, rippled in a yellowish mist, reflected little but her black braid on her breast, the sallow shadows of her face. About Chet she was now more sad than bitter, but the whole matter of looks—her looks, other women's looks, Chet's women's looks, and men's—still hurt, was still tender. He had shown her too well what she already knew—that she was getting older and that she could do nothing about it that would matter, or that wouldn't shame her later on. Her frown lines were indelible, she'd joked about them. She had lost weight, she could thumb her waistband out more than an inch. She looked okay. Different, but okay.

Livingstone must have thought so. Who but him had seen her dressed up, and then undressed?

She'd come to like the ghost images in the house mirrors—like the old photos that spiritualists concocted to evoke the dead.

She remembered suddenly her mother braiding her hair, a tender morning ritual that nevertheless brought warm, involuntary tears to her eyes, the alternately gentle, then sharp tugging of her scalp—affection and anger in one motion—the tight neat plaits of hair Anna would later finger absently as she read a book or daydreamed or chatted with a friend. But that sting stayed with her, as if her mother's unhappiness, in the shadows of the tallest trees in the world, were woven into her daughter's hair.

She remembered too those weeks at home she couldn't sleep, alone by choice in the back room she'd turned into studio and bedroom, leaving Chet upstairs in the old bed, the first step toward leaving him entirely. So often awake, she'd found a tiny FM station, squeezed obscurely into some megahertz slot so slender it was like tuning into outer space. After midnight it ceased playing the eccentric instrumentals the stoned, whispering DJ had collected in his hippie wanderings, his own personal stash, as he liked to say. He'd slip away somewhere and the broadcast would shift to auto-pilot: nothing but the sounds of surf breaking slowly over and over. A mike had been placed on a coastal shore and recorded hours of sea and wind, sometimes a muted foghorn, the rush and hiss of water through sand, shingle, in soothing, successive waves. She'd lain with her eyes half-closed and sooner or later she drifted out to sea, a swell rose high enough and reached far enough to bear her away. It might have started there, alone in that back room, her journey here. The sea had salted her dreams.

XX.

SHE WOKE MUCH earlier the next morning. Now the bale, her awareness of it, seemed to alter the house. It felt intrusive, disturbing, an alien object in the humble atmosphere of her kitchen. But to inform the police, bring the Mounties and all that fuss to her home, to the road? She would have to get rid of it. Of course. Red Murdock would know how, wouldn't he?

Anna spread a wool blanket over the bale, disguised it further by pushing it against the wall and scattering atop it magazines and dishtowels. While eggs were boiling and tumbling in a pan, she sat in her room and tried to read, sipping tea. She could forget it was there for a few minutes until its shape, somehow heavier, denser, crept into her mind.

She checked the back door. Across the strait St. Aubin's hills were dim in early fog. She strained her eyes toward the shore: no one. Gulls rose from the pond, teetered in the wind before sheering off seaward. No vessels on the strait, not the white boat either. She wished she were sure it was Livingstone's. Had to be. So.

Out in her field, goldfinches, flowers on wings, radiant in the moist green foliage, the tall neglected grass, the thick dark leaves of the old maple. A mourning dove, lost high in the branches, cooed monotonously. She would carry on as usual.

Anna searched her room for the figure drawing of Breagh, she'd wanted to bring it to her house, realizing it was now a kind of offering, though she hoped Breagh would never see it that way. But it wasn't underneath the big table where she remembered it. Had she moved it somewhere else?

All right. She had pulled home a thing possibly dangerous, sought after, risky. She had to make decisions, she was in charge of it now. Even setting it adrift again in the dark was not a simple act. But she could make something new happen, or not happen, and she liked that.

SHE RARELY SAW anyone at her shore, up from the point as it was, almost never during the week, and summer people, most of them, had waterfront of their own. But straightening up from weeding her garden she was struck by the sight of a man there where the bank was low, almost level with the sea. She could see him only from the waist up as he moved slowly along the stones, toward the point, his head down. She at first thought Murdock and, pleased, started to wave, but that was not his profile, not hunched, and wouldn't he have stopped anyway, at least looked up? Then he disappeared below the bank, behind the small stand of stunted spruce. When the man reappeared, he was higher along the shoreline that separated the pond from the strait, too far to make out much of him, only to notice that he'd stopped and seemed to be looking out at the sea. He stood there, hands at his sides, without moving, a still figure. She was about to turn away when she realized he was not staring out at the water but in her direction, at the house, at her.

She flushed with self-consciousness, trying to imagine what face, what kind of eyes, were taking her in. Whose? She didn't recognize anything about him. He couldn't know her, she was from away. She mirrored his stillness, as if that would make her less visible, less vulnerable to any judgment of her. But when he did not move and she could feel the seconds mounting, she shivered: she did not want to flee, that might invite him, seeing she was afraid. And why? Because they were sharing a sightline and she could think of no good reason why? She turned slowly, casually perusing the horizon before heading for the house. In the kitchen, she moved unhurriedly about it, washing carrots she'd pulled, peeling overcooked, hard-boiled eggs. She would not look, she would not put her face in the window, this was absurd, it was daylight, but why were her hands trembling? Crazy weather brought craziness, and that made her fear that if she *didn't* look, he might be coming up the path to her door. She *had* to look: and he was still standing as before, but then he did turn away toward the point. She watched until he sank from view.

She drank a little brandy straight from the bottle. How foolish to be so shaken! But she stayed at the door for several minutes before she locked it and closed the curtains.

Trying to calm herself, she passed some time in her workroom, touching up a sketch of a dead gull splayed on the sand, but too aware of why she was doing this, she quit and strode defiantly outside, down as far as the old orchard where she stood amid the trees. Ridiculous. No one had been *anywhere* around after that storm. Not a boat. Not a person.

"I'D LIKE YOUR help with something, Murdock. Could you come over?"

"Emergency?"

"Not exactly. It's not for the telephone, though."

"Over when?"

"Soon. This evening?"

"I'll see you then, Anna."

She would have invited him for supper, but there it would be, in the way of their meal.

Anna toweled off the dark creases of the bale where salt had dried. Maybe a drowned body would have been preferable to this, less complicated. Now she wanted to lie. *Oh, no, it was nothing special, Murdock, just a dead animal in my garden, and now something must have carried it away. . . .* No. Not to Murdock. He was her friend, her ally.

The postcard to Chet lay unmailed. They still had matters to settle, but that was not what she'd bought the card for, a bright view of Cape Breton Island's west coast where she hadn't yet driven, rocky in a grand way that would remind him of Big Sur, mountainous, a broad blue sea. Just an impression or two, summer called for that. She owed him no special language anymore, that energy and love that long ago filled her letters when she had tried to bring him, in words, to wherever she was. The message on the address side was postcard boilerplate, no access at all to her life. Should she mention, in code, the incredible stash that had probably washed into her arms? She *felt* it. *Real* news. His delight and envy would be spontaneous, genuine, out of their shared past, how could that backwater where you are offer such a landfall? But no, no details like that, and never in *pen,* not anymore. And the man at the shore? How much weight should she give to him? Murdock would know, she had to pull him in.

At her garden, Anna tugged out green onions but kept straightening up to gaze toward the sea. She beat dirt from the bulbs, then flung the onions away and headed toward the shore, through the ancient apple trees bearing stubbornly their first green fruit, through the tall grasses laced with thorny stalks of wild roses.

The Black Rock cliffs caught the sun, a molten line along the high ridge behind her. Waves mixed calmly through the stones.

If he instead of her were to cut open the bale, that would assure her innocence, would it not? Murdock too, curious about it, would have taken such flotsam to his house, who wouldn't, wrapped as it was, taped, obviously important? Unlike Murdock, however, she knew what it was.

She walked to where she could just see his house up the shore field, then she turned back, suddenly unwilling to meet him on his way, casually, cheerily, as she sometimes had. She crossed over to the pond, smoothly dark, another mood entirely from the sea. Gulls clustered and dozed, immobile in precise reflections. She pitched pebbles into the pond, scattering the gulls from their rest, then returned to the house to wait for him.

"WHATEVER IT IS, she's wrapped good," Red Murdock said. He wore a light-blue cotton shirt, neatly pressed, and fresh jeans. He slid his hands over the bale, its plastic, its thick tape. "She floated."

"I wonder how long," Anna said. Because the bale took up much of the table, they stood side by side, regarding it. She knew how its contents would look, smell, taste, what kind of ambience it could bring to a room. How would she tell him now that she might want to keep some of it? How much or how little, and the consequences she imagined, had varied with her moods since yesterday. It was all a risk, but new, unexpected, and somehow invigorating, despite the man at the shore whose stare still ghosted through her mind. She handed him the worn kitchen knife and he sawed at the tape.

"That could use a stone," Red Murdock said.

"A stone?"

"I meant the knife." He slashed through layers of plastic. "My granny used this. I used to keep an edge on it."

Murdock withdrew a brick-shaped packet, sniffed it. He took from his back pocket his own knife, then carefully sliced the translucent wrap as he might have gutted a fish. He extracted two weedy strands, immediately fragrant. Tops, all flowers. *Sinsemilla,* Anna shaped with her lips. Expensive as gold now, but someone at parties might have had a little in the old days, days for which she felt a sentimental rush, so superior to the "nickel bags," cleaning twenty bucks' worth of pot in the lid of a shoebox, seeds dense as BBs sliding back and forth (I could start a plantation with these, Chet would say, disgusted), gathering with a few grad student friends on the floor of someone's flat, a candle guttering in sandalwood, passing a joint around and talking talking talking about their peeves and joys, going quiet by turns, distracted by music in the room and in their heads, by the constantly shifting sexual tension, who you were with, who you would like to be with if circumstances allowed.

"That what I think it is?" Red Murdock said, placing the brick on the table.

"It's what the Mounties asked us to watch for, Murdock. It's worth some money all right." She untangled a long cola, sticky with resin, and put it to his nose like a flower. "Marijuana. Pot, grass, weed, boo, tea. Wacky tobacky."

"You know about this stuff then?"

"Part of my era, Murdock. College days, and after. It's what we had fun on. Like liquor for you, I suppose."

He sniffed it. "What's it do?"

"I guess it depends. It can make you feel better than you might otherwise. High, euphoric. Some people overdo it, like they do with booze, with anything. But that's always the way, isn't it? It's much kinder to your mind than liquor, I can tell you that. It takes me out of déjà vu."

"It won't be kind if they catch you."

"Who would catch me in my house? The Royal Canadian Mounted Police?"

"I couldn't say anyone would. But you might've been seen, hauling her home."

"Unlikely, don't you think? Late in the day, after a big storm? The shore was deserted, like it usually is. I didn't notice anyone up or down the beach."

Murdock closed his pocketknife and sat down slowly. "Anyone can be seen there from a long way off."

"Are you trying to frighten me?"

"No need to be frightened, I think. Just something you should know."

Anna poked the colas into the packet, folded it shut, pushed it into the bale, as if that would take them both two steps back.

"Well, there was a man on my beach this morning," she said, casually. "Looking toward the house, at me. I thought, what would he want, staring so long?"

"How can you be sure his eyes were on you?"

"I guess I'm not sure. But I wondered what brought him here, today."

"Hard to tell, Anna. Sometimes people come from a long way to walk the shore. Could be anybody. Maybe the Mounties'll give you a medal when you turn this in."

"You think so?"

"Would get it out of your life anyway. Mine too." He smiled.

"It's not really *in* yours, is it, Murdock? It needn't be. I won't tell anyone you sniffed some marijuana."

"But I know about it. I know you. So I'd be concerned, wouldn't I?"

Out Anna's window green onions hung in a bunch from the porch post, beating in the wind. He'd brought her a small basket of beach peas he'd picked from the shore. Her pickling cucumbers were start-ing. There was an outdated *Globe and Mail* on the daybed, a Saturday edition she'd been nursing.

"Suppose I didn't," she said. "Suppose I held on to it, hid it away."

"My Lord, that's a whack of drugs you're looking at, girl. What do you mean to do with it?"

"I don't know, Murdock, exactly. To be honest with you." After the day Livingstone had come by, perhaps into her morning walks, into the routine of cooking and tending to herself, studying moods of sky and sea and self, even into the reading and drawing, there had crept a taste of boredom she was afraid of because it seemed wrong, so against what she valued here, the work she had done. The old house and its wild sea fields, the small discoveries, the lovely yellow-red irises that suddenly bloomed below the kitchen window where their bladed leaves had been lost in grass, the twisted apple trees leafing out, the black fox that strolled past her back steps as casually as a neighborhood dog, a dead rabbit in its muzzle. But there it was, sometimes, a hint of ennui, her staring off at a blank rainy ocean, a book as limp in her hands as the rabbit in the fox's mouth. Did she really miss flea markets, art films, concerts on campus, small parties with old friends with whom she could get pleasantly loose and gabby and high, openings at Melissa's gallery?

"You don't want them to think you were after selling it," Red Murdock said solemnly. "They'd hang you for that."

"Oh, no, not sell it, never. But surely they wouldn't hang me, Murdock, just for finding it? Livingstone says sentences are ridiculously light here."

"You wouldn't look good in jail, Anna, I don't care what Livingstone says. You didn't tell him, did you?"

"About this? I barely know him, I've only seen him once since . . ."

She took a swallow from the wine she'd poured before Murdock arrived. His attitude made her stubborn, and she could not explain herself to him. "Look, Murdock, it just . . . washed up. I didn't order it, I happened upon it."

"But here it is. In your kitchen."

"Like a fugitive, isn't it? I wonder where it came from. Did the boat sink? Did they have to toss it overboard? It's had a long journey, maybe from South America, the West Coast, California. How did it end up here? Don't you want to know the story?"

"I think I've heard it before. It was liquor then." Red Murdock opened the back door, stared out at ocean light the color of slate.

"The storm brought you a bale of dope, me a boat," he said.

"A boat? You're safer with that gift, I guess. Not a police matter, is it."

"She got blown to my shore and I salvaged her out," he said.

"Well, there you are, Murdock. Salvage. If not our beaches, someone else's."

"Suppose them who owns that come looking for it?" he said.

"How would they know?"

"People like that know more than you think." He closed the door.

"I guess I'd have to call on you, then. Murdock to the rescue."

He turned to her. "Listen, put it away somewhere for the night, eh? God, you can't leave it out like this."

She had an authority now, of some kind: she could act or not act, say no or yes and there would be definite consequences. She knew things about what was in that bale that Murdock did not. And now it was hers. "Okay. Give me a hand."

He followed her upstairs to the spare bedroom, bearing the bale in his arms. Anna knelt inside the closet, yanking clothes from the deep, camphorous trunk, heaping behind her a dark wool suit, trousers, shirts, a blanket. She beckoned to him. "Here," she said. "This is perfect."

"No such thing." He dropped the bale inside with a disapproving grunt and stepped away. Anna covered it with clothing, shut the lid, the closet door. They stood awkwardly in the waning light.

"The bedrooms are small," she said.

"We only slept in them. Mostly."

"Me too. It's warm up here. Mostly."

"You sit in that chair?" Red Murdock said. The old varnish of the rocker was nearly black in the evening light. Anna raised the window slightly, a breeze quickly cool on her skin. Her eyes went to that spot on the shore where she'd seen the man: no one.

"I like to look out from it," she said.

He tugged at the bed's thin coverlet. Under it, Anna knew, was a hard, bare mattress. She'd lain on it occasionally, arms at her sides, staring up at the stained ceiling like a penitent. This was her thinking room sometimes, spare and unforgiving.

"What do you look at?" he said.

"Whatever's out there," she said. "You know what's out there. I don't."

"I used to. I'm not so sure anymore."

"Has the view changed that much?"

"Oh, Lord." He touched the rocker, set it creaking softly, then stopped it. "Before the bridge went up, people'd row across sometimes, if it wasn't too rough, they didn't always take the ferry. There was this young fella here liked to do it, he'd skip the ferry if he could. Kept a small boat at the shore there. He took her back and forth, he had work in the summer on the other side, a farm. His uncle was old, you see, confined to this house, and anxious about him, and so he'd watch for him late every afternoon, from that chair, until the nephew was in sight, rowing home. One day the young fella, a few drinks in him and fed up with his uncle always at the window like an old woman, he laid down in his boat when it got near where the uncle could see it. Hid himself in the bottom and let the boat drift like, so his uncle'd think he'd drowned. But the man was so struck by the empty boat his heart just quit, gave out, right here. Died in that rocker, right there by the window."

"That was cruel," Anna said.

"He didn't mean it. You don't think when you're young."

"Yes, I know."

She followed him out, embarrassed when he glanced into her bedroom with its unruly bed and tossed clothing. She hadn't slept well and left it turned out on this particular morning.

"You can call me up if you like," he said at the door. "If you need any more advice you don't want to hear."

"I don't want to make trouble for you, Murdock."

"It's your own trouble I'm thinking of."

"It's just you and me," she said. "Isn't it?"

"For now, girl. For now."

XXI.

IN THE REAR of his work shed Red Murdock planed a board he'd cut for the thwart. The skiff, keel down on sawhorses, took up too much space, he ought to finish it or move it outside. Shavings, releasing a scent of spruce, curled out of the plane and dropped like hair to the floor. He'd lost heart to work on it. As soon as he'd seen the skiff the day after that hard squall, laden with water, near to drowning in the swells, he'd felt his uncle's panic, what the sight of an empty, drifting boat must have done to him all that long time ago, trapped in a rocking chair. The clarity had stunned Murdock for a step or two, as it often did now, and then he'd calmed himself and thought, I will get this boat, I will fix it and row it.

He'd waded into the surf still washing high and whirled a small grappling hook over its gunnel, hauling it near enough to grab and drag clear. He'd tipped the water out, turned it keel-up on the rocks: she'd taken a knocking, but not a bad boat. No oars or nothing. A busted thwart, a spread plank. Sound, on the whole. Some refastening, caulking, a coat of good paint. Must've got away from somebody in the storm. He hadn't seen a boat like it around here since he'd given up his own. Trim it up, see how she'd go, why not. Rosaire's name on the gunnels, the stern. He'd promised her one, that he'd teach her to row. You could row here safe enough, if you watched the weather, if you knew the tricks of it, the water itself, he told her.

Someone hadn't known, though. And maybe it had carried a bit of cargo. For MacDermid's Cove.

But he was not in the mood to work wood this morning, his or anyone else's. Five cigarettes a day he'd been keeping himself to since he'd put aside his pipe, for the cost and because he was tired of the packets' bold warnings about strokes and heart disease and death, thank God he had his granny's arteries. Now he was smoking one after the other, as he had after Rosaire died. He was trying to hold on to the Anna he knew before yesterday, and while he worked at his tool bench, he almost could. But what had he known of her anyway? Some days she seemed settled in, like she had no future but here, just the way she was living now. Then that damned bale tumbled out of the sea.

Murdock lit another Export, grinding the match out carefully into the earthen floor. He was not in a hurry, nothing in his life could rush him now. But any pause today seemed to bring Anna's kitchen to mind, the dull knife sawing the tape, the stuff inside packed like rough tobacco. Jesus, it was over there in the old house right now. He knew how polite a Mountie could be just before he collared you. Predicted rain had not come but the air was sticky, windless. Out the double doors of the shed, flung wide, the sea was pressed flat by the gray weight of the sky.

He unvised the board and sighted along its edge toward the open door. He'd seen a fiberglass boat with a red hull this morning. No insignia but he was sure it was the Mounties. They wouldn't chase much down with that rig if the weather got dirty, only a big outboard. Just an every-now-and-then patrol. Still.

He'd felt angry with Anna: he didn't want to be pushed and pulled, or tangled in a woman's affairs, not after Rosaire. It bothered him that

she wouldn't get rid of the stuff quick, that it was there in his grandmother's house, tucked away in his mother's trunk. It was help she
asked for, not advice.

If she were not pretty, if she were small or mean or a bad neighbor,
would he turn her in? Probably not. He couldn't rear up like a minister
and tell the woman what to do. She didn't expect that of him besides,
she wouldn't have had him cut open the bale. He was not high-minded
about this drug business, had not paid it much notice except when it was
in the news, its lurid causes and effects, but then the local rumors began,
people at Sandy Morrison's old house near the wharf, cars in and out
a lot late at night, party noise, tires tearing gravel. Willard going nuts,
about them, about his dog, still. But the drugs had seemed to *come at*
them here from away, and that was part of the problem: tied into movies and the TV, and those caught up in it didn't care anymore about
their own people, they answered to criminals way off somewhere. It
made local men act differently than they might have once. Bootlegging
liquor, the profit was here in their own hands, or in later years they
bought booze at the Liquor Commission and resold it for double to
thirsty men caught short on a Saturday night or Sunday. It all stayed
here, the money, such as it was, and nobody pulled guns, they didn't act
like gangsters. God, in the old days, men were working all the time, the
money was terrible but they worked like hell. If a man was not working,
there was a dangerous hole to fill. But the hard fellas were hard differently now, with the drugs sometimes they just didn't give a damn about
anyone's life. The stakes went beyond your name, who you were and
who you knew, what family you belonged to. But here in what was left
of Cape Seal? Hard to imagine what they called a Drug Problem. Even
so, he had to wonder. Anna's bundle didn't drop out of the sky.

Murdock had seen drunkenness all his life, after all, seen it good and seen it crazy, been whacked out himself at times, woken up face down in dirt. But he'd sung with it too, danced under it, drawn out some good talk he would never hear again. It was just what you knew, a man in the country, you got half cut and you let whatever happened happen. But this other stuff they lit up, sniffed up, put into pills, he couldn't see any good in it.

Before last night, except for a fella he'd traded moonshine to offering him a smoke of marijuana he declined, saying, Whatever it does I'm too old for it, he had never *seen* drugs. Now he'd seen it in her hands, smelled it, heard her talk about it. Upstairs now, under his uncle's moth-holed suit, shiny in the knees and elbows. That bed she slept in he had slept in many times. Her bare feet padded over the same floor. The white iron bedstead looked more frail than he remembered.

Seeing her suddenly on the shore on a warm afternoon, stepping slowly from rock to rock, searching for objects—that could lift him up, some days. . . . He had come to like that, having Anna not far away. Now it was like a strange man had moved in with her and it gave him a knotted feeling in his gut. Had Livingstone, damn him, gotten to her somehow?

Her naked in that drawing drifted into his mind more than once, he had to admit. Not just that it was clearly her, unclothed, but that she had done it there in that room where his grandmother used to sit, she had stood there undressed in the window light long enough to make that picture of herself. In an ordinary day. What did she get from such a likeness? A drawing was always for somebody else, wasn't it? Maybe not. He wondered, as he sometimes had with Rosaire, what it would be like if he could, for even a few moments, see things exactly the way she did, in the atmosphere of her own mind, what brought and kept her here, made her what she was.

He was disgusted that he had tightened up in front of her, that the whole affair had shaken him some. He had no cause to be righteous about what these drugs did or why they were liked so, he knew that. Alcohol was not soda pop, if you overdid it you paid a price, long-term or temporary—look at poor Connie, for God's sake—and the word "high" meant the same thing everywhere, it didn't matter what got you up there, you were glad for it, whatever worked would do. He understood that, that didn't trouble him. But with booze, everybody seemed to know the rules. Who was going to die for that? Maybe the spaces it had to fill were bigger than they used to be.

The new thwart fit snug and he fastened it with brass screws. This boat had good lines, she would sit in the water sweetly. A smuggler's boat, he'd bet money on it, you could haul three or four of those bales in her, and they'd probably got who knew how many ashore before she swamped. They might have lost more than one over the side, washed ashore maybe other places along these waters, people puzzling over them, then wrestling with what they'd found. Some would turn it in, some wouldn't, if they knew there was money to be had. Hard to blame them, here cash had always been scarce. Nevertheless, he'd never know for sure. You couldn't connect any of this to MacDermid's, not this boat either, nothing remained there but what had always been. Maybe just as well for Anna Starling.

Red Murdock flicked his cigarette outside and turned the boat over to start scraping the hull. He'd been about to cast the boat back out to sea, shove it off to sink somewhere. But here it was, he would make it good anyway, respectable, paint it a fresh clean white. Trim the gunnels in blue. Blue was Rosaire's color, blue was her eyes. He said her name aloud and all of her appeal seemed to rush his heart, staggering him for a moment, so deeply did he want her.

ANNA HEARD SWIMMERS, they seemed further off than the shallow cove behind the point. Their voices and play were comforting, protective. She wouldn't swim today. She sat down on a large, flat stone at the water's edge.

The tide had left kelp, cinnamon and dark yellow, like bands of thick, shed skin. Swells, faint shadows on a metallic sea, broke softly and fell back, crackling through the shoreline gravel, small, polite versions of the waves of last week. Civility would do. Calm. The slow rustle and slide of stone.

There was the red boat again, the one she'd noticed yesterday, meandering along the channel, stopping here and there. They weren't fishing, the two men, and they didn't seem to be heading in or out, but they did cast a heavy line, pull something up, toss it back. Her binoculars were in the kitchen but she thought that underneath their orange life jackets she could see khaki, and she had never noticed a fisherman here in a life jacket. The red boat rose and fell lazily, like the afternoon, as if the boat were merely part of its motion, a daub of color against the bluffs of Black Rock Head toward which it now turned, cutting a wake.

Would Livingstone want to know about it? Might be a Mountie boat. Too late? Too bad. She would never tell him, not anything, even if she knew where he was. If that dirty white boat was his, it was nowhere in these waters today.

She fished in her jacket for the cigarettes Red Murdock forgot the other night, two of which she had smoked. She lit a third, certain she wouldn't crave them again. There was no reason to suppose any link between that boat and herself, between what they might be searching for and what she'd hidden in her house. Had they suspected, they would be on her shore right now, wouldn't they? But they never even looked her way. She turned the cigarette packet over in her hand, read the stark white-on-black warnings, English one side, French the other, "strokes" and "heart disease," then "*des maladies du coeur.*" Ailments of the heart. No wonder she'd quit.

The red boat was now just that, someone fishing in the distance perhaps or cruising around. The sun had turned the water blue and friendly. Her shoulders were warmed, her hair. Red Murdock hadn't been around since they stuffed the bale into that heavy old trunk with *S. MacL.* stenciled on it. Was he wary of her now, afraid to be involved? The sea looked benign, everything—water, cliffs, the low table of Bird Island. Flat calm, leveled. Maybe she was in this alone.

Anna closed the card to Chet without adding another line. She could not sustain a greeting card voice, the neutral cheeriness she'd opened it with. Too tense, restless. She didn't know what she wanted to write to anyone at home, on the back of a pictorial scene, the cliffs of Cap Rouge, up the west coast where she would love to run off to for an afternoon, if she did not have something at home that begged for her attention.

Behind her, the sand dissolved into the golden summer grass of the point, shivering with wind. In it pieces of antlered driftwood crouched, prehistoric, they startled her sometimes, skeletal, hunkered there like crazy animals. Driftwood could fool you—a duck at the edge of the pond? A heron frozen in the shallows? Some unknown creature poised in the sea oats? She'd done many sketches of them. Not today.

There was her home above the pond, up the small hill, the mountain rising beyond it in a faint, cool haze. She felt differently about it from here: as if she were taking in a piece of the landscape, a faded red house with a steep-pitched roof, one of its white shutters torn away in the storm. Who lives *there?* she might ask, and what does she do? A woman from away, or a certain man on the beach, might answer, She is hiding a few thousand dollars' worth of marijuana somewhere in her house.

Long swells that Murdock called rollers had arisen, as if some great vessel had passed unseen behind the horizon, the waves spread higher and louder through the stones. Surf had roamed high, scattering stone and wood far back into the rough sand, joining old trees and limbs and trunks, as far as the pond where, bone bare, they tangled in the iron-tinted water. She'd thought an afternoon like this could only ease her mind, weather she loved.

Not quite. She shaded her eyes toward the old wharf a quarter-mile west, just visible jutting out into the strait. The other night she'd heard whooping at a bonfire on the shore below. Kids, teenagers? Faces firelit, moving in and out of the flickering light. Willard's enemies? Hers? They've got the devil in them, Willard had said. But she'd seen no stranger on her shore even though she had often looked for one.

ANNA OPENED THE closet trunk and teased out a single flower top, like lifting jewelry from a treasure chest, then sealed the bale up again. With the curtains drawn, amused that she could still do it so deftly, she slowly rolled a joint in a small square of tracing paper, twisting it tight in her fingers. She lit it with a kitchen match she struck on the bed frame. Sweet weed, despite the harsh paper, as sweet to the taste as the point's grass to the eye. Primo. Two deep hits and she tamped it out in a Mason jar lid, spread the curtains wide and sat in the rocker, rocking gently, lulled, smiling. Something pleasantly illicit about being indoors like this on a lovely afternoon. Like sex with hot sun at the window. She should get back into the dog drawing while she had this vision, this piercing, intense recall.

Red Murdock's cat crossed the field below, freezing suddenly as a goldfinch shot from a thistle bud, then resumed its deceptively casual stroll, its gray fur soon diffused in the weeds. That cat would never come to her, she tried to entice it with tidbits in her most coaxing voice, but it would watch her from a distance calmly, unafraid, something or someone else on its mind. She should get a cat, she'd love the company, a warm bundle of fur in her lap. But then, how long was she to remain here? Was that a question that was opening, or closing?

She fixed her eyes on a sailboat cutting past the point, heeled over in the same wind lifting her curtains, pulling in the yells of children at the swimming beach, their exuberance remembered from her childhood, though she played only on the cold edges of the Pacific. Languid in the warm room, she closed her eyes. Stony grass, oh, yes. The Blue-Eyed Elf was upon her, denizen of her own tales, dancing in her mind. Maybe Red Murdock had a version of that sprite, out of some excess of his youth, underneath his reticence. But it wouldn't be old Blue-Eyes, those ice-blue marbles under his brow, helping her juggle her own, soaring, nostalgic high, stitching past into present. No sense to the sequence of memories, one tumbled into the next, yet each one made crystalline sense, sheer sensuous clarity its own truth, it could put her *there* or *here* in a wink.

Now a gnawing concern: how deeply did *Murdock* care that she had marijuana hidden in a bedroom closet? She wanted to keep the stash, but only for a while. As he'd said, *for now*. Now was what she was in. Just give it up, watch it float away? No. Not yet. She rocked faster.

XXII.

R ED MURDOCK WAS glad to see Anna at his back door near dark, holding out his packet of cigarettes, one of which she was smoking. A moon the color of buttermilk was low and large behind her, a sliver of cloud lidding it like an eye.

"Peaceful, isn't it?" she said. "Look."

In the window frame a green spider, big as a grape, was knitting up its web, trembling in the wind. He asked her if she would like a drink.

"That hooch you said you make?"

"Hooch?" She had never tasted his liquor anyway. "Women have liked it."

"Thanks, Murdock, it's not what I need right now." She turned toward him, smiling, a smile with shades to it. "Listen, I'll have a drink of your stuff with you, if you'll share some of mine with me."

"Yours?" Anna took from the pocket of her blouse a joint with a twirl on one end. Red Murdock nodded.

"Ah," he said. "*That* stuff." He sighed. Not the same as a drink of his liquor, not at all. They had, he and this woman, shared a few things these last months and shared them well. But she hadn't mentioned the contraband in her closet and he hoped that somehow it was gone. Her dark eyes seemed to be sizing him up, and he did not want her to see him as old-fashioned, as just country. "Why?" he said.

"Why do you drink, Murdock?"

"Not for fun, not anymore."

"But it must give you something you like, you enjoy. Doesn't it? And you like drinking with other people?"

"Not so much now."

"Thanks."

"I didn't mean you."

Anna lit the joint, held the smoke, breathed it out. "Don't look at me as if I were shooting heroin, Murdock. This isn't anything wild."

"I wouldn't know just what it was."

"Here. I just want you to understand its appeal, why I might like it. *You* might like it."

"You go ahead yourself. I'll get a bottle of mine from the basement."

"No, listen, I mean it. Don't be silly now. *You,* and *me.*"

"You don't give a man much choice." He accepted it, scowling as he puffed.

"It's not a cigar, Murdock," she said. "Take it in gently and hold it a little. . . . There. That's the way."

He told her he didn't feel a thing, that an unfiltered Export did more than this, but down in the cellar his head suddenly went light and his feet wandered a bit before he set them carefully down. He studied the light bulb swaying at eye level and his mind seemed to sway as well, slowly, broadly, everything clear but demanding more attention than he would usually give it. He listened to a drop of water, a single distinct spat somewhere in the dark crawl space, and for a few moments it magnified into a leak but his sense told him no, it's condensation from a water pipe or a little weeping around a joint, nothing for worry. He smiled, and then more widely. A little giddy. *Guanach*, his dad would say. How did her funny cigarette get that name? He started up the stairs but had to back down because he forgot the jar of liquor. Up we go. He couldn't seem to quit grinning. His eyes burned a little, like he'd been on the water in the sun. He asked Anna if she would take his moonshine mixed with pop and she said sure.

"Murdock, I thought you died in that basement."

"I'm old enough. I could've."

He poked noisily around the kitchen for a bottle of ginger ale until he could stop smiling. He had no idea if anything was amusing at all or just everything, but did not care so long as he didn't look foolish. He measured out the drinks, held each one to the light, frowning like a chemist. It seemed important that all this be done exactly right, without rush, and he almost forgot Anna was in the room. He had framed her forge drawing and hung it on the wall and he studied it now with new attention, its powerful colors and shades, they seemed to have sound: the raised arm and the fist gripping the hammer, they were supposed to be his (weren't they?), the flamelike light, the interior dark like a cave.

"You don't *feel* old, do you?" Anna said.

"Not this minute."

She'd pulled him into the flow of her mind, it seemed like. Things sang in his head. Her voice a ripple of light, of sound. The drums in his own life had quit, he knew that. There had always been some music he'd hummed to without thinking. He could taste the excitement of it, the life of it, and Rosaire had brought it back to him. God, how he would love to have her with him, in his arms, tell her every damn little thing tumbling through his mind.

He didn't know what to talk about while he was feeling this way. I'm getting lighter day by day, Rosaire said, everything else heavier. See those little things of mine, Murdock? I couldn't even pick up that paperweight over there. Pretty though, isn't it, that crystal? Not that little marble box you gave me either, couldn't lift it now. I'll lift it for you, he said. No, she said, that's not the same thing. I love you though. . . .

His sight drifted toward a back window: Black Rock Head, blunt in the sea's blue darkness. Down the strait, a boat light swung. There was an early star, solid as the head of a spike. He wanted to know more about Anna, he hadn't guessed he would. Her hair, glistening black in the ceiling light, had been teased by the wind, it was always fetching, her eyes dark and ambiguous under long lashes. She had put on lipstick, he didn't remember seeing it before.

He said, reeling a little but catching himself, "This makes me your partner in crime, looks like. We're in this together." His voice was joking, he smiled, but his heart seemed to be beating loud enough to hear: she was from away, and she had brought that thing into Granny's kitchen, that domestic place he'd known all his life.

Anna smiled. "Anyway, what are we *in?* Something deep and mysterious, I hope."

Suddenly he was unsure of her tone, her intentions. Was she having him on?

"We should haul that bale back where it came from," he said, then hearing his own gruffness, went on more lightly, "we could row her out and drop her, you know, let somebody else have the headache of it."

"But I *want* the headache of it, Murdock. For a little while. I want to see what it's like just to . . . have it."

"It isn't just you."

"For God's sake, Murdock, I'd never implicate you. It's in my house, not yours." She touched his hand.

"My grandmother's house. I'd go to sleep hearing her down in the kitchen, baking something maybe, or just fussing about. She used a spinning wheel, for God's sake. A conch."

He drank his liquor quickly, open to its masking heat. It was different from the smoke and he wanted to tell her how. Then he wanted to tell her a detail of his father's only suit, that in the black gabardine cloth its pinstripe had been all but invisible. This was all tied up with *her,* with her company. Something came into his nerves, he felt it but he couldn't describe it, some kind of gentle force had him, like filings lining up over a magnet. Warm. Like fine memories, like touch. His mind was easy with it now, he wasn't afraid. She had relaxed and talked and he wanted to tell her things too, and his enthusiasm for it made his thoughts shift swiftly, each one as in need of telling as the next. Like the day Anna had baked him oatmeal cookies and he'd sat in his kitchen that evening with a cup of tea, the cookie tasted good, for a first go, but as he was chewing he felt a hair on his tongue. He pulled slowly through his teeth a strand of fine black hair and laid it carefully, without disgust, on the white saucer, trying to pinpoint its taste, the odd feeling it gave him. He'd imagined her at the old table, bent over a bowl, mixing the batter, her dark braid loosed in the effort of that homely task.

"Suppose we dumped the bale and it washed back in here, on *your* shore?" Anna said. "Now that would be funny."

"I'm not laughing."

"Okay, sort of funny. Where is your boat anyway, the one you salvaged?"

"She's ready. I'd row her anywhere," Red Murdock said. Many times these last months he had felt like pulling toward the ocean alone, rowing out there until he couldn't lift an oar, taking whatever came until it was all nothing but expanse, then he would drift. He wouldn't lie in the bottom this time, not like he did that day, his poor uncle anxious for the sight of him, not because he had loved Murdock so much but because he wanted to feel normal again, unafraid.

"Where do you suppose it came from?" Anna said.

"I couldn't say. She's not from here."

"You'd think someone would be looking for it."

"You know what I miss?" he said suddenly. "Swordfish hearts. Been a damned long time since I've had me some hearts. Almost as big as a deer heart. He hunted swordfish, my dad, and Uncle Hugh. He could fling a harpoon, I'll tell you. Sometimes they got tuna too they couldn't give away, giants, in those days."

"Where did you get your tattoo?" Anna said. She had hold of his forearm, touching the faded blue maple leaf.

He rolled his sleeve up further. The tattoo looked somehow fresh to him, new. The air seemed warm, even the breeze from the window.

"Halifax. I decked on a cargo boat for a while, way back."

"My husband got one a year ago. A phoenix with an arrow through its heart." She pulled out another of Murdock's cigarettes and lit it. "He and his girlfriend, high on pot and dinner wine. Romantic, I suppose, and maybe it was. You know, a little thrill. Sly glances from students and secretaries. He liked that. Then a colleague said, You never did time, did you? And the feminist theorist in the office next door told him it was aggressive, like drumming your chest, she said.

I told him it was sexy in a ratty sort of way. The girlfriend's was an elaborate butterfly."

Red Murdock nearly said, as a helpful link of information, that a bosun he'd sailed with, an ex–petty officer, had a green horsefly tattooed on the head of his prick. Instead he thought, it must have hurt like blazes, the man was not that big.

"Chet, my husband, sold his solid, safe Volvo sedan and bought a Harley-Davidson motorcycle." She could see it, smell its exhaust. A simple-minded Freudian machine, gleaming between his thighs. From those high handlebars he'd slung his thin physique. On a downtown street one morning she had suddenly seen him blare by, hearing the Harley first, the chesty accelerating stroke of its engine, then looking up to spot his ponytail flying, his chin high, and she had actually admired him for those two or three seconds, that rushed grainy image of him, a person he might have been, braver, bolder in some way that mattered, but could never be except for mere moments in his wife's eyes, she who had been his lover once, at maybe the best time of her life, of his life. Did Alicia Snow know that, would she reckon with it? Anna knew things about Chet that Alicia would never know or notice because she wasn't looking for them. But now Anna wondered how fair this memory of him was, how she might easily exaggerate its vividness, mock it. Surely he could call up selective memories of her, embarrassing, unflattering. Had he? "His girlfriend liked to ride on the seat behind him. I never would've."

Murdock, barely listening, poured himself half a glass. It sat warm inside him awhile and then spread quietly into his head, seeped into his tongue. *Tha'm pathadh orm,* his dad used to say, I'm thirsty. Nobody here now but old Malcolm down the Cape had the Gaelic.

Red Murdock used to go down there and listen to him, just tossing out a line, a phrase, words clustering around a name, an incident, comforting sounds that Malcolm took and wove into a conversation.

So much had slipped through his fingers. And Rosaire.

"Chet's seeing a therapist," Anna said, as if she were talking to someone who was following his life.

"Why, did he hurt himself?"

"Well . . . yes. As far as I'm concerned, he did."

Red Murdock smiled politely. He didn't care about this Chet or who he was seeing. The sea was rushing the stones of the shore, a loud stirring. Ah, the trunk in the closet: it fixed and sobered his attention. The time to discuss it seemed to have passed somehow, and Anna, still garrulous, was telling him about the strange and appealing dresses Breagh had sewn, what they might do for the right women.

"How about yourself?" he said.

"I don't draw that kind of attention."

"You don't want to, or you can't?"

"Oh, any woman wants to, I suppose."

Murdock pushed toward her the untouched glass of his liquor. "Your turn."

"Fair enough." She downed it in one swallow, surprised that its heat was smooth, not searing as she'd expected. She leaned back, her eyes glistening.

"That's booze all right," she said. "I'm spinning."

"Don't shut your eyes then."

"Oh, I've done that already, Murdock, many times. Did you ever by any chance read *The Death of Ivan Ilych*? Tolstoy?"

"I haven't. Doesn't mean I wouldn't. Books were never much to hand."

"I was thinking of the story, you said one day your friend's death left you not caring about things, objects, we really only want them when we're not sick, when no one's dying. . . ."

"We're always dying, it seems to me now."

"Ivan Ilych is the man's name, he's dying slowly. A Russian man. Cancer."

"Yes."

"Material things, they no longer matter to him, getting them, having them. What comes to matter is his servant who gives him relief from his pain. This peasant just sits at the foot of the bed and lets Ivan rest his legs on his shoulders while he listens to Ivan talk. That simple act relieved the man's pain."

"I don't know what that's like."

"Tolstoy could help, you know, spiritual pain, that's what he does. . . ."

"From the outside I know, but not further in, not where the real pain is. They're alone with that. *She* was."

"What was she like, your . . . ?"

"That's hard to talk about."

"I'm sorry."

"I mean it's hard to call a woman up . . . for someone else. The way I knew her."

"I shouldn't have mentioned it."

"Needn't be sorry." He closed his eyes and touched his fingers to them. "She's in my head. I don't know where she comes from, or where she is now, but that's where I have her."

They both went quiet, their eyes toward the sea window.

"Oh, she'd wear Breagh's dresses right enough," Murdock said, his voice low, "she loved clothes, you know? That hurts, she told me,

I have nothing to wear but this silly gown with the ass out of it, day after day. Some getup for the dying, eh? You wouldn't catch anyone capering around in this. Get Breagh over here, she said, sew me something bright.' "

The long ray of the Black Rock lighthouse was swirling slowly over the sea, and the dark land behind it. The whirligig on the back porch chattered to life in a sudden breeze.

"Have you seen anything of Livingstone Campbell?" Anna said.

"No more than I'd care to. His buddy went flying by this morning, in that gypsy pickup of his," Murdock said.

"Billy?"

"That's him. Livingstone's making more than music, I'm thinking."

"Like what?"

"A lot of activity the other night down at Sandy's, cars, late. They woke Willard up. He saw Livingstone driving off, then they all left but Billy. Breagh, she might've had enough of his tunes anyway."

"Oh?" Anna felt elated for a few moments—a feeling that could go nowhere, she knew, except to lighten her guilt.

"She's seeing a teacher, now and then, she told me over the phone. I like him a lot, she says, I like talking with him. Teaches English, I think she said. Over at that university college, in Sydney."

"Good luck to her. She'll need it."

Murdock lit a cigarette, blew smoke at the ceiling.

"Livingstone must never, Anna, get wind of what you've got."

Anna smiled slightly. "Too late for that."

"What do you mean?"

"I don't mean I told him. Did you know he and Billy have a boat? It's pretty big, a dingy white."

"That's theirs, is it? Saw it, a while ago. I don't think they've got a clue about boats."

"Maybe other things?"

"Maybe."

Anna stood up from the table. She tapped out one cigarette from Murdock's pack, showed it to him before slipping it in her pocket. "For later," she said. "I'd like to draw your portrait, Murdock. Could I? I don't mean right now, but sometime soon."

"What would you do with a thing like that?"

"I have a collection of faces from here. Yours is special."

"That's kind. Well, after we've settled with your house guest. Let's hope his pals aren't looking for him."

"Can I call you if they are?"

"Right away. I'll be there fast. You walked? I'll drive you home."

"I don't mind the dark, Murdock. I know the way."

"Do you? I'm not so sure."

He could tell by the way she took hold of the door that he would have to let her. He lifted a flashlight off a wall hook. "Take it. Even you can fall."

Murdock waited until she should have reached her house, then he got into his van and started down the road. At the first curve his headlights picked up someone approaching on the shoulder, and the instant he knew it was Connie, the man leapt away and stumbled into the trees. Murdock braked and rolled down the window, calling his name out. Never known him to run from anybody, Connie, but God knew what alcohol was doing to him by now, what ravages it was exacting. He waited, idling, but heard nothing from the woods but two barred owls tossing hoos back and forth, staking their territory.

At Anna's, he crept down the driveway, his headlights killed, keeping back in the trees. The moon was high and white over the water, a wide shadow as defined as daytime beneath the high crown of the silver poplar, it had popped up wild when his grandmother was already old and she let the seedling flourish because, she said, It's a fast tree and that's all I have time for. There was a light in Anna's workroom and when he saw another come on in the bathroom, he relaxed at the wheel. A few minutes later it went off. Behind the house, moonlight washed cleanly through goldenrod and daisies. His attention fixed hard on that field, as if he were seeing it for the first time.

RED MURDOCK WALKED the beach late the next morning, looking for whatever he could find that might have something to say. He hadn't slept well, so much had reeled through his head, Connie ducking away like a convict, he needed the sharp, cool air. Anna was nowhere in sight, and that was okay, he didn't want to meet her, not this morning: he had to persuade her somehow to give up that bale and he didn't know what tack to take now without offending her, without pushing too hard. At his feet lay a lobster trap the storm had crushed, clogged with stony seaweed: could be the man lost a lot of gear in that blow last week, but this wasn't what Murdock was looking for.

The Dutchman's tour boat was heading out from the St. Aubin shore to Bird Island, a sign the seas were down. Be seasick passengers anyway before they got to the birds. Binoculars flashed at the rocks where Red Murdock was standing. All he could see was a string of sunglasses and caps along the bulwarks, sometimes the mirror flare of a panning lens. Lookers, not watchers. They didn't see much really, nothing they could keep, just snapshots. And ordinarily he wouldn't give them a thought, but now any eyes felt suspect, any person aiming themselves at this shore.

Lord Jesus, he'd been here so long, and the MacLennan houses far longer. His dad had seen sail here, schooners, and local rigs of their own. A boat could come in right off the point there, riding the tide, and you wouldn't hear a thing but maybe a voice, the soft shaking of canvas.

When he'd last come upon Anna, suddenly around the turn of shore, he felt strongly the simple pleasure of her looks, complicated by an old desire, the thought of touching her. It had sneaked into him. Here, on this familiar beach, where everything had said Rosaire. He had let the feeling pass—it was not one he could keep, should keep. She was from away and would always be from away. She had an armload of dope in her house and would not let go of it. Yet. Yet.

Was it his duty to keep the family flame clean, clear of smoke, of soot? He had borne it without question, he'd become after all the last man home, and if you didn't get away somewhere, you found your-self standing alone some Sunday afternoon in the middle of an empty kitchen, everyone gone for good, dead or living, and memories of them at every turn. How would his own MacLennans be remembered, how would he cap that off? He couldn't take it lightly, the respect his father had, his grandparents, his uncles and aunts, their names had nothing awful attached to them. Red Murdock MacLennan was known as a certain kind of man, and how he saw himself had a lot to do with how others saw him. He couldn't change that, it was banked, he could only trade on it, and keep the risks small. Having Rosaire stay over for nights had been gossiped but easily forgiven, lapses of the flesh fit into everyone's kind of forgiveness, and weren't they delicious to discuss? But dope was outside of things, not a community sin known and understood but one of garish headlines, handcuffs, sinister figures in poor lighting. People saw you, and they saw *you*. No need to rattle that. If he could help it. Some lines he would have liked to cross, but had not, wasn't sure he ever could. . . .

AFTER HE GRABBED his mail that afternoon, and jammed the bills into his hip pocket and shut the mailbox, Murdock gazed down the road in both directions out of long habit, not that you'd hail a person or a vehicle much anymore. Things being what they were, better to see it empty. That a dead crow near the shoulder? He would toss it into the brush, he didn't like to see them flattened, but he drew nearer and it wasn't a bird but a man's black shoe, its laces busted, the tongue gagging out. He picked it up: pretty worn, heel rubber nearly gone, the leather cracked from soakings. Whose trash did this fall out of?

He heard the flies then, twirling up out of the ditch, and he stepped nearer, looked over the evening primroses shut to the sun. Jesus. A man face down at the bottom, why the hell the highway department had ditched so deeply he did not know, had to be four feet or more. Was that Connie, for God's sake? He didn't want to believe it. But there was the black coat. Stained khaki trousers hiked up his calves. A torn white sock half-peeled off a foot shockingly pale, the limbs twisted, the disturbing angle of the neck that said it was broken.

He slid carefully into the ditch, into its wet clay smell, and stooped in the shallow water, rain runoff, and lifted a shoulder: a muddied, muddled face, the back of his head a sticky mat of blood. Connie, what have you come to, boy?

Murdock stood up, a bit dizzy, and gazed around him: nothing but summer sounds, what you'd expect on a dead-end road: nosy crows overhead hopping and gabbing in the high branches, insect buzz from the roadside brush, wind tugging a thin eddy of road dust. Connie couldn't just have fallen, you didn't damage yourself like this tumbling into a deep ditch, a car must have hit him. And then just *left* him? Nobody on this stretch would do that, not even to a deer. If the Mounties weren't here before, they'd have to be now. He reached down and laid his hand on Connie's matted hair: a poor end, boy. Lord. Who would run you down and leave you? Why did you flee last night? Didn't know it was my truck, me? I never knew you afraid.

Murdock didn't want to leave him there, his face in ditch water, but the police might prefer it that way. He climbed out and hurried toward the phone.

XXIII.

I T WAS THE way the man was stepping, as if he had never walked on a stony beach, that caught Anna's eye while her mind was somewhere else. He'd appeared around the lower point, his arms winged out like a kid's on skates. A fine rain glistened over everything and that made it strange to see him here, mid-week, an afternoon of gray damp. He crept near the water to yank at a piece of dark plastic in the sand. She wanted to run, to be out of sight, but held herself erect, an air of proprietorship about her. She regretted she could not drive him off with a shout, a threat. She endured his approach when he spotted her, his hands coming down to his sides. By the time he reached her, she saw who he was and he had a cigarette lit in his mouth.

"This your place, Anna Starling?" he said, through smoke. She glanced behind her where he was looking: just her house up high, the wide path, the vegetables blooming in her garden.

"You know it is, Billy." She might have said no, just to confuse him.

"Never seen it from this way." He poked his aviator sunglasses higher on his nose.

"Not from your boat?"

He stared at her, shook his head slowly. "Uh-uh."

She measured him, rain inching down her face. His head was thick with curls from the drizzle, and his sunglasses did not convey the menace he might have intended. He seemed to be inflating his potbelly for her benefit. She could never understand the pride men took in that, lugging it around like a prized rock. He rearranged his foothold so he could stand relaxed. Binoculars hung like a pendant against his chest.

"Are you watching birds?" she said. "The island out there is full of them."

"No, I'm not after birds."

She knelt down and resumed unwinding fishing line from a driftwood piece she'd fancied. She hated his standing there stupidly.

"What brings you here then, Billy?" After yesterday's disturbing accident up near Murdock's, he was a troubling presence.

"You spend a lot of time on the beach here? Nice view. Shit, I wouldn't want to *swim* here."

"You wouldn't, no. It's deep. A swift current out there."

She uncurled the string from the wood more slowly.

"You're not much for the gab, are you?" he said.

"Gab away, Billy. I don't mind."

But he clattered carefully off, stopping now and then to squat over something. She could tell his attention remained on her, so she was not surprised when he looped back. She stood up with the driftwood under her arm, fingering its satiny grain. She wouldn't mind seeing the red boat out there. Canadian law and order. A Mountie in a scarlet coat. Or Murdock.

"We lost something off our boat," he said. He waved vaguely toward the ocean, Bird Island.

"A lobster trap? I saw one up . . ."

"No." He unsnapped a button of his denim jacket. "No, it's . . . a bundle, like, wrapped in green plastic. You know. Gear."

She took a long slow breath, wary of details or lies. She smiled, tilted her head at him. "Art is all I'm interested in. Natural objects."

"Art?"

"Pieces of old metal. Sometimes wood. Natural sculptures. Stones. I hope you find what you're looking for. Lots of people use this beach."

He looked slowly up and down the shore. "All I've seen is you."

"Sorry."

"See, it's that Liv and me, we got to find this gear, you know? It belonged to some other guys and they really want it. Need it." He shaded his eyes unnecessarily and looked across the water. "You'd let us know, wouldn't you? If you was to find it?"

"Of course," she said. "It's yours after all, isn't it?"

"Yeah. It sure is."

She listened to the stones shifting under his steps as he set off toward Murdock's shore.

All the way up her path, lingering casually to pinch leaves off a tomato plant, her knees were a little weak. She was already unnerved by yesterday's events, the sirens that froze her, their wails rising beyond the trees, so near on this dead-end road, then diminishing toward Murdock's. Coming for *who?* Then she thought fire, then someone stricken, maybe Murdock, he was not young. She called him, the phone rang and rang before he picked it up, sounding tense and weary. I can't talk now, Anna, a Mountie is here, an ambulance. Connie was killed up on the road. Car hit him, it looks like. I would hate to think, Anna said, this has anything to do with me, with, you know. . . . I don't know, he said, just what it has to do with. The constable's having a look up there. Nobody saw or heard anything. Anna said, I wanted to be sure you were all right, that was the main thing. There was a pause and she could hear him breathing, he must have rushed to the phone. I'm okay, he'd said, but an old friend is dead, and I don't know but I might have saved him.

She had so wanted to believe that the bale had drifted from a long way off, that no one here where she lived had a claim to it, but everything was constricting dizzily. She drank a glass of water, then walked through the woods to her mailbox as she would on any afternoon. Lowering the lid, she hoped for a letter that would take her somewhere else, but she felt nothing in the box, not even a flyer. She let her hand rest in the cool tin while she caught her breath: no one but Murdock knew what she'd found. How could they? Her hair was dense with fine rain and she pulled her hood up. A truck approached, heading out, its windshield fogged. The driver tapped the horn, waved, she waved, people did that here, they didn't need to know you, and whoever it was did not. Breagh knew her. But she was up north, or down north, as they said here. Anna hadn't seen her in a long while, and wished she could visit her and talk about inconsequential things, play the drawing game with Lorna, Anna starting it off with a crude figure on a sheet of paper, Lorna attaching something to it, however her whimsy moved her, and on they'd go, laughing as the figure grew more absurd, silly, grotesque. Anna was home too much, her lights burning, her radio playing the CBC's eclectic menu, her car parked under the silver poplar with its high, dramatic branches. But Billy on the beach? Too close to home.

Upstairs, Anna wrestled the bale out of the trunk and carried it down to the kitchen. She drew back the old hooked rug, swept up the dust underneath. The trap door was heavier than it looked, but she pulled it up and flopped it open. She wouldn't climb down into that musty, vegetal air. Something rotted there? Old potatoes? Damp cardboard? Sweating, she pushed the bale over the edge of the opening, watched it bounce once on the wooden steps and disappear into the darkness. Good. Much better. Once she laid the rug down—stained, a bit soiled—and smoothed it with her foot, the floor was as it had been.

SHE LEFT THE muddy road and its jarring holes and followed Red Murdock's drive, which, like hers, twisted through woods, then opened out to the old house and outbuildings and fields, more cleared than her own. She had not come to it from this direction before, only from the shore behind it. They had neither of them met up since she weaved home three nights ago, sweeping her way with his flashlight, a little paranoid about her visibility in the moonlight, she shut it off before she reached her path. She and Murdock had seemed to sheer off from each other that evening, as if at a certain point what they really needed was to be alone. The grass, probably, grass could do that, and Murdock's moonshine or whatever it was that had left a sharp ache behind her eyes. She had hoped, while heading there, that something would resolve itself, but by the time she left she'd had no idea what she wanted to be resolved, needed to be, only that she'd believed smoking grass would, like a potion, put them on the same wavelength and all would dissolve into a congenial ease and frankness and something new.

Behind a small gabled building there was an upturned boat, its hull brilliant white against the grayed shingles. The house had a small front porch, but when she'd been inside, everything felt turned toward the sea, and Murdock too would be somewhere in the house with his back to the road, he was not in the woodshop with its smells of oil, fresh wood, thinner.

The back yard was familiar enough, the forge, the wild grass of the sloping field. She startled him when she tapped on the kitchen window. He beckoned her inside. In the sink lay fish, cleaned and filleted. She could smell them on his hand as he offered her a smoke.

"I'm not hungry today," he said. Liquor drifted off his words.

"I'm so sorry about Connie," Anna said. "That's terrible. You said he was hit?"

"Of course he was a Jesus drinker. Still, it's odd, I don't like it. The constable, he knows Connie, had run-ins with him. How deep is he going to dig? Drunk men fall down. But they don't get busted up like that."

"Is he coming back?"

"He's still got people to talk to. Nobody heard nothing. You worried?"

"Not especially. It happened a long way from me."

"*It?* Not all of it. Look what you got at home."

He stood up at the sink, staring at the fish there. "I pulled in a few sculpin this afternoon, seemed like a good thing to do, fish for a while. Ugly little bastards, I always feel sorry for them. Good eating. Listen, I don't know. Something moving through here hasn't been here before. Left him like a dog in a ditch."

"Any guesses?"

"You'd run out of guesses in a hurry. He staggered in and out of that pack down at Sandy's. But then what?"

"Good thing you found him. Would coyotes have bothered him?"

"Just think how we'd taste. They're too smart."

His kitchen had seemed so pleasant to Anna in sea light, clean and spare, but that ambience was gone. She wanted this to be an incident totally separate from her own, to which she could offer an outsider's sympathy.

"Look at the sea out there, Anna. Dead still. The weather feels strange, eh? The rain so straight down flat. Somebody had him as a lookout, I think. Maybe Livingstone, or his pals. Why he came back here, I don't know. Wanted to tell me something maybe, that's what he did, he'd come see me. Oh, Connie could blurt out the wrong things sometimes, when he got oiled up. Talked too little, or too much, when he got older."

Anna closed her eyes for a moment. "What did you tell the Mountie?"

"Not everything, not with you hiding that stuff, Anna. We'd have them nosing all over. How many got their fingers in this, I don't know. It isn't just Livingstone and Billy."

"So Connie's connected to me?" she said reflexively, knowing it was merely rhetorical, that she didn't really want an answer.

"You've stumbled into it, Anna, whatever it is." He took a glass from the cupboard and poured her a whisky. "Here."

She raised the glass. "To your friend Connie. I'm sorry." They drank the whisky down.

"You have to turn that marijuana in, Anna."

"Murdock, I can't turn that dope in now. I'd be embroiled in all this, I don't want that. I can't work. I'm barely working."

"Then you have to turn it out, girl."

"You make it sound so easy."

"None of it's easy anymore, Anna. It'll get harder if you wait."

"I had a conversation with young Billy on the beach," she said.

"Beachcombing was he?"

"I think he was looking for something already combed."

Red Murdock frowned. "Like what you've got stowed away?"

"He wasn't that specific. But close."

"Jesus. What kind of talk was it?"

"What could he suspect? It's a long shoreline. He doesn't know a thing about my house."

"Livingstone does."

Her face went warm and he stared at her frankly, but without accusation, and though questions rushed her mind, there seemed no point in asking them.

"Your house, you know, it isn't hard to break into," he said.

"I'm sure a good shoulder to the door would do it. And those old windows have no locks. But would Billy? Livingstone?"

"Someone else who's in this might. Got to be others."

"There are."

"You can't leave that bale upstairs, Anna. We've got to move it."

"Are you trying to scare me?"

"They have an eye on your house, I'm afraid. Maybe it's time you *were* scared."

"*They*. Ominous word sometimes, isn't it? I don't want to be scared just because I'm a woman."

"Common sense."

"Not much excitement in common sense, is there?"

"Is excitement what you're after?"

"I won't let them bully me. Out of nothing more than suspicion? I'm supposed to just roll over?"

"God damn it, Anna! Do what you want!"

He got up and put his back to her. He stared out where a dark curtain of rain was moving in from the sea, flowing with wind.

"Oh, Murdock," she said, turning the empty whisky glass in her fingers. "I'm sorry."

"Have some sense about it. That's all I'm asking."

"I do have enough sense to ask could I keep some of my drawings here, in your house? Just in case. I would hate like hell to lose them."

"I'll look after them." He faced her, gave her a slight smile. "Does that include the nude one?"

"Of me? Murdock, I'm flattered you'd ask."

"Good." He tipped his glass toward her. He sat again, leaned forward under the trawler lamp that hung above the table. "We used to sit here and talk," he said, "under this cabin sort of light. Like in our own boat, that's what it was like. Sat here smoking cigarettes." He laughed, shook his head. "Smoked *cigarettes*. Can you believe it?"

"Do you mean her?" Anna said, nodding toward the photo of them on the wall.

"Her it was. Connie always liked her. Who *didn't* like her? I'd wring their necks."

Anna stood up. "You know what I'd like to do, Murdock? Drive up north, see Breagh and Lorna. Would that be awful? Am I running away?"

"Might be good to stay away from the house for a bit."

"Just for a couple hours or so."

"Ask her if she knows where Livingstone is while you're at it. Lock up and I'll go down there later," he said, "have a look around."

"Murdock, remember, if I should get busted or something, it's all on me, nothing on you."

"Oh, I'm in it too, dear."

She started for the front door but he stopped her with his hand. "You have to leave the same door you came in, Anna. Bad luck."

She turned and hugged him, felt his hesitation give way and he took her hard in his arms. "Ah, Anna Starling," he said. "What are we going to do with you?"

ANNA FLED NORTH, over her mountain into clearing weather, avoiding the ferry at Englishtown for the longer route around St. Ann's Bay, beautiful in any weather, its coves and inlets, the old houses high above the water, silvery in occasional flashes of sun, through the Tarbot valley to the Cabot Trail highway and up the east coast, the Atlantic never long out of view, it was like flinging open a door to a fresh wind. Of course this was escape, leaving matters with Red Murdock, as if when she returned he would have vanquished the curious, the dangerous, laid some protective shield around the house, shown that a man was there, not a woman on her own. *For Now:* the motto on their coat of arms.

When she'd come up this way in early spring there'd been hardly a tourist vehicle, but she was soon stuck behind a motor home all the way to the Wreck Cove General Store where she stopped to ask the woman at the counter if she knew of Breagh's shop, Peerless Apparel.

"Oh, yes," she said, "they're nice girls, nice, those two. Maybe three miles on you'll see it, on the water side. They come in now and again with the little girl, a sweetheart."

"Yes, I know her," Anna said—feeling for the first time the pleasure of telling a stranger they shared acquaintances here, and with a woman who knew nothing about who Anna was, here or beyond. Or cared.

Just off the highway, not far from a white church and its churchyard, Anna spotted the old schoolhouse, its shingles painted soft green and the trim in yellow, shades reflected in the art nouveau script above the door: *Peerless Apparel: Original Clothing for Women, and* (as if an afterthought) *Men.* No cars in the small lot out front but Breagh's and an older van. Out back, a scrim of wind-stunted spruce and then the ocean, gray, jumping calmly with whitecaps. A plump blonde woman in jeans was leading Lorna out the door, and Anna stopped in front of them.

"Hello, Lorna," she said. Lorna squinted up as if she didn't know her and that chilled Anna for a moment. But then how well could she read the glance of a child, even Melissa's girls, who were older? She introduced herself to the woman, who offered her hand.

"Isobel," she said, "Breagh's partner. You're the Anna from California?" The woman wore a blouse of colorful quilt patches draped over an ample bosom and she laughed easily when Lorna tugged at her hand. "She's mentioned you, a neighbor. Long way from home, eh?"

"Yes, Isobel, but I feel at home *here*." She might have said that with conviction not long ago, but now she could barely conceal its ambiguity. "Breagh mentioned me favorably, I hope."

Isobel gave her an easy smile but said no more.

"Your business off to a good start?"

"Tourist season, Anna. Seven days a week. Breagh and Lorna crash in the back there. A couple cots, a bathroom. She loves the beach, eh, Lorna? It's friendly, sandy, no high cliffs, like home."

"Lorna? We could draw pictures again," Anna said. She felt the tension in her voice but she couldn't control it. "Would you like that?"

The little girl considered this, staring at her sandals. "We have to get Popsicles," she said.

"Yes, we're off to the general store," Isobel said, laughing. "You go right on in, Anna. Herself's in the rear there."

IN THE BIG, high-ceilinged room, the tall school windows were raised and a breeze rustled the racks of clothing, hangers tinkled. The walls and wainscoting had a fresh, warm coat of pale yellow paint, a mature hue bright in a way this room had never been. Wares were arrayed—hats and scarves and shawls, a few sturdy sweaters—on two long trestle tables of stout pine, left over surely from the school. There was a round wood stove further back that looked older than Anna's, well used, how well could it have warmed a room like this, the kids on the outskirts? Anna made her way through the clothing toward Breagh at the far end of a table, bent over a shoulder bag, sewing by hand a bright blue strap to lemon-yellow cloth dashed with forget-me-nots. She pulled the needle through high and held it as she glanced up.

"Oh, it's Anna Starling."

"Hello, Breagh." Anna felt suddenly like a customer, some tourist who'd pulled in on a whim. "I haven't seen you in a while."

"Did you want to?"

"Why would you say that?"

"I thought maybe it's Livingstone you'd be wanting to see, off the road somewhere."

"You're wrong, then. It's very much you I needed to see. Oh, I might have a couple questions to ask Livingstone Campbell, if I ran into him."

"Oh? I'd love to hear what they'd be."

"Why are you so cool to me?" Anna had to ask even though she knew the answer, she'd face it however she could.

Breagh set aside her sewing. She stood up, tall and lovely in a dark green gypsy blouse of soft cotton, cinched with a wide black belt, its silver buckle incised with a Celtic horse, her full skirt crimson, its hem just above high black boots. Anna had missed the sight of her on those wet, gray days, the energy in that absurdly lovely hair: there was nothing passive or complacent about her beauty, she made no great thing of it, used no makeup but touches of mascara that startled the green of her eyes.

"Livingstone told me about it, about you and him."

"Oh." There was an empty chair near her and Anna sat down slowly. A door in the rear said *Private*, and tacked underneath were two child's drawings, one a light blue fish possibly, dolphin-like, in a watercolor wash, the other on orange paper, black, frantic figures too small to decipher. "It's not as if he knows that much to tell. About *me*, I mean."

"He wasn't making it up, was he? Your hot night?"

"What in God's name made him tell you?"

"He was drinking. That helped, that and your drawing of me. Why did you give that to him? It was supposed to be mine, and it's on his damn bedroom wall, so he says."

"I didn't, I wouldn't. He must have taken it, Breagh, when I wasn't home. It's been missing. I didn't know where it went. And I never invited him to my house."

"You must have had it out in plain sight?"

"No, no. It was under a table, I was touching it up to give you. He might have been looking for something else. . . ."

"Like what?"

"Drugs maybe . . ."

"Oh, go 'way! In your *house?* He's got his own contacts, believe me, unless you've been up to something else I don't know about."

"I'm just guessing, Breagh. He does have a history of just wandering in, doesn't he?"

"Billy, more likely. Now I'm up on his wall for his buddies to leer at."

"Is that why he did it?"

"A little blackmail in it, maybe. Well, I know you're not lesbians, he says to me, you two. I says, what the hell are you talking about? I mean, he says, I've had you, and I've had her. Is that so? I says, tell me more, I'm dying. He starts in, I don't know if it's all true, he likes stories."

"It just happened, that's all. Once. Not planned or calculated, not on my part. He stopped by on his own, that Saturday night. We had some wine, a little pot . . . what can I say."

"Not much, girl. Not now." Breagh shuffled the clothes on a rack, talking over her shoulder. "Just once? Doesn't sound like Liv. Sorry."

"A long time afterward, we talked, nothing more. He seemed more interested in what he could see of the shoreline." Anna looked past Breagh through a back window where, on the far horizon, a container ship, boxy and dull, seemed immobile.

"Oh, I could see it coming," Breagh said. "He gets curious about a woman, he used to say, and he has to find out what she tastes like."

"He said that to *please* you?"

"He was talking about me at the time. That's what I thought."

"Would you have done different than I did, Breagh? If he'd showed up at your door on a Saturday night carrying wine? Be honest."

"Honest? Sure, maybe not, if I didn't know him better. But that's not the point, and you know it."

"It wasn't an affair, Breagh."

"Good for you."

"Not really. I had no designs on him, believe me."

"I thought you were straight up."

"Older? Sensible? Like a schoolteacher's shoes?"

"Just different. Someone I could trust, if it came to that. Jesus, Anna. You fairly jumped in bed with him."

"That's his version? Not that mine would make any difference. I'm sorry, I wish it had never happened." That was not entirely true, but true enough to say it: she regretted the consequences, not, even now, the evening itself. Trust. Oh, that hurt. This was not what she'd hoped to be talking about on this particular afternoon, here by the sea. Breagh's disgust with her was disheartening, isolating. How lovely it would have been to tell her everything about the bale of weed, as she had about falling into the winter pond, every detail of its appearance, what had happened since, to find humor in it, to listen to how Breagh, as a woman from here, would respond to what Anna had done, and not done, she would have sheltered in her judgment, advice, whether or not she agreed with it. She felt older, trapped, unlikely now to salvage anything good.

"You heard about Connie?" Anna said.

"Molly phoned. And Murdock, later. Connie, poor devil. Bound for a bad end, that fella. Liv gave him work, pocket money. He was never a criminal or anything like that. Murdock asked me then if Livingstone ever came to your house. Why? I said. So I can warn her about him, he says. He might be foolish sometimes, but he's not dangerous, I told him, and you might want to warn *him* while you're at it."

"I didn't think I was dangerous. I should feel good about that, but I don't. That's a lovely pendant you're wearing."

Distracted, Breagh touched the chunk of amber that hung from a gold chain. "Murdock. His girlfriend's. There's an insect in it."

"You didn't tell him about . . . ?"

"I came close, yes I did. I know you like him."

"Don't you?"

"Of course! Oh, hell!"

Breagh moved to a window, raised it high and stood in its wind pushing her hands through her hair. The ocean beyond was broad and gray and restless. Below her, a weed-ridden playground held a little red swing. "If Liv told me about you," she said, "what's he told others about *me?* I hate that."

"Some men will do that. They enjoy it."

"Women don't? He seemed angry with you. Been edgy anyway since a while, lean on him a little and he flies off."

"Something's been going on at Cape Seal, Breagh. Connie was tied up in it some way, I don't know. Maybe smuggling, that boat he and Billy . . ." Anna wanted an opening to spin it all out, but she couldn't make one, it seemed wearisome, overcoming Breagh's hostility, getting past her anger. "Do you love him?"

"I'm not *through* with him. Okay? Maybe I should be, but I'm not."

"Yes. I know how that goes. You dated a college professor, Murdock said."

"We're friends. So far. Nice to talk with a man about something different."

"Murdock says Livingstone's desk is finished. You expecting him here?"

"His *desk?* I know a man who'd get more use out of that." Breagh faced the window, hands on her hips. "I don't know what to expect."

She lowered the window to her waist and turned around. "What did you mean, smuggling? Smuggling what?"

"I guess dope. Somebody landed it in MacDermid's Cove, Murdock thinks. Livingstone might have been in on it somehow, he said. From his boat."

"You're not just saying that to . . . ?"

"Talk to Murdock, Breagh, I don't know."

Breagh sat down and shoved her sewing aside. "Jesus. It's not like he's above it or anything. Foolishness. Who knows about this?"

"At the Cape? Maybe no one else. Not the Mounties at least, but they're looking into Connie's death, looking for a car that might've hit him. Murdock suspects the smuggling, but there's no evidence left, in the cove. Anywhere. But . . ."

"But what?"

"The smugglers might've lost cargo, Murdock says, overboard. Billy, I think, believes that I found some, that it washed up on my beach. Where he got that idea I couldn't tell you."

"He said that to you?"

"He implied it. I can fill in the blanks. Some odd things have happened around my house. I'm not sure who it is."

"Them and that damned boat . . . Billy, worthless bugger that he is. God, they had me keeping an eye out, eh? I didn't know, I didn't much care at the time what he was up to. Poaching a few lobsters, I thought. I'll see him again, he'll be by, sooner or later. We'll talk. Yes."

"Please don't let on I'm the one who told you. I didn't want to pull you into this anyway."

"Oh, I was pulled in a long time ago, I think. It explains a few things."

"I suppose I should get back, Breagh. Murdock's . . . I should give him a hand." Anna stood up, fingering a scarf she would have bought. "I really miss seeing you and Lorna," she said. "A lot. I guess I'm an evil influence now."

"We're not talking about evil, Anna, nothing grand as all that. Garden variety stuff. Loyalty." She sat down at the table. "Lorna thought Liv was the greatest thing since candy, he's got a way with kids. Funny, isn't it?"

"I'm sorry."

"Me too." Breagh turned back to her stitching.

Anna stepped outside and waited on the small porch hoping she might catch Lorna coming back. She could feel Breagh in the room behind her, aware that this was what a mother might do, fret and wait. But the little girl did not show up, and when a car with Alberta plates pulled into a parking space, she left.

XXIV.

MURDOCK DID NOT want his grandmother's house broken into, by anyone. He parked underneath the poplar tree and got out.

A SCULPTURE SAT out in the front yard, metal in angles of anger or confusion, it seemed to him, rusted scraps Anna epoxied together. A long barn-door hinge and pin, iron from a buggy frame, a small plow blade, wheel spokes, a copper scuttle handle, other strange bits that had caught her eye. They must have meant something to her that he could not see, could not grasp. I'll show you how to weld if you like, he'd told her, you can do bigger pieces. She was keen, and he to teach her, but then the storm, and that bundle of trouble.

Murdock scanned the lawn Willard had mown out of the field thick with goldenrod and fading daisies and blue asters mixed with the last of the old timothy and browntop, its purplish heads shining with moisture, all sweeping down through Queen Anne's lace to the pond silvery in the rainy light, the bar of stony sand diking it from the sea and its darker, moving water: no one there. Nor on the grass ground, as they used to call it, the flat field behind the point, cleared in his youth of flotsam and stones, where men would knock together on a weekend a wooden platform and people would dance the nails out of her. His feet and Connie's feet had thumped those boards, round

dancing or square dancing, they had bonfires and there were good fid-
dlers up and down the Island, and in the wee dark hours men step-
danced in the headlights of the last car until the lights went yellow and
it had to be pushed to get it a start home. They'd invited girls into their
arms, a stammer didn't hold Connie back, not then, he was a handsome boy, and how many words anyway did it take to get a girl out
on the floor with you? And the ones who drank, you'd slip away later
into the trees with, back and forth for swigs of liquor, whether the girl
stayed with you or not. A beginning, to what they never knew, but for
Connie, and anyone like him, he was choosing the partner he'd always
be faithful to: a bottle in his pocket or behind his belt. That was when
of course their people were here in numbers, and they all had a stake
in each other's lives, you knew everyone from the Cape to the highway—Careys and Stewarts and Gunns and Dunlops and MacNeils and
Drohans and MacKenzies—no one broke into your home, the doors
unlocked anyway, and no strangers took over a house and led a secret
life there, and no man, not even an alcoholic on his last legs, would be
cut down on the road and left there.

Anna was right, he tried the back door and it gave to his shoulder,
the latch plate tore easily out of the wood. Granny's house. How many
repairs had he done for her in her later years?

Tense about Anna's privacy, he stepped quietly through the
kitchen, struck by her things. He stomped his foot and felt the hollowness under the rug. Was Granny's churn still in the cellar? Used to
be. A vase-like crock, and the wooden stopper and the dasher's handle
running up through the small hole in it, she working up and down
the plunger with its wooden disk, gazing out the window, thinking
of something different in the middle of a dull task, her iron-gray hair

falling into wisps, and just before the thick cream turned to butter, she'd give him a glass of it with a big spoonful of sugar.

He turned a few pages in the book she had been reading, not noticing the words, they didn't matter. She'd tidied nothing today, left everything as it was, too much of her lay carelessly about, for any-one's eyes. Yet as he walked the rooms downstairs he felt a surprising tenderness toward her: something of herself she'd always kept out of sight, and, whatever it was, here he was protecting it.

He could carry the bale out the front door, hide it in his van. Up the mountain a ways he knew a small lake that would hold it until it rot. Not as risky as the sea, and it would be done with.

He slid his palm along the banister as he climbed, its maple oiled smooth by many hands, his great-grandfather had made it, and the newel post and balustrades. On the landing wall the old wood-framed photo of that man still hung—chin-whiskered, in a high-lapelled black coat, but if you looked closely, his eyes, pale and gentle, belied the severe gaze Murdock had avoided as a boy. He paused at her bed-room door: sheets spilling, her bed gaping with window light, a pillow crushed on the floor. He'd forgotten how it felt to be immersed in the intimacy of a woman's bedroom, of her scents, the hints of her tastes and habits, the clothes she wore, the objects she chose to surround her as she slept. Rosaire too had been slow to make a sprawling bed, Oh, it just speaks of the night before, she said, I like that. Last night had been hot. Upstairs here it was always hot in high summer, hard to sleep sometimes. He used to lie in that little bedroom, the raised window bereft of air, and kill the big, slow flies on the ceiling with a long rub-ber band, his grandmother scolded him for the dark spots, threatening to make him scrub them clean, but she never did, she was soft with him, he would be, after all, the last man home and she loved him. I'll bake you some raisin bannock, will I, darlin'? Will we walk you down for a swim, dear? Where had that feeling gone, of being adored and tended to? What a place to hide, what warmth, what comfort, and he could never have it again, from anyone—a love without responsibility, without debt. He had given back to her what he wished, nothing more was asked of him but to return her affection. . . . At some moment near the last, he had squeezed Rosaire's wrist, harder than he should have, he was trying to keep her from spinning dizzily away from him, he'd never have bruised her but now he wanted to see blood marks, hear her say, No, no, that hurts. But instead he touched his lips to her hand, to its dry, frightening coolness.

He was hesitant to enter Anna's room, to touch her flung clothing, here where he himself had tossed in the heat, and slept under quilts when the window was frosted. Somehow she'd know, he would leave a trace.

She might turn against him anyway for what he was about to do. *It wasn't your business, Murdock, you didn't ask me.* There wasn't time for asking, and he didn't want Livingstone or Billy or any of their kind to get a hold of that dope.

He opened the spare-room closet. The trunk was underneath clothes she'd recently hung there. Whose initials on the trunk? Anna had asked him. My mother's, she left us in a hurry for a man in Boston, didn't have time to pack a trunk. What she left behind, most of it, my dad flung on a burn pile, poked the flames until there was nothing but metal bits, zippers and buttons.

At first the voices seemed to come from the shore but when he rushed to the window, there was a young man, and a girl, in the yard already, she laughing at Anna's drenched, limp scarecrow, and before Red Murdock could duck, the man saw him and turned by instinct to run. Catching himself, he gave a false and hearty wave.

Red Murdock stepped out back into the soft rain just as he would have at his own door. He didn't want to fuss about private property, act suspicious, there was too much of that now, trespassing signs nailed on trees.

"You're her husband, I guess?" he said to Red Murdock, "the woman who lives here?" The friendliness of his voice had an urgent strain to it. His sunglasses were huge pupils of purple. "I met her on the beach one day."

"She's gone for a while. Just having a walk, are you?"

"Me and Rita there, yeah."

The girl wore a pink jacket, its hood down, her blonde hair streaming over her eyes. A smile touched her lips for a second. "We're taking a break from fishing."

"What're you getting?" Red Murdock said. He was aware of the Black Rock lighthouse, a deep wail every thirty seconds, a stab of light in mist.

"Pollock," the man said, too quickly. "Off the old wharf back there."

"Pollock have a lot of blood in them. But you get that blood out quick, and they're a good meal."

"She said it was all right to cut through your property. Your wife."

"No harm there. You're not dressed for the rain much."

"Doesn't matter." The man tilted his head up, taking in the house. "You got a nice spot here. What a view, eh, Rita?"

"Terrific. You must see a lot out there." She leaned her head grace-fully to the side, squeezing her hair into a dripping braid. "Stuff washes up here, I bet."

"Like any shore. Well, you walk as you wish," Red Murdock said. "I'm busy in the house."

They backed away before they turned onto the path to the shore. Had no intention of cutting through, neither of them. From the kitchen, obscured by the door curtain, Murdock watched the man scoop up an apple and pitch it like a baseball into the orchard. The girl was older than Red Murdock had thought, her walk was a woman's, sure of how she looked. Now he'd have to be certain they were well gone.

He fetched his tool box and was unscrewing the door latch when he heard Anna's car.

"What's wrong?" she said, coming breathless up the back steps.

"A friend from the beach was here. A fella with a shaved head."

"He broke in?"

"Me. As you said, this lock's no good."

Anna looked down at the empty shore. "What did he say?"

"He said he could cut through here, that you told him."

Anna touched the broken latch. "He's lying. I don't know anyone like that."

"He had a young woman with him. Girlfriend, I suppose."

"Charming. A couple."

"He thinks I belong to the place, that we're married, and maybe that suits us, you know. It won't hurt."

"He was blowing smoke. If he's in with Livingstone, he knows who I am."

"I wouldn't make much of a husband anyway."

"Oh, I think you'd more than do, Murdock. I'm sure your late friend thought so."

"She didn't," he said, smiling. "She knew better. But I did for her." He slowly drove a screw into the latch plate. "That dope, Anna, we have to get rid of it. Today."

"In daylight? With those people around?"

"After dark."

Get rid of it. That sounded so easy, but the bale's power was undeniable. Even between her and Murdock it was a force, and she wasn't sure she wanted to give it up entirely, just toss it away, now that Livingstone was after it. With her foot she drew a slow circle over the rug like the beginning of a dance. "We could hide it better," she said.

"Look, Anna, they know that stuff washed ashore, our shore. They might just be guessing about you, but that doesn't make things any better."

After her talk with Breagh, Anna felt pushed, cornered, the outsider. "The guy with the shaved head, he did have a girl with him. Why would he be dangerous? He wasn't sneaking around at night."

"Night isn't here yet."

Anna took off her rain jacket and flung it on a chair. She ran water into a pot and set it on the stove. Murdock watched her, a crank drill poised in his hand.

"Anna . . . ?"

"Husbands usually stay for supper," she said.

"There's nothing usual about any of this. That's not a bale of hay upstairs."

"Just not tonight?" she said. "Please? I'm tired out. I feel like I've been pulled around by my hair."

"I'll finish your door then," he said, his face hardening. "You need a stronger lock. I don't think they even make them that strong."

THE PASTA ANNA boiled, now a cold nest in a colander, had not raised her appetite. Murdock had left without a word after he finished the door. He was angry and that made her feel worse, she'd driven him away. She opened the expensive bottle of California wine she'd been saving, for something, someone. From the kitchen table she could keep an eye on the back field, the shore, the path. The rain grew fainter and fainter until it was just still, moist air, and then a wind came up out of the east, cool, full of sound, waggling the sticks of her sluggish scarecrow, its denim shirt soaked. She'd put out in the grass a bowl of leftover dessert and the ravens were at it immediately, their beaks tipped with whipped cream like kids at a party. Who would come here now, in this weather, seeing her at home? That stranger and his girlfriend? Did they even know she had a root cellar? Did Billy? Why should she give in to someone after her weed? She wasn't going to cower, to hell with them. Let Livingstone stew for a while. Murdock, of course, would not understand.

She was back and forth at the rear windows, staring out. She had let the house slide a bit, and her work. All she had left were two blank sketchpads and the dog drawing, but she could not pick up a pencil or a charcoal stick without Livingstone rising in her throat, his cruel, unnecessary betrayal.

Curled up in a chair, she tried to concentrate on a novel, but the words streamed by like water. She couldn't even escape into someone else's language, but she picked up a letter from Melissa, the handwriting, bold and elegant, soothed her. *I love the pen drawings on the gray paper, with just touches of white shading. The crows at the dead rabbit, the blood and the white fur, terrific. You've done good animals here but nothing like these. The lines are strong, powerful. I know you have Dürer in mind, they have that kind of sharp stillness, empathy, awe, such careful observation. I sold the red fox, beautiful. I imagine him lying there in the sunlit snow like a dog, full of your leftovers. You must've had time to sketch him well, you finished it so fine, the detail. Your best work ever, I hope you feel that way about it. The woman wants it framed so I'll do that for her. I'm keeping your money like you asked, any time you want a check for it just say so and it's in the mail.*

Anna wanted to reply, but the bale seemed to dull her wit, her invention—she hardly spoke about it except for Murdock, yet it altered everything she did, like sudden, spectacular wealth. It had seemed at first such a luxury to have that sweet smoke at her disposal, all hers, so valuable, a universal currency, and now there were people, not very far away, determined to get it back. But who had guessed it was *here* in her house? Then again, she was the woman from away, from California, a likely suspect. And she had toked up with Livingstone Campbell. . . .

At least the lock was new.

She smoked half a joint in plain view at her table, killing it in a yellow rose teacup she'd filled with sand. Then she pored through a jumble of old photographs she had found moldering in a shoebox, all from times when cameras were not common possessions. She'd worked her way through them slowly as if she were squinting through a microscope, imagining histories, however vague or inauthentic, for the faces there. A few were tiny prints probably from the nineteen teens, in sharp sepias: a woman, maybe Anna's age, in a long wool coat and tight-fitting hat, the ubiquitous spruce behind her draped

with snow, she bent awkwardly forward in a white clearing, maybe
pond ice, where a man held her arms to steady her, maybe her first
time on skates. In another, a dark collie leaned with affection into a
woman's skirt, a mown field behind them (dogs seemed beloved wherever they appeared). She wore a nautical dress—a white jumper with a
dark neckerchief and a long dark skirt, likely navy, and on the back of
the photograph she'd written: *Myself taken away from the house last
fall. I am fatter in the other pictures I think.* Who was she addressing?
What hopes did she have in their reaction? What did she mean, "away
from the house"? Two middle-aged smiling women at either handle
of a long crosscut saw resting on a sawhorsed log, a loose pile of cut
wood beside them: they weren't posing so much as pausing at a task
they were well familiar with. No men to do it? Or did they take it on
themselves, just another domestic necessity? A boy, maybe seven or
eight, putting up his dukes for the camera but looking aside (Connie?
He had the thick dark hair). Anna dwelled on three dark, surreal figures in heavy snow, too indistinct to single out the faces, they were
framed by a black sky and a black foreground—a murky dream from
a Bergman film: on the back, *Snowshovelling 1930.* A ship, its three
sails filled but ghostly faint, was passing down what might be the strait
behind the house, *August 1917* in pencil, a world war not yet over.
She examined closely a photo of a soldier who'd served in it, in his
kilted uniform, at relaxed attention for this posed postcard, his bon-
net jaunty, his large farmer's hands at his sides, a slight self-conscious
smile on his lips as if he were both proud and a little doubtful. On
the back he'd written: *Mama I never thought I'd miss the haymaking.
Knit me socks please. Love Rod.* Under it, in another hand, *Cpl. R.
MacAskill, killed at Ypres.*

Anna's mother had taken but a handful of snapshots that she could remember, and preserved even fewer. Anna had one of herself, still in pigtails, with her dad on a Pacific beach, huge rocks behind them, mist from a hard surf swirling in the air, and another in their surrounding woods, resting her head against the soft, warm bark of an enormous redwood.

She looked hard for Red Murdock and thought he was there in a few dim black-and-whites, a young man on a boat, maybe the old ferry, shirtless, arms crossed firmly over his bare chest, not out of arrogance (his smile cancelled that) but because he was entirely at ease with himself: there was nothing about him that said I need your help to know who I am. Anna turned the photos slowly, absorbed: was that his philandering mother, pulling her hem up to reveal her shapely legs? Who was the handsome guy, dark as an Italian, holding a baby girl? The four elderly men in black suits, soberly graying, seated on a row of chairs placed in a field, deciduous trees in full leaf behind them and, further on, the sea? Everything about them said a Presbyterian Sunday afternoon, said Gaelic was in their mouths.

She had persuaded herself she wanted to get by on this shore, in this place, alone, and she had. Not because of its simplicity or purity, since it was not simple or pure, but rather its old complexities which she sometimes sensed acutely, in this house and elsewhere, she had preferred them to her own, they had informed everything she drew.

Did she hear a car? She willed the sound away, if there was one. Dusk: *entre chien et loup*. Between the dog and the wolf.

She got up and went from window to window. The bale in the cellar was like a radioactive core: anywhere in the house she could sense its soft vibration. Why had she let Murdock leave that way, in that mood? She wouldn't run to him, she couldn't. The rattling call of a kingfisher came up from the pond. She felt watched. The field would be dark before long. Trees were swaying shapes in the wind, she felt terribly alone.

XXV.

THE MORNING OF Connie Sinclair's memorial, Murdock car- ried a piece of water-carved limestone up to his clearing in the mountain woods, a handsome stone he'd dug out of a brook where water, over many years, had worked it into graceful curves and hol- lows. He knew Rosaire would like it. This was what the settlers had done in their early graveyards, sited near water where they could be reached in all seasons: marked graves with undressed stones picked from the shore or wherever a pleasing rock revealed itself. Murdock set the brass canister holding half her ashes into the small hole and filled it in, tamping the earth down gently with his foot. The rest would stay with him at home, in the beautiful box. Two places at once, my dear woman, how about that? Can't do that while we're living. Be damned handy if we could.

This was the day of ashes.

Tired from his climb, he sat on the bench, pleased with the look of the stone. Like a sculpture. Did Anna ever carve in stone?

Last night he had lain awake for a long time. He had the feeling she would leave before long, somehow, in some fashion. If she did, she wouldn't know October when night frost stiffened the grasses, and the sun, as it rose into the morning, melted away the winter there, you could forget a while longer that it was coming. She wouldn't see a bliz- zard rage for three days and drift high as the telephone wires where birds had roosted, disheveled by the wind. She wouldn't be dancing by her stove, or his either. But she still had moves to make whether she reached for his hand or not.

He shouldered the shovel and took his time down through the woods. Sun filtered through the crowns of trees, the maples and birches, the barest hint of autumn there, a subtle cast to the light, a tinge of melancholy, he always felt it late in summer, before the first red in leaves, and geese took to the air in long, fluttering vees, arrowing southward.

THERE WAS TIME before the cemetery to drag the skiff, the hull fresh white with a stripe of royal blue along the gunnels, to his shore. He'd found in a forge tin his dad's old punch that incised a small heart shape into wood, and before he painted her he'd whacked that mark into the hull just aft of the stem, one port, one starboard. He circled the boat, looking it over, running his fingers along *Rosaire* on the stern, the nameless boat was his to name. The afternoon had turned hot along the dry stones above the high-water mark. The wind had dropped. Seaweed, burned black, brittle and sharp to the touch, crunched underfoot. A grasshopper hidden in a clump of beach grass made a thin chirping sound. More like a desert today than a northern shore. The skiff was too out in the open here, he didn't know who might be watching.

Under a bare sun, through a sea of undulating glare, he rowed to MacDermid's Cove, where, sweating and winded, he hauled her up, sheltered her where she wouldn't be easily seen. She'd handled nicely, responded well, cutting cleanly through the light chop, and the long oars Donald John had given him—I won't be putting my back to these anymore, Murdock Ruagh—felt good in his hands. Full moon and calm tonight was the prediction, wind down, hardly a breeze, but shut your eyes to sun one minute here and you might open them to rain the next. Be better without moonlight, but he was determined to slit that bale wide open and dump its guts into the sea. He had stowed a gray wool blanket and two life vests. He would take Anna with him, out of her house.

He and Connie and the MacDermid boys, they had played on this beach, took out their dad Robbie's boat on the sly, learned to row that way, just small they were, then. Older, half-cut, they staggered in swimming some summer nights, slept out into morning, sometimes with a girl, when they were lucky. He and Rosaire had swum here too one night under a high moon, shed their clothing and waded slowly in, she fearful of crabs or fish or eels, but they had felt on their feet only the soft stroke of eelgrass, tasted later the salt on each other's skin.

Now the sea was lazy, teasing the shore, barely breathing. In the shallows seaweed swayed dreamily. Somebody had capsized in this skiff, not a good oarsman, dangerous waters for an open boat, you'd have to know them. And no one here had been watching, had they? Donald John and Molly's big window would be dark that time of night, Willard gone home to sleep in his church. Hell, they had all slept through it, himself, all of them. If he'd only moved sooner the day Anna drove north to see Breagh, he could have spirited that dope away.

Murdock fussed about the skiff, checking the oars, the oarlocks, the killicks he'd secured her with, stone anchors Robbie's father had made, *calaich,* they'd hold her, the tide wouldn't reach here anyway. He shook out the blanket and tucked it under the stern seat. This was where Anna would sit, facing him. After supper, he would wait for nightfall to come back here, hoping no other hulls were cutting water, then pull for Anna's beach, for Anna Starling.

Feeling someone's presence, Murdock squinted up at the shore-bank path: Livingstone was looking down at him, his face shaded by a black cowboy hat cocked over sunglasses.

"Nice boat, Murdock."

"What're you doing here?"

"Could ask you the same thing, couldn't I?" He pointed up at the cliff edge of Murdock's eastern field. "I stopped by your place to see you."

He worked his way down carefully in the high-heeled boots, a cigarette in his mouth. He wore a jacket of rich brown leather, fringe dangling from the sleeves, but up close he looked scruffy, dusty, the boots dirty with mud and damp sand, he must have walked down from the gate. His beard needed trimming, as did his long hair, and the lenses of his glasses were oily with finger smudge.

"A buddy of mine had a boat very like this one," he said, stepping close to it, rapping the hull with a knuckle. "He lost her out there that storm we had."

"Is that so? Funny I never heard of it. If he had any sense, he wouldn't have been out there. How did he get ashore, swim?"

"Fisherman. Towing it at the time. Had some gear in it though. You seen anything washed up along here?"

"He wasn't fishing and you know it. How'd you find out I had this boat here?"

He tossed away his cigarette, whipped the sunglasses off and massaged them between finger and thumb. His eyes were bloodshot and danced. "I know people here, Murdock, just like you do. Anyway, you know how it is. Everybody's got binoculars, cheap or pricey. People over there"—he nodded toward St. Aubin—"see people over here."

"Maybe. But some of them belong here and some of them don't."

"Like Anna Starling, you mean?"

"Leave her out of this."

"*This?* Is that possible? She lives on the shore. Not too far from here."

"You know what I mean. Friends of yours sniffing around. And then there's Connie."

"Connie was a juicer."

"That's not all he was, not the whole of him. Somebody met up with him up on the road. You know who it was, don't you."

"Not any more than you do. You get a drunk stumbling along in the dark . . ."

Murdock grabbed his lapels and yanked him close, his jacket releasing a sweaty smell of leather.

"Listen, you bastard. Connie would make two of you. You used him for this caper here, on this beach. Were you done with him? Is that it?"

"Who the hell told you that? Connie? He ran his mouth when he was loaded, he made up stories . . ."

"About Willard's dog? Making him kill it so you'd give him booze?"

"Let go of me, Murdock."

He shoved him away. "Glad to!"

Livingstone straightened his clothes, his hat. He grabbed a stone in his fist and threw it hard into the water. "Shit! I'll tell you one thing,

Murdock." He pointed to the boat. "The fella that owned that, he wants what he lost from it, he's pissed. Him and some others. My ass is on the line here. I have to drive to Sydney today, now. If I don't have what they want, I don't get my money, just grief for a bonus."

"I can't help you. I don't want to help you."

"Somebody better."

"Like who?"

Livingstone looked away across the water. "If I was sure, I'd go there now."

"You'd better be more than sure."

"I'm not the only one in this, Murdock."

"You're the only one I know. You and Billy Buchanan. Tell them to stay away from her. She's got nothing of yours."

"Well. . . ." Livingstone grinned. He pulled out a cigarette and lit it. "That's not exactly true, Murdock. I left a little something with her, back in the cold weather."

"You get by on lies. Why would I believe you?"

"Ask her. She tells the truth. I like that about her."

"Good. Then believe her now."

"Wish I could."

Murdock pulled a rope from the boat, uncoiled it. "Look what you brought into this place. You proud of that?"

"Hey! Folks smuggled liquor right into this cove, I know that much. Old Robbie here had a hand in it, and your own dad, your own people. They better than me?"

"Yes. They were. They all drank the liquor. They knew what it was. Nobody got killed over it."

"Different time, Murdock."

"Is that all you can say? It's that simple? Connie is dead."

"I've got to get out of here." He started to back away.

"I bet you do. I know what happened, Livingstone. What you landed here."

"Where is it? And what washed ashore at your granny's? You going to turn me in?"

"Stay away from Anna Starling."

"I told you, it's not just me! Jesus. There's damn few houses along here, Murdock. Hers is one of them."

"Bad guesses, that's all you've got. With the tides here, that stuff could have washed in anywhere."

"So, you know what we're searching for, what it looks like?"

"Billy described it, to Anna."

"Billy! God, he's useless, *useless!*"

Murdock tossed the coiled rope into the boat. "There's a service for Connie in a little while. I don't suppose you'll be there."

"Hanging around here now is a bad idea, Murdock."

"It is. In your case."

"I'll send Billy. He's sleeping it off."

"Sure you will."

He watched Livingstone pick his way up the bank path toward the woods, pause to whack sand from a cuff. "Don't row that thing too far, Murdock!" he called back. "You're a long way from help!"

"I could row you to hell, Livingstone!"

"But you couldn't row *back!* Don't forget your nitro, old man!"

Old man. Okay. Jesus, he'd like to put a leash on that young pup's neck. He'd known Livingstone since he was a tyke, known his father, killed in a mine accident, and his mother, a calm, pretty woman concerned about her kids. Distasteful to be the one who turned him in. And how much evidence was there to set against his denials, apart from Anna's little prize in her closet? Left something with her in the cold months, did he? Revenge would be sweet, for dancing with Anna Starling on a winter night, in the light of a candle, dancing her off God knew where. But too much was uncertain. Where were the witnesses? Once the bundles left here, they could be hidden in any town, or more likely trucked off the Island. And Anna's bale had no name and address.

THEY WERE COMING up the hill on a foggy morning, in ones and twos for Connie Sinclair's memorial, not many, tramping slowly up the narrow cemetery road along the wet grass of the treadway, he could hear their voices soft in the damp air. Red Murdock, the first there, opened the green wrought-iron gate fastened with a loop of rope. He hadn't been here since Rosaire was alive. He meandered toward the MacLennan graves in the northeast corner, the oldest a humble limestone whose name went back a hundred and thirty years to the Isle of Lewis in Scotland, so blurred you'd have to kneel and make it out with your fingers. His granny's was partly obscured by a bush of scarlet peonies Murdock had transplanted there years ago. *Loved and Remembered,* that's all she'd wanted. His father's was red granite too, polished, his name stood out, but there was no woman's along with it as on others. *Until the day breaks and the shadows flee away.* Murdock had long wondered where his mother lay, among what faraway people. Did her stone mention this place that had shaped so much of her? Doubtful. She'd wanted only to get away, to cut herself off. He, the last of these MacLennans, had made no provision for his own burial, he didn't care anymore, someone would take him up and put him where he needed to be. Rosaire had told him to plant her ashes wherever he wished, and he had. Through a thin row of spruce, mist, white as steam, hung over the water.

Rosaire. Her wonderful, physical self.

Down below at the point, the beach where Anna swam every day was empty, and he regretted he had not stopped at her house, disgusted though he was with her stubbornness, the risk she refused to free herself from. He had thought she would come around if he left her alone for a day or so, let the danger sink in, but he'd heard nothing from her and that worried him. She was on his mind too much anyway. What was the right thing to do? What line in her life should he cross? He had walked to her shorebank three times and seen her once up above kneeling at her garden, another going up her path in a swimsuit that she looked more than all right in. But he hadn't wanted to talk to her, it was as if someone he didn't care for was standing between them and couldn't be ignored, not if they were to get back to where they had been. What was occurring up here on the hill this morning of course had nothing to do with her, not in any direct way at least. . . .

There were voices behind him and he turned to them, the greetings began, people he hadn't seen in a long while took hold of his hand.

The Ferguson brothers from the other side, lean Johnny, his hair kinky gray, and older Willy all but bald, a shine of damp on his big amiable scalp. Some others in from town, Al McCulloch, Connie's distant cousin, a big, quiet man, and Sally MacCuish, silver-haired and rounder, still pretty, smoking furiously, dropping her cigarette to hug him, and, when they were younger, hug him she had. Murdock had a soft spot for Sal, she was fun and kind and loved a man in her arms, but she was a talker who'd pull back in the middle of sex just to tell you she'd got a speeding ticket, she couldn't keep the mood, daily life wouldn't let go of her long enough. She'd slept with Connie too, always liked him, and someone said to her, You must have some great pillow talk with that fella, and Sal said, A good man, he doesn't have to say a word.

A hard-bitten woman from The Mines hung back pulling on a cigarette, her companion a skinny pale man beside her, old drinking pals of Connie who used to visit him. You'd hear them up the hill shouting drunk. At least they'd showed.

"They could just as easily pickled him," Sam Cunningham said, "cheaper too."

The men huddled around him laughed low, they knew Connie wouldn't give a damn what they said. Yes, he'd bowed his head and prayed like the rest of them when it suited, so were they raised, but to Connie funerals and wakes had been just another reason, for a man who no longer needed any, to drink himself dumb. But they all wanted to hear how Murdock found him, since rumors had raced around—Connie had been shot before he fell into the ditch, that he had taken his life, that he'd had a stroke—but Murdock didn't feed the gossip, he gave them only the bare bones, nothing they could chew on: the Mounties were looking for a vehicle that might have struck him, but what had they to run with? No one saw or heard a thing. He did not mention that Connie might have helped out drug smugglers, he didn't want to open that nest of hornets. Anna had already been stung.

"A full ashtray in the Legion bar, all that's left of him now, old Con," said Willy, nodding toward the small varnished box with a brass plate and handles. It sat on the turf beside a high snowball bush past its blooming. Murdock could have made a better box, had he been asked, had there been time. But who would have asked him? Connie had no one in Cape Seal now but Peter Ingraham, an old buddy, who had arranged this modest memorial.

"Calmed him down some though, didn't it?" Archie Fleming said. "No Roaring Connie this morning."

"There's nothing half-assed about ashes," Johnny said.

"Are you going under whole?" Archie said, turning to Sal.

"Oh," Sal said, "I don't even think about that," her high cheeks blushing as if he'd asked what underwear she was wearing.

"Better decide soon, girl, we're not none of us getting young," George Fraser said. "I'm not keen, myself, to be burnt like the Sunday papers."

"You'll feed the worms then, boy," Johnny said.

"You seen those caskets they make now? By the time a worm chews through that, you won't be worrying and neither will anybody else."

"Poor Connie," Sal said. "You couldn't reach him those last years, not at all."

"If you couldn't reach him, Sal, nobody could."

"It's ashes for Connie anyway. He didn't want the big hole."

"I don't think he wanted to die in a ditch either," Murdock said.

"It was quick anyway. Not a bad way to go," Sal said.

"He wasn't ready to go, I don't think," Murdock said. "And how quick was it? We don't know."

"Going along the road, looking for another drink, I suppose," Johnny said.

"No," Murdock said. "It wasn't just that."

He moved away toward Donald John and Molly when he saw them making their way up the hill.

"Where's Willard?" Murdock said.

"Oh, he's coming on slow. There he is," Molly said. They waited until he waved them toward him, off to the side on the grass.

"Listen," he said, pausing for breath. "They've got Billy Buchanan."

"Who's got him?" Donald John said, shifting his cane.

"Mounties. Took him away a little while ago."

"Just him?" Murdock said.

"At Sandy's alone, nobody but him. Some of that gang that used to come and go tore out yesterday, no sign of them."

"Took him what for?" Molly said.

"Billy's truck, you see, he liked to show it off, eh? You know, you've seen it out front the house there, that proud pile of metal. But then he takes to hiding it in the little backyard there, you could barely spy the ass end of her. I think that's odd, I says to the constable when he come to my door, looking into Connie's case. He said show me. We go over. There's Billy in the house making like he's not home. The constable, he checks the pickup, looks it over real slow, careful, doesn't say a word. Then he rousts Billy out. He was a wreck, face all puffy, like he hadn't slept in a year."

Someone yelled over to them they were starting soon, and Murdock raised a hand, "We're coming!"

"Go on, Willard," Donald John said.

"The Mountie says, There's blood in your headlight rim, Billy. You want to talk about it? Terrible liar, Billy, twisted himself in knots. Next thing you know there's tears down his cheeks, he didn't mean to, an accident. Some hard fellas at the house had it in for Connie, they told Billy go fetch him, bring him back. Billy sees him on the road, late, up by your place, Murdock."

"Yes, we almost run over him one night, he staggered in front of the car," Molly said.

"But Billy's drunk himself, see, he clips Connie with the truck too hard, sends him flying into the ditch. Just wanted to knock him over like, he said, Connie could fight like a bastard, you know? So he panicked, took off. Anyway, the Mountie cuffed him, put him in the car."

"Haven't seen Livingstone?" Murdock said.

"Billy might've warned him. He had time before the constable banged on his door. They was dealing drugs there, at Sandy's."

"Is it all over then?" Molly said. "Are they all off the road?"

"We'll see," Murdock said, certain someone would be back for that goddamned bale, smugglers or police. Depended what they pumped out of Billy, how much he wanted to tell and how soon he told it.

"They won't be at Sandy's anymore, that's something," Donald John said. He pointed his cane at the gathering in the cemetery. "Looks like Peter's ready."

There was no minister for Connie's interment, so the remarks fell to Peter Ingraham, his last and final pal. Peter, known as a bit of a poet, a man fluent with words, greeted everyone with an earnest handshake and moved quickly into the cemetery where he stood, in his clean second-hand suit, near the graves of other Sinclairs. His thin black hair was damp and combed slick.

"My friends, you know," he said, "I couldn't make a poem for this day, this morning. Some kind of nice rhyme, it wouldn't do, I think, not for Connie. Sometimes we can't match one side of a man to the other, hard to think of nice words that'd come together, in some sweet way. But that's all right, for a man of contradictions. He could be a charmer or a bastard, you could love him and you could want to wring his neck. But that's over. It's easy to be righteous about a drinking man, isn't it though? But this is Con's time, this morning, here in this spot where we're gathered. Did he not love to run here as a boy, swim right down there at the point? This water, these woods, this mountain, he knew them, and they knew him. He went away, and he came back. So it is fitting he should find his rest here, in this place. There are better deaths than Connie met, we all of us know. But if he was next to me now, he'd be whispering, Peter, cut it short, boy, Jesus, I'm terrible thirsty. Connie, your thirst is over." Peter raised his face to the soft mist. "Oh, merciful God, forgive Connie Sinclair, forgive us, sad sinners that we are. You have taken our friend to your eternal heart. He is washed clean. He was a good man brought low by a weakness, and the weaknesses of others, and who among us has never been? Amen."

Murdock joined the mumbled amens, wondering if they would dare return, Livingstone, his pals. Not before nightfall, even were they sure Anna had what they wanted. They would stay out of sight for a while, with Billy in the cooler, maybe squawking away.

His attention wandered to the beach in the lee of the point: a dark-haired woman was unwrapping a towel from her waist. Anna. There she was. A great feeling of relief rose in him, and, he had to recognize as well, desire, a yearning from his dreams. He had never seen her swim though he knew she did. He watched her pause at the water's edge, her head lowered as she took a cautious step. The skin of her back was darker now from the sun. She dove and he could just hear her limbs thrashing the water. How he'd loved in the morning to kiss Rosaire's back, the smooth curve of her spine, then hold her in a blissful spoon—another small thing desperately missed, it slipped unbidden into his mind.

The small crowd broke and took up talking, in twos and threes, about anything at all, this part of Connie was done with, they had living to do. But already people were drifting toward Willard, closing around him, and Molly and Donald John: they had information now, the latest word.

Murdock hung back. One thing he was certain of: you didn't meet anyone on the other side, loved or unloved, this was the only side there was. Con's ashes sat in a shiny wooden box pearled with damp, a thick white birch leafed overhead. Long lost to the sky by now, Connie's smoke, it had thinned out to what, to where? Nowhere? He was rooted here, but no family mourned him on this occasion. And here was he, Red Murdock MacLennan, who, with all his faults and failings, could do with the rest of this foggy morning whatever he damn well pleased. That's all death was about, wasn't it, for the living? I can keep going?

He'd brought Rosaire here after they got serious, just to show her the names, and though he'd joked about it, Come meet the dead of my family, she had to know who he belonged to and his ties to these families from around. On that evening, long before she took sick, when he stood with her in the chilly dusk, she had read aloud, because she liked it, an inscription on a gravestone for a woman near her age who'd died in 1904: *Thy sun shall no more go down, neither shall thy moon withdraw itself, for thy Lord shall be thy everlasting light, and the days of thy mourning shall be ended.* Rosaire and himself were quiet then, and what after all was to be said? Suddenly she pulled his face to hers and kissed him hard on the mouth. But we are *alive,* she said, me and you together.

Rosaire. Woman of my life.

People touched him and wandered away, he murmured goodbye, goodbye, see you after, take care of yourselves. Anna was gone from the shore but he could see where her feet had disturbed the sand. He had to seek her out soon, say to her, Let's carry that stuff away for good, Anna, it's time.

XXVI.

MURDOCK WAS CHANGING out of his suitclothes when the phone rang and he ran downstairs in his shirttail and shorts. He was glad to hear Anna's voice.

"I saw the people up there at the cemetery," she said. "I wish I'd gone. I didn't know."

"You swam. I saw you."

"I feel better now with this wind blowing the sun around, it's so warm. I was watching shadows of leaves flickering on my floor, everything full of clean light, and I thought, how could anything bad happen?"

"We don't know what's coming down or when, Anna."

"Someone rang me up today, two different times. They hung up when I answered. Not a salesman, I would guess."

He told her about Billy, about Livingstone and the people who were unhappy with him. "We won't see him, I don't think, not while the sun is up. Might see somebody else, of course. If Billy doesn't talk."

"I need a bigger scarecrow, I guess."

"How about me?"

"Oh, Murdock, you're my husband, remember? You should be here anyway. You could answer the phone in your deep voice."

"Come over here this evening. We'll plan our next move."

"I would love to do that. I'm ready. I've been packing up my draw-ings, I'm mailing them in town this afternoon and . . ." Her voice lost its cheerfulness, as if she were not yet sure what this meant. Murdock suddenly felt foolish standing there in his underwear.

"Come any time that suits you, Anna."

HER CAR ROCKED slowly down the road to Red Murdock's, she could feel a splash here and there in the floorboards, her headlights begging something to lurch from the trees. She almost wished for some noisy confrontation that would shake loose the solemn weight of the evening. Near suppertime there'd been a quick white squall, pelting rain for a few minutes, then the late sun rushed out behind it, mag-nified by a bare washed sky, everything sparkling, window screens beaded with drops. The moon was just an ivory glow behind the St. Aubin hills in the south.

She could have done without the joint, its paranoid intensity, a full moon might have been enough. Too late now. Nevertheless, she remained cool, all considered, unalarmed, down the length of his dark driveway. In the back seat lay the rolled-up drawings she had not mailed to Melissa. Beside her a bottle of red wine rocked on the seat. She had locked her doors, but why? It hardly mattered.

"How are you now?" Murdock said, letting her in the kitchen door. He was wearing a yellow rain jumper, unfastened, its rubber slick with damp like his face.

"I'm glad to be here."

He finished coiling a thin rope and placed it on the table where an oil lamp burned.

"That's nice," Anna said, setting down the wine. "I love the old lamplight," catching it in her open hand.

"Doesn't attract much attention," he said, peering out the back window.

"It attracts me. The womanmoth."

"Clear enough to row now, and flat calm. Where the boat is, we can get to her without a flashlight."

"It's Saturday night, Murdock."

"Won't be easier on Sunday, or Monday either. It's time, Anna. You don't have to come with me, if you'd rather not."

"Of course I'll come with you. I couldn't *not* come with you." She realized her voice was trembling and she groped in her pocket for the roach. "Could I have a light please?"

Red Murdock sighed. He pulled off his jumper and let it drop to the floor behind him, poured himself a glass of liquor and sat across from her. He reached over the table with a flaring wooden match. She offered him a hit but he raised his hand. "That's no help to me," he said. He watched her lips purse the joint.

"You smoked that with Livingstone, did you?" he said.

Anna squinted at him, let her breath out slowly. "I don't care about Livingstone Campbell, Murdock. I just want to sit here, for a little while," she said. "Do you mind? It's a peaceful night."

"I like you sitting here. Fine with me."

"Anything new about Breagh?"

"She came and went the other evening, in a hurry. I wanted to see Lorna, so they stopped by. I had a wooden car for her. She likes cars. Breagh doesn't know all what's going on and why would I tell her now? She couldn't get hold of Livingstone, wondered if I'd seen him."

"The man of the hour."

Anna watched him light a cigarette. She thought he looked older, tired perhaps. Maybe it was the red-gray stubble.

"You must've been hot in that. Your shirt is soaked."

"A sticky night." He lifted his glass and emptied it in one swallow. "Iron for the spine," he said.

Anna took a quick hit but the roach was cold. "Oh," she said, rising, "your kitty! He always runs from me over at my place." Cloud sat in his chair by the stove showing no inclination to run anywhere, his sleepy eyes registering her.

"He's different outdoors, he's wary," Murdock said. "Like the rest of us."

Anna approached the cat carefully, and when he didn't bolt she worked her hands gently under him and, smiling, took him in her arms, petting his head, tickling his chin, whispering. She sat back down, cradling him in her lap, stroking him into a loud purr.

"He'd never let me do that," Murdock said. "You have the touch he's been missing."

"I took a few mailing tubes to The Mines this afternoon and posted them. They're safely gone."

"Is that what makes things safe? Going?"

"I don't know, Murdock. But when I got back from my swim, someone had been in the house. Just little indications, you know, nothing glaring. Things in my workroom somewhat out of place, a drawer not quite shut. Upstairs the closet was open, a sleeve was hanging out under the trunk lid. . . ."

"They got it then?"

"I'd moved it to the old cellar, Murdock, it's still there."

"Christ!" He crushed out his cigarette. The cat leapt from Anna's lap and disappeared. "I wish to hell they'd found it, hauled it off!"

"But maybe now they won't be back? I almost wish they'd turned the house inside out."

"They have to lay low, with Billy locked up. But they're not done with you." He leaned his head back on the high-backed chair, closed his eyes. She wanted to touch his face, soothe it with her fingers. She squeezed the roach in her hand and stuck it in a pocket.

"Murdock, I'm sorry," she said quietly. "I had a longing for old times, the feel of them. When I smoke, I can sort of get there, you see? I wanted to remember how I *felt,* what I knew then. You don't know what I mean."

He looked at her across the lamplight. "Maybe I do," he said. "I hope you got there."

He picked up the wine and rummaged around in a drawer, finally holding up a corkscrew triumphantly. "She enjoyed wine," he said. "And we enjoyed each other. I think I can say that to you." He uncorked the bottle and Anna couldn't see what he was pouring the wine into until he set it in front of her: the teak goblet.

"Thank you, Murdock." She sipped it, smiling. "Mmm. Big, and berrylike, with, I think, a slight aftertaste of the Atlantic Ocean."

"That's the wine for us then, Anna Starling. That's where we're going. When you're finished, we'll walk up the beach, eh? While we can? I'll row her down to your shore. Shouldn't take long . . ."

Anna drank quickly. "To our voyage," she said, raising the goblet. "Murdock, I'm sorry about the dope. But you have to admit it's in a good hiding place, isn't it?"

"It isn't if you grew up in the country."

"I see."

She got up and walked slowly around the kitchen, in the dusky perimeter of light, pausing to place her finger on the pastel drawing of the forge, the heat of its fires, rattling gently the cobalt bottles along the sill, a filleting knife on the sink top that teetered when she touched the blade, and she ticked it a few times like a clock.

THEY SET OFF through the sea field, the tall grass, into the moonlit dark. Wet beach stones, awkward even in daylight, wobbled and slipped under their boots. Low swells were sifting the gravel like long sighs. Anna trailed a few steps behind him. A breeze off the sea cooled his face and he halted when she tugged at his arm.

"Did you see that up there?" she said in a loud whisper. Above the point, a set of car lights latticed the spruce trees along the cemetery road and went out.

"Probably parkers. Lovers maybe. Saturday night, Anna." He was aware of a single star, dim as a nailhead, and then a boat a hundred yards or so offshore, barely making headway at a low, idling rumble. They wouldn't be fishing, unless it was a pleasure boat, and if they were coming home, it wouldn't be at a couple knots. Her starboard light bobbed in the darkness as the engine slipped into neutral and revved a bit. Something splashed near the white hull. The moon was high and very white in a break of cloud and the boat's shadow slid up and down. Damn them.

"That boat out there," he said. She was beside him now. "I'm leery of it."

"Are they heading for here, do you think? Are they Mounties? God, I would hate getting us busted, that would be awful. They could go ahead and hang me."

"Not a Mountie boat. Wouldn't be after you anyway, or me either, not by sea. They don't know a thing about us."

"Isn't it white? It looks a kind of white to me. Livingstone and Billy's boat!"

"They wouldn't be in it then, and they don't own the boat, somebody else does. That's Livingstone's problem. He doesn't own anything, and he won't when this is over. But they've scotched my plan. Best to get off the beach. They can see us, but not who we are."

"We could watch from my house," Anna said. "We could wait there."

"We'll walk then. See if you've had any visitors."

He took her by the hand and led her over the familiar rocks that had slid and tumbled all these years under his feet, storms and tides jumbling them, always on the move, boulders shifting so slowly you barely noticed them sinking deeper in the sand, and still he could follow them without falling, even in the dark he never fell, and that was good, he was proud of it. They didn't speak as they went, the sea the only sound, its long breaths, a gasp of gravel, a pause, another. Who was this woman whose hand was in his? Where were they going? It was like he had caught hold of her passing by. The boat, whoever was manning it, was not coming for them, not here. He helped Anna up the short bank, up the path he had trod so many times to the red house, across the shorn patch of lawn. Under the frenzied moths of the back-door light, monkshood bloomed like blue and white bits of china. He knew she was scared, he could feel it in her skin, and he drew her hand to his lips quickly, it was what he felt like doing at that moment, he never broke stride, he had no regrets. She squeezed his hand before she released it, unlocked the door and stepped inside, and Murdock turned away to set his eyes toward the water. He had to pay attention, he had to take heed of the unordinary, Connie had not, he had let himself be run down. Rosaire, God love her, nothing had been ordinary anymore once she knew, and he knew, that she was dying. He kissed her brow one afternoon as he was leaving, and she said, sleepy but alert, Murdock, that has the feel of a final kiss to it. He turned back to her and kissed her mouth, her warm, feverish lips. My Murdock, she said. Wasn't the very sharpness of love in knowing you would lose it, had to lose it someday, along with every act that made it sweet and good? Always underneath it, like a cold hidden spring, there ran the force of separation, the powerful chill would hit you, sometime.

The boat had a small searchlight going now, a shaft of light driven down into the water, not aimed at the shore, and he heard Anna's voice behind him, "Murdock, come inside, they'll see you."

"One minute." He took out a small pair of binoculars he'd tucked inside his jacket, directing them up toward the cemetery: he could barely make out the markings, the parked car was a Mountie's.

"I don't know if that's good or bad, Anna," he said. "We'll think good, what with the boat out there to catch his attention. And we won't give him anything to look at."

Murdock went from room to room with the flashlight, Anna behind him pointing out what was amiss. He finished by flipping the rug back and then lifting the cellar door, putting the beam on the bale that lay a few feet from the steps, fixing it there as if he'd exposed a housebreaker.

"We'll get rid of that tomorrow, so help me God," he said.

They stood inside the back door, just the sound of their breathing in the darkness, moths clinging like petals to the screen.

"We're okay," he said. "That boat is heading off, no visitors from there. We can ease back." Wasn't that one dispiriting consequence of getting old, worry and easy fright? But fear was part of love anyway. Fear gave it its point, its cut: as a boy, he had felt it that night in his bed, his mother absent from the kitchen below, his father pacing, weeping, raging at himself and her in the oil-lamp light, while Murdock lay overhead afraid to move, to make a sound lest his dad be obliged to tell him what she had done.

But how could you love without risk, how could you stir your heart in that way without it?

Anna switched on the ceiling light, looked at him, then turned it off.

"I just wanted to see you," she said.

"You can't stay the night alone," he said.

"I know."

Murdock took her face in his hands and pressed his mouth to hers. They stood there in each other's arms listening to the old house creak as it cooled in the night wind. Just slightly, almost imperceptibly, they swayed to it.

THE NEXT MORNING, Anna, carrying her sandals, walked barefoot through the fine cool sand of the point. She nudged the charred spokes of a driftwood fire, its smoke no more than steam. Crushed beer cans, a few butts. But for that, the shore was clean. Late-night revelers? Had the patrol car watched them? They'd heard nothing during the night, she and Murdock, but each other.

She was not afraid, she would not hide. She would have her swim as she had every day in the lee of the point. Murdock was not far and he'd be back, she knew that, they were in this together.

The high grass of the point's broad field drooped with fine-spun moisture, running brilliantly through the gray air to alder bushes and the rushes bordering the pond. She glanced back at the red house, then undressed slowly, as she had last night, but with Murdock helping, tugging gently at her clothes, blouse, jeans, today more conscious than usual of her body, feeling strong in her black swimsuit, she could stroke out near the eddy now, flirt with its pull as it curled around the point. At her feet lay the thick heel of a bottle, abraded into foggy green stone. A wine-colored jellyfish pulsed in the shallows but she waded past it, the water moving in cold circles up her legs. A soda can flashed in the bottom sand. She stopped, sifting water slowly through her hands. He had unbuttoned his shirt and draped it neatly over the back of a chair, then his jeans, slowly unclothing himself, as if he were preparing to bathe or swim, pale but for his darker face and forearms, lean, somehow chaste, she thought. He had touched her face, a gentle tarry smell on his hands, like rope on a wharf. She had skimmed her fingers over the muscle of his shoulders, his chest, felt him tremble along the hard ridge of his back, his pleasure seemed to flow through her, out of his own unselfpitying solitude, she took it gladly into herself, and not until much later, when she awoke suddenly and felt him next to her, did she remember that the name he'd whispered was one not her own. She didn't care, that didn't diminish anything, every touch had been sincere. In the dark, her face to his, everything for a while felt locked out except for the space they lay in, holding each other, to Anna it had all come down to these moments, a pure feeling of invincibility that could never last. In the warmth, in whispers, she told him about the bridge and the dog, how cold it all had been but was finally leaving her. He said he was sure that was the worst thing Connie ever did, and how awful to go to his grave with it.

It was barely light when he kissed her and left, I'll be back later, I'll bring your car, he said, but ring me quick if there's anything unusual.

She dove, groaning in the cold water, but after a few hard strokes she felt good and she turned on her back and floated, breathing in the pearl-white sky, oddly at ease, unmoored. Tonight they would take the marijuana up, she and Murdock, ferry it off to sea. And what more would go with it? She was afraid something of her maybe, of them, once the tension had dissolved. They had in a sense, the two of them, smoked it all, every grain of it, burned it all away.

As she climbed the path home, the well-tramped grass of her comings and goings, and turned out of the spruce grove and into the field, the house looked as it always had, from this distance, gazing seaward from the hill, stolid, weather-wracked. She wanted to keep this morning as it was, and the night before. She stopped. The spare-room window was raised high as she'd left it, open like a shout, the pale green curtain flapped crazily in its mouth. She studied the house as she might draw it again, its details, angles, shadings, what point of view it would offer now, what perspective, here on the outside as she was, at this spot. She took one slow step and then another. Her metal sculptures lay hidden some in the grass, taller now, Willard had not mown. One had come apart, just fallen in pieces. At the steps she pressed her damp towel to her face and then broke off two lemon-yellow lilies to sketch. By evening they'd be shut and spent, their petals mush.

The kitchen was tidied except for things set out for supper. Chanterelles she'd picked among the spruce above the road, her own gnarly-fingered carrots waiting to be rinsed of their clay, basmati rice she hoped he'd like, a sturdy yellow onion. In the fridge, the fish she'd bought in town yesterday, the chilled bottle of Australian chardonnay. She had prepared for a guest, yet it seemed more than that, as if she were putting the whole house in order. She couldn't remember anymore exactly how it had looked the day she stepped into its cold front hall, or just where items had been in the kitchen, what she'd grabbed from cupboards. But bit by bit her mark was disappearing, she was gathering her belongings, an act that had seemed casual for a while, natural, as if it were happening unconsciously, guided by . . . what? By the season, by the changing light? She was not a cottage person, fleeing summer's end. She didn't *want* to leave, she didn't want to be *made* to leave. Murdock had been here, had spent the night with her. She had to step back, slow down. The woman from away.

In her room, she cleared her art equipment off the oak table where they would eat. She had packed the skates early; they'd hung on her studio wall, waiting for ice. The antique lamp was to go to Breagh, sometime. She could see Lorna beneath its mosaic light, musing on its colors, pulling them, with that fierce frown of concentration, into her drawings. One sketchpad was stowed behind the fat chair, handy for whatever urged her to capture it. The dog drawing sat on its big clipboard, she had plunged back into it early this morning, she'd seen a way, she thought, to finish it, to make it whole, now that she knew who'd flung that animal into the air, and why. He had paid for it, dearly, he was part of the picture.

The kitchen rug was in place just as she and Murdock had left it the night before. How serious was her own crime of concealment, of possession? It had been opened, some was missing, she could not claim ignorance or good intentions delayed. The Mounties would have come last night had they known, had Billy told them it might be somewhere in the house, Murdock said, they wouldn't have waited in their cruiser for long. And Livingstone and the rest of them would be hiding, you won't see them here in daylight anymore, Anna, not those creatures.

Even so, she walked reluctantly to the mailbox, she wanted to show herself, composed. Along the driveway a ruffed grouse startled her when she sent it beating in a feathery commotion through the underbrush. Jittery, she almost turned back but kept on, not expecting mail of any consequence. But there in the box lay a letter, a vanilla envelope, addressed in Chet's impulsive, forward-slanted hand. She wouldn't read it now, she didn't want to be yanked back there, not today, if she could manage it.

Into the afternoon Anna worked on the drawing, recalling Connie on the road that night, his dark, shambling figure from behind in the blaze of headlights, tormented already by what he had done. What she wanted in those lines and shades and hatchings, a kinetic fusion of shapes, was coming, she knew she would finish it, be done with it now any hour she wished.

XXVII.

WHEN HE CAME in the back door in the afternoon and saw her waiting for him, wearing a full skirt of black cotton and a yellow blouse, he smiled, took her waist in his hands, drew her to him, kissed her.

"All quiet?" he said. "No travelling salesmen?"

"A red squirrel climbed the screen. I didn't ask what he was selling."

"Don't let him inside, he'll winter in your walls."

"Maybe we should pull that rug back and go away for the night. I'll put a sign on the front door, 'Check the Cellar.'"

"Tempting. But let's not hand it to them, Anna. Not now. I don't want Livingstone walking away with anything. I don't think he will, Willard says the Mounties are looking for him, and that means the rest of them too."

"That puts them off us then?"

"He hasn't been located. He won't be easy, Livingstone."

"They know where he lives."

"You can hide poorly in the city, in the country you can disappear. For a while. Livingstone grew up across the water there."

"You mean they won't find him?"

"Not right away. RCMP, they're spread pretty thin."

"I thought I knew him a little," Anna said.

"We missed things. All of us."

She took his hand and pulled him gently out the back door, into the field flowing with goldenrod beyond its prime, greening faintly like the goldfinches past their mating, they bobbed on flower tops, then dipped away toward the trees. Bull thistles released into the wind their downy seeds, a gust ballooned Anna's skirt and she let go his hand to press it down.

"See those, Murdock?" She had set two kitchen chairs a few feet apart in the lawn grass. "I want you to sit in that one and I'm going to do a portrait of you. No arguments."

He shook his head but let her sit him down. "Is this what husbands do?" he said.

"For a little, early on."

Watching a gypsum freighter outbound, registered in Panama, he waited while she went for the sketchpad and then sat across from him, propping it on her knees. "Now look off east, toward the sea. And keep still if you can, please."

"That'll be hard, you close by, and the wind in your clothing."

The sun was bright and Anna felt its heat in her skirt as she drew first the shape of his face, the high cheekbones and deep-set eyes, the cleft of his chin, then penciled in details, the creases and lines of his years, the slight smile she knew was for her, his tight, almost kinky hair barely ruffled by the wind. His gaze was aimed up the coast where in the far distance Cape Smokey thrust into the Atlantic. Everything felt broad and wide, the high, balding slope of the mountain behind them, the strait stretching seaward and inward beyond the bridge. Anna felt as if she could soar in any direction, be lifted away. She didn't care who was watching them here by the field, they couldn't be harmed by anyone. She worked quickly and deftly, she'd seen this face close, traced it with her fingers.

"Murdock?" she said, catching him cast his eyes seaward. The freighter's wake churned white and faded quickly gray into the water. "Have you ever been to California?"

"I've been hardly anywhere. Just ports. In and out. I don't like to be a stranger."

"Well, you're not. Anymore. Would you travel for me?"

He didn't answer. He made his eyes slits of distant concentration. "I would, in a way. A long way."

"But not to California."

He smiled. "I'd be hopeless there."

"Lots of hopeless there already, Murdock."

"I'll make it one less."

When the sketch was finished enough to show him, he stood behind her, his hand on her shoulder.

"I won't look that good again ever," he said.

They walked down the path, without purpose, unhurried, past the arthritic apple trees and the fruit rotting in the grass under their canopies, wasps digging in the mashed flesh. The stones of the shore, scattered by the last tide, lay in an array of rounded textures, black swirled with white, rust veined with yellow, the rose granites, the smooth, dark grays. Anna picked them up, dropped them back, Murdock just behind her, turning now and then to keep the house in sight.

"Look, Murdock! How did it get here?" Just below the high-tide line, in the sandy gravel, a short sunflower had germinated and was blooming gaily, its incongruousness almost comical, its brash good cheer, but to Anna delightful, so unexpected, she had seen no sunflowers anywhere around.

"A bird dropped a seed, probably, or an animal," Murdock said. "People grow them in gardens."

They stopped at the point just shy of the lee where the higher field behind them obscured the house. Along the shore an eddy ran seaward like a rippled stream, but beyond it a strip of water was calm, so laden was it with seaweed, and beyond that the ever-widening channel was ebbing, broken by shoals. They sat on a beach log side by side, their legs touching. Aware of a house on the other side of the water where tiny figures ran along the shore, they didn't embrace, didn't kiss, Anna could feel his yearning, like her own, held in check. He stared ahead, squinting at the glare. Anna brushed a bit of sand off his knee.

"You're free to leave after tonight," he said. "I know it's pulling at you, Anna, like that tide out there. I can see it in your work. In your eyes."

"Free? I don't feel that way. I made a mess of things."

"We're after clearing it up, your corner of it. I'll take care of the rest. If there's any spillover, it won't reach you."

"And you?"

"I live here. The good and the bad. That's the way it's always been."

"I got a letter from my husband. He's going to marry the woman he's with now. So we have some steps to take, Chet and me. The last waltz."

"There you are."

"I want to come back here, Murdock."

"You think so? It'll be pretty much the same. I'll be here."

"That's what I like—the same, and you'll be here. I still have a lot of drawing to do."

"You do, but not just in Cape Seal. Don't hear me wrong. I'd love to see you down the beach on a gray morning."

She wanted to resist, tell him no, the best work she'd ever done was infused with here, that was true, she wasn't finished. But the art was here, the meaning was there. She took his hand firmly in hers and said nothing. A flock of gulls, spooked by something, rose from the pond behind them in a great chattering swirl, then settled again one by one out in the water.

"I can't look at you without wanting you," he said. "I am happy and sad at the same time. How can that be?"

"We could go back," Anna said. "We could lie down for a while."

He turned to her, solemn for a few moments. "We could," he said. He smiled. "I need the nap. After all, I'm rowing tonight."

IN THE SPARE bedroom they lay side by side, dozy now with the heat of the afternoon. The pillows smelled of old wood. Sun played through the dancing curtains, over their perspiring skin. His hand lay on her belly and he moved it lower, brushed it lightly over the dark hair there. Anna, her eyes shut, smiled and took his hand to her lips and kissed it. He kissed her breast and then sat up.

"I'd better fetch our boat while we have the day," he said. "When it's dark, we go."

She watched him dress. He drew his jeans up his lanky body, pulled over his wide shoulders a denim shirt, buttoned it slowly, tucked it in. He ran his hands through his hair. He looked out the window before lowering it. "That bed makes quite a racket," he said quietly. "I forgot."

"I don't think anyone was listening. I did forget to lock the door."

"I'll lock it behind me." He squeezed her foot as he passed the bed. At the door he paused, his back to her. "It won't ever look the same," he said. "This room."

Anna lay as she was and listened until he closed the front door. A sentinel crow spotted him and cried from the high poplar. The van started up and faded away. She took in the room around her, the rocker by the window and the small chest of drawers painted white. Everything about the spare bedroom was as it had been, except for herself lying naked here. Who else had lain in this room on an August afternoon? The ill? Not likely a woman and her lover, her husband, the days would have been taken up with rural tasks, they wouldn't have climbed the stairs and stripped off their clothing in the middle of the day, though surely passion ran its course elsewhere, on the sand, in the cool moss of the woods. Later, the woman of the house might descend into the cellar with a pail of milk still warm from the cow. Anna remembered the sepia photograph, a woman squatting on a milking stool, her forehead pressed against the cow's dark flank, her fists sending two clean streams of milk into a bucket, how somber she'd looked, pensive and awkward in her long white dress, its skirt jammed between her thighs, and something on the back of the picture in Gaelic with an exclamation mark, not written, Anna thought, by her.

She looked at her clothing heaped on the floor. The wind felt cooler and, aware of her nakedness, she drew over her the thin coverlet. What was she resuming when she wheeled from this bed? Something bittersweet, all the more because she would not have it again, never, in any way, like this, like here, not possible, all these things that touched her. She took a deep breath, drew in the mix of air, and held it until it dizzied her. Every time she put her hand to blank paper, all of this was in there, in what moved her hand—room, house, shore, sea, the fragrant woods, the dark pond, the scattered flotsam, the wandering animals, their skulls and bones. Never would these drawings have come out of her anywhere else, never at home, never on that street, in that house, in that California garden flowering in some way every day of the year. Murdock was right: she had work to do there, where nothing stayed pretty much the same.

She would have to dress for tonight, for a boat, for the end of the marijuana, sitting down there where potatoes should be, apples, not that double-edged gift from the sea.

MURDOCK DROVE TO Breagh's first, up her driveway, and even though he saw no car, hers or anyone's, he knocked on the door, walked around back, hooded his eyes at the windows. Just a hunch, that Livingstone might have kipped here, the last house on the road. A pair of jeans and a child's red overalls flapped on a clothesline running from the house to Dougal's deer fence. He was glad she was clear of this. Livingstone could be hiding anywhere right now, up any of a dozen unused driveways, logging roads, whatever, or holed up somewhere in Sydney waiting for a chance at Anna's house. Murdock faced the ocean: the land was high here, well above a broad sweep of afternoon blue. Good wind and water could drive the dross from a man's mind.

HE SHOVED OFF from his shore and stepped into the skiff, grabbing an oar and poling the boat through the brief shallows. The water dropped off dark suddenly and he trimmed the oars and pulled out a distance before turning toward Anna's, the splash of the blades break-ing only briefly the wind-roughed surface. There was a bit of a lop but he liked the slight thump as the boat punched through waves, the feel of it, the fine spray on the back of his neck. He was thinking of Anna, he was filled with her, the sight of her on that sun-drenched bed, her skin pale where she'd worn a swimsuit, where he'd kissed and tasted her, but his mind slipped back to his visit at Donald John and Molly's not long ago where he'd told Willard it was time to stop talking about his lost dog, because he had Connie on his mind, how killing the dog became a torture to him, greater almost than Willard's loss, I like dogs too, he said, but you've got to get past it, Willard, mourning like that, months and months. And Molly said, Are you past it *yourself?* And Murdock, to kill the subject, said yes, there comes a point you have to move on. But that was a lie, he had not, could not close that door Rosaire kept coming through, though not as often with the same crip-pling power as she had. She had flared to life yesterday and he'd lost himself in that fantasy for a night. He was grateful for it, no denying, it brought a joy he would never know again except in the mirror of memory, it settled his heart in a good place, calmed him. Now the pleasure of lying with Anna, of having her in his hands, seemed to slide away with every stroke of the oars, and he was just rowing, getting from here to there over water the way they used to.

Clouds white as snow bulged and sailed seaward into new shapes. The wind was southwest but should drop around suppertime as the land began to cool, and they'd have a smooth sea in the evening. Not far astern a cormorant surfaced from a dive, black and sleek, then fled, its rudimentary wings thrashing inches above the water as it bore like a projectile toward Bird Island. The oarlocks clattered hypnotically, he was soon soothed by his motions, the rustle of water along the hull, the rhythm of his own breathing. A small ketch passed south of him outbound, driving hard, its sails filled, and soon he rocked in her wake. He was sweating now, a little thirsty. Somehow he wanted Anna to stay, impossible though it was, selfish, into the mountain's blazing autumn, into another winter she might now be ready for, he would have the sight of her, the chance of her company, clear of what had washed unbidden onto her shore. Rosaire, his dear Rosaire, she would understand this. She was always generous that way, about the world. What did he owe her now? Love, the love he had given only to her, forever. He pulled hard for Granny's beach.

XXVIII.

ANNA HAD SPREAD a lace cloth, marred with a few coin-sized holes, over the big table in her room. She'd poured two glasses of white wine and placed two lit candles, waxed to tea saucers, in the center. She'd had three glasses of wine before he arrived, nervous but pleased. Murdock sat across from her. On their plates were servings of swordfish and rice with chives that had bloomed in lavender near the back door. She'd made a salad from her own garden.

"I couldn't get hearts," she said.

"They'd all be small now, Anna. The big heart swordfish are gone."

He raised his wine. "Here's to you, Anna. In all ways."

"Returned, Murdock. Many times over."

"Safe home."

They ate quietly at first, trying to ignore evidence of her departure. She had moved two shipping boxes to the parlor out of sight, but the walls were bare of her drawings and none of her belongings were slung about. Although neither said so, they were both half-listening for sounds. Anna glanced toward the kitchen: Murdock had set the bale near the back door, but the old brown blanket could not obscure its presence, its demands. She had hoped that their meal would be, as much as they could make it, festive, but around the edges of it they were attuned to the telephone or the purr of an engine in the driveway.

"This divorce business," Murdock said. "Is it a hard go? Bitter?"

"I don't want it bitter, or prolonged. We'll do it civilly. There's no children, after all. Not even a cat to fight over. Stuff to divvy up. Who cares about that? Not me, not Ivan Ilyich."

Knowing that Chet would marry Alicia Snow, that he would take up again that kind of life with her, all its snares and responsibilities, gave Anna a feeling of peace, as if, storm-tossed, she'd come to a shore all her own.

"My mother might've, I suppose, divorced my dad," Murdock said. "There wasn't much of that in those days, not here. You lived through your grievances. Was running away better or worse?"

"Worse for you, I'd think."

"I'll never know. Like a lot of things."

"Did you ever eat by candle growing up, Murdock?"

"Ate by Aladdin lamp, didn't have lights until, hell, the sixties, out this end, electrical. My mother might've used candles in Boston, entertaining. We didn't know just what she did, only that she wasn't doing it with us." He pinched a bit of tablecloth. "No wine stains in this."

"My father liked candlelight. In a certain mood he'd get my mother to leave the lights off for supper. I can't see my food, she'd say, this is silly. Sometimes I didn't know why he loved her, but I know he did. I know that now."

Out the window Anna could see, in the southwest, the upper half of a moon emerging above St. Aubin's hills, faint yet in the early dusk.

"When should we leave, Murdock?" She wanted to get it over with, to return, enjoy this time with him. "We have to see our way without flashlights, don't we?"

"We won't rush away. We'll have a moon. You've made a fine meal here, Anna. Let's drink to that."

They raised their wine and touched glasses. She brought out ice cream covered in maple syrup and walnuts, the very food that had seized her when she was stoned, that unyielding hunger, voracious, almost sexual. At home, a joint would have made the rounds already. Murdock joked that he didn't use maple syrup like this, too dear.

"It's delicious on almost anything, isn't it?" Anna said. "I'll send that portrait I did of you, Murdock. Finish it when I get there. Pen over pencil."

"It's kind of sober next to the other one. Hammer and fire, I liked that."

"Speaking of fire." Anna snuffed out the candle wicks, remembering Willard's old house, last century's newspapers balled-up in the walls, rural vengeance, fire, and she would be the cause of it.

"We'll leave the rug rolled back, open the trap door," Murdock said. "Leave the lights on. No spot they can't find, look they high or low. Too late. They'll know that soon enough."

"Why 'they'?"

"Could be just Livingstone. Could be nobody."

After she dropped Livingstone's sweater on the daybed, she followed Murdock outside, the bale in his arms, there was still enough light to see the path they both knew so well, though their breath was louder than usual. Their hurried pounding steps roused a small bird asleep in the wild roses. Ahead of them the moon was creeping higher over the hills of St. Aubin. Somewhere back in the mountain woods rose up a thin chorus of yipping, like dogs. Murdock paused as they neared the shore. "Coyotes," he said. "They've got a kill."

He'd hauled the boat up on flat sandstones where the path came out of the bank, but from this spot, because of the shorebank trees, they couldn't see the house or who might come there. Soft swells crackled through the gravel and he steadied the boat while Anna climbed inside. When she was on the stern seat, he dumped the bale in. As he took hold of the bow, his fingers brushed the heart-shaped mark he had hammered into the wood, and that hitched him, just for a second. Then he shoved off, the water soaking his shoes before he jumped in and grabbed the oars.

"We'll get out a good ways, Anna," he said, breathing hard already from their rushed walk to the shore, "before we chuck it." He bent deeply into his strokes and the shore fell away astern, he didn't look up toward the house, the water was calm and each dip of the blades seemed the only sound there was, clean, he was into it now, steady, a good clip, he'd put some distance out until he had to rest. Anna was half-turned in her seat, looking back.

"I don't see anyone," she said. There was kitchen light in a rear window, framed in the white shutters.

Red Murdock slowed his strokes but kept them moving out to sea. His wake was true and he liked that, white, trailing straight. He knew where the shoals were, he'd steer them clear. He wanted to talk even if he didn't have the breath for it, not quite, he didn't know just what he should say to Anna Starling, what she might, on this occasion, want to hear.

"See that brook?" he said. "Cutting down through your little woods? My grandmother . . . used to wash clothes there . . . that was her water." A seabird took flight ahead of them, its wingsound like the whip of a saw. "She'd build a fire under a big iron pot . . . pour in buckets from that cold brook until . . . she had a good head of steam."

On the shore where Anna's path ended, a flashlight flared and darted back and forth, frantically up and down the beach.

"One day a spark got into the dry roof . . . started to burn a hole in the shingles. Well . . ." Above the ridge of the mountain a black cloud stretched languidly into the very last of the light there. "Who was to help her, no man around? . . . She soaked a big quilt in the brook, my granny . . . then she climbed a ladder, we always had a ladder there then . . . she flung that wet quilt over the burning hole." The flashlight was now aimed ineffectually toward the boat, Murdock could not tell who was behind it, just a figure against the shorebank. "She carried buckets down that ladder and up again . . . pouring them onto it. She put the fire out. . . . By God, she did. By herself."

"See that flashlight?" Anna said, pointing back toward her shore. "I should've brought the glasses."

"That light can't reach us, nobody there can."

The darkness seemed to accelerate as they moved further out, leaving the red house behind, and then Murdock's, and MacDermid's Cove, and further on Donald John and Molly's, and Breagh's as the cliffs got higher. A wash of dark blue was inking into the horizon.

"There's nothing for them to find," Anna said.

Murdock took three more strokes before he shipped the oars. He bent over, catching his breath. "It's probably Livingstone behind that flashlight, and he won't be there when we get back. He wouldn't destroy anything."

She scooped her hand slowly through the water a few times. "I'd like to think he wouldn't."

"Ever since a boy, he could see Granny's house on the other shore."

The moon was waxing pale in the west, shimmering faintly down the sea.

"Me and Connie, years ago, just young, rowed a dory out here, all the way to Bird Island. You could load that tub to the gunnels with fish, she'd take a good sea and get you back home. Light and cloud and storm. Excitement. Fear, sometimes. I miss it."

"Is this a good boat?"

"Tight as a bottle."

Murdock's knife clicked open and he set to work on the bale, slicing hard through the plastic in several places. He pulled out one brick at a time and slashed it open wide so that the colas were well exposed, like gurry, then he flung it overboard. Anna watched him, he didn't ask her to help him, he would do it himself just for the satisfaction, he wished Livingstone was watching right now, that he could see this far.

"What was her name, Murdock?" Anna said.

He paused and looked back at the land, the mountainside a collection of shadows, small black valleys he knew, the odd clearing of moonlight.

"Rosaire," he said. "Her name is Rosaire."

Anna reached over and took a brick from his hand, she plucked out strands of marijuana and tossed them like flowers into the water, barely visible as they drifted away, then another and another.

"Let them smoke that, eh?" Murdock said. "Sea weed, they can choke on it."

They worked on silently until the garbage-bag wrapping was empty and he crammed it into a small bundle and shoved it under the bow. They watched the litter bob clear of the boat as Murdock took up the oars and resumed rowing, just enough to put them under way.

"That moon," Anna said. "A man I cared about a lot pointed its seas out to me once, named them. I didn't forget. Mare Serenitatis, Mare Tranquillitatis, Mare Cognitum. They pull me somewhere way back in my life, Murdock, just hearing them."

"They're all dry," he said. "This is our sea."

"It's beautiful."

"Beautiful for a while."

Gentle rollers began to breathe under them, rising from the open ocean so slowly at first, with such grace, Murdock hardly felt their long, quiet rhythm, coming from a long way off, heralding wind, storm. A cool breeze came up, flowed over them, and he shivered. He could not see Anna clearly. He brought the bow around slowly until light ribboned out behind them, and the moon was in her face.

The author wishes to thank Diane Bradbury
for a warm house in winter.